Fred pointed his ... s play to shoot McCarth... ...d, but he couldn't bring himself to squeeze all the way. Back-shooting just wasn't in him. For that matter, shooting any-one wasn't in him. He drew back, bowed his head, and closed his eyes. What good was a lawman who couldn't shoot anybody? The answer was obvious. The lawman wasn't any good at all.

Fred had never felt so worthless. He almost decided to get out of there while he still could and let the kid handle things alone. But no. That wouldn't be right ei-ther. He was the one wearing a badge.

Opening his eyes, he stared at the Smith & Wesson. He wasn't a gun hand. He hardly ever practiced. That old saw about not being able to hit the broad side of a barn—that was him. He holstered it.

Fred knew what he had to do. His mouth went dry and he broke out in a sweat. It was plumb loco. But he couldn't see any other way. Jamming his hat back on, he took a deep breath and stepped into the aisle and over to the other stall.

McCarthy didn't hear him until he was almost on top of him. Wheeling on his heels, McCarthy pointed his Colt at Fred's head. "No, you don't! I will by God shoot you dead."

Ralph Compton

THE EVIL
MEN DO

A Ralph Compton Novel
by David Robbins

A SIGNET BOOK

SIGNET
Published by the Penguin Group
Penguin Group (USA) LLC, 375 Hudson Street,
New York, New York 10014

USA | Canada | UK | Ireland | Australia | New Zealand | India | South Africa | China
penguin.com
A Penguin Random House Company

First published by Signet, an imprint of New American Library,
a division of Penguin Group (USA) LLC

First Printing, February 2015

ISBN 978-0-451-47222-9

Printed in the United States of America
10 9 8 7 6 5 4 3 2 1

THE IMMORTAL COWBOY

This is respectfully dedicated to the "American Cowboy." His was the saga sparked by the turmoil that followed the Civil War, and the passing of more than a century has by no means diminished the flame.

True, the old days and the old ways are but treasured memories, and the old trails have grown dim with the ravages of time, but the spirit of the cowboy lives on.

In my travels—to Texas, Oklahoma, Kansas, Nebraska, Colorado, Wyoming, New Mexico, and Arizona—I always find something that reminds me of the Old West. While I am walking these plains and mountains for the first time, there is this feeling that a part of me is eternal, that I have known these old trails before. I believe it is the undying spirit of the frontier calling me, through the mind's eye, to step back into time. What is the appeal of the Old West of the American frontier?

It has been epitomized by some as the dark and bloody period in American history. Its heroes—Crockett, Bowie, Hickok, Earp—have been reviled and criticized. Yet the Old West lives on, larger than life.

It has become a symbol of freedom, when there was always another mountain to climb and another river to cross; when a dispute between two men was settled not with expensive lawyers, but with fists, knives, or guns. Barbaric? Maybe. But some things never change. When the cowboy rode into the pages of American history, he left behind a legacy that lives within the hearts of us all.

—*Ralph Compton*

Chapter 1

The homestead wasn't much. A cabin, a barn, and acres of corn.

Twilight had turned the sky slate gray when the three men drew rein on a low rise to the west. The tallest leaned on his saddle horn, his green eyes narrowing. "What do we have here?" His wide-brimmed brown hat and vest were caked with the dust of many miles. On his right hip in a triple-loop holster was a Remington with walnut grips.

"Nothin' much," said the rider on his right. Short and stocky, he hadn't washed his hat and store-bought duds in a year of Sundays. Grime darkened his stubble. He pulled at his left ear where the lobe had been before he lost it to a Ute arrow and frowned. "Just another sodbuster."

The last rider always wore black clothes to match his dark skin. It made him hard to see at night, which came in handy when people were trying to put lead into him. "Sodbusters got food," he said. "Sodbusters got watches and rings."

"That they do, Lute," the tall rider agreed, and gigged his roan. "What say we go invite ourselves to supper?"

"Ah, hell, Dunn," the short man said. "We've got grub."

"You turnin' soft on us, Tucker?" Dunn asked, giving him a sharp glance.

"You know better," Tucker said. "I was just hopin' to go a ways before we got the law after us again."

"We do this right, they won't be."

A yellow dog barked as they approached and the cabin door opened, framing the farmer. Skinny as a rail, he wore a loose-fitting homespun shirt and bib overalls. "Who's there?" he hollered. In his hands was a shotgun, and he wagged it menacingly.

"Look at him," Dunn said, and laughed a cold laugh.

"Sheep come in all sizes, don't they?" Lute said.

"Don't let on," Dunn warned. "You be friendly until I say it's time not to be. The same with you, Tucker."

"When do I ever cause you grief?" Tucker replied.

"You know better," Dunn said. "You ever did, you'd have a window in your skull before you could blink."

"You never threaten Lute like that," Tucker said.

"Lute and me been together a good long spell," Dunn said. "We're like peas in a pod, him and me. There's nothin' we like more than snuffin' wicks and helpin' ourselves to what other folks have."

"I know that," Tucker said.

The farmer stepped out and raised his shotgun to his shoulder. "Who are you and what do you want?" he called out.

"Friendly cuss," Dunn said so only Lute and Tucker heard. Then, raising his voice, he yelled, "We're plumb friendly, mister. Just passin' through. We'd be grateful for some food and coffee if you have any to spare."

"That's close enough," the farmer said, putting his cheek to the shotgun. "A man can't be too careful these days."

Drawing rein, Dunn smiled and held his hands up, palms out. "Didn't you hear we're friendly?"

"You seem to be," the farmer said.

Dunn gazed about them. "Nice place you have here. Didn't expect to find a farm this far from anywhere."

The farmer lowered the shotgun but only partway. "I'm James. James Larn. Out of Springfield."

"Pleased to meet you," Dunn said. "These are my pards, Lute and Tuck. Tuck is short for Tucker and Lute for Luthor."

"Gents," James Larn said.

"How about that food?" Dunn said, and patted his stomach. "Would you happen to have any to spare? We're low on supplies and haven't hardly ate in two days."

"We can pay you," Tucker quickly said. "Not much, mind. But I have a dollar and it's yours."

James Larn let the shotgun's muzzle dip toward the ground. "Shucks, we'd feed you for free, but I won't say no if you want to give us that dollar."

"We?" Dunn said.

"My wife and my boy are inside," Larn said, switching the shotgun from his hand to the crook of his elbow. "Fayette is my missus. The boy ain't but a few months old and we can't make up our minds what to name him."

"Can't wait to meet them," Dunn said. Swinging down, he let the reins dangle and stretched.

"Been on the trail awhile, have you?" Larn asked.

"Feels like forever," Tucker said. He dismounted and scratched at his stubble. "What is that I smell?"

"Soup," Larn said. "Potato soup, to be exact. With carrots and peas. We ate the last of our meat a couple of days ago. I've been meanin' to go huntin' but haven't had the time."

"Soup is great," Tucker said. "A bowl would do me right fine."

"I usually have three or four," Larn said.

"As thin as you are?"

"I could eat five meals a day and not gain a pound," Larn boasted. "It's just how I am."

Lute alighted and wrapped his reins around his saddle horn. Turning, he took a step, but the farmer held out his hand.

"You'll have to eat out here, I'm afraid," James Larn said.

Dunn was swatting dust from his shirt and stopped. "Why's that? He's as hungry as we are."

"Likely so," Larn said, "but he's not the same color."

"Well, now," Dunn said. "You're one of those who doesn't cotton to blacks, I take it?"

"It's not me so much," Larn said. "My wife is a mite finicky about who she lets inside."

"So she's one of those?" Tucker said.

"Don't think poorly of her," Larn said. "She lost her grandpa to some colored soldiers back during the War Between the States, and to this day she can't look at a black without gettin' all teary-eyed."

The female of the place chose that moment to emerge, holding an infant bundled in a cloth. Only the baby's face poked out. "How do you do, gentlemen?"

Tucker gave a slight start. "Mrs. Larn. That's a cute sprout you've got there."

James Larn said with fatherly pride, "He hasn't given us a lick of trouble. Doesn't cry a lot or keep us up nights, or nothin' like that."

"Good for him," Tucker said.

Dunn came over and smiled at the baby. "Look at him. Some say babies are cute, but I'd never want one of my own."

"Never say never," Fayette Larn said. "If my pa taught me anything, it's that each day brings its own surprises."

"Listen to you, ma'am," Dunn said. "But ain't it the truth?" He motioned at Lute. "Which reminds me. Your husband told us you'd rather our friend here should stay outside. I'd take it as a favor if he could come in with the rest of us."

"I'm sorry. No," Fayette said. "It would bring back painful memories. I've shed enough tears over my grandpa. He was near and dear to me as a person can be."

"Lute is my pard," Dunn said.

"I'm sorry. I can't help how I feel."

"Makes two of us," Dunn said.

Tucker glanced sharply at him, then said to the woman,

"The war was more than twenty years ago, ma'am. I should think you'd be cried out by now. Can't you make an exception in our case?"

"Some sorrows run too deep," Fayette said. She mustered a smile for Lute. "Nothin' personal, you understand, mister?"

Lute didn't say anything.

"Did you hear me?" Fayette asked.

"He heard you, ma'am," Dunn said. "Didn't you, Lute?"

"I heard her," Lute said.

James Larn took his wife's arm and ushered her indoors, saying, "Come on in, gents. The soup will be a few minutes yet and we can get better acquainted."

The cabin's furnishings were as plain as the occupants. In addition to an oak table and chairs, a rocking chair sat by the stone hearth. A bear-hide rug lay on the floor and the skin of a bobcat hung on a wall.

"Nice home you have here, missus," Tucker said.

"Shucks, it's nothin' special," Fayette said. "But it's ours, free and clear, and that counts for something."

Nodding, James Larn leaned his shotgun against the wall. "Or it will be once we've paid it off." He claimed the chair at the head of the table. "Have a seat, fellers. Make yourselves comfortable."

"Don't mind if we do," Dunn said.

Tucker couldn't take his eyes off the bundle in Fayette's arm. "A baby, by golly. I hardly ever get this close to one."

"Folks have babies all the time," James Larn said.

"We haven't run into any with a tyke as little as yours," Tucker said. "Kids, yes. But we've been lucky with no babies."

"What a strange thing to say," Fayette said, bending to kiss the baby's cheek. "That's not luck. Babies are the sweetest darlings on God's green earth. Just holdin' one makes a body feel good."

Tucker looked across the table at Dunn, whose face might as well have been chiseled from granite. "A baby changes everything."

"I don't see what," Dunn said.

Fayette laughed. "That's only because you've never been a papa. Trust me. When a baby comes into your world, nothin' is ever the same. Your whole life is rearranged forever."

"I like mine as it is."

James Larn held out his hands. "Why don't you give him to me, hon, so you can ladle out the soup when it's done?"

"It almost is." Fayette gently deposited the baby in her husband's arms and went to the big-bellied stove.

Tucker sniffed, and beamed. "Sure smells good, Mrs. Larn. I can't recollect the last time I had home cookin'."

"It's just soup," Fayette said.

Dunn leaned back in his chair, tilting it so it balanced on its back legs. "How long have you been farmin'?"

"Going on three years this fall," James Larn answered. "Hard to believe. Time flies so damn fast."

"No cussin'," Fayette said.

"Sorry, dear."

"Got any neighbors hereabouts?" Dunn asked.

"Not for five to six miles," Larn said. "We hankered to be off by ourselves where we can do as we please."

"You did," Fayette said while stirring. "I'd have been fine closer to Springfield or some other town."

"I like my privacy," Larn said.

"I miss going to a general store or a dress shop. I miss talkin' with other ladies."

Larn grinned and winked at Tucker and Dunn, then said to his wife, "You're female. You can't help missing it."

"My ma had her own millinery shop years ago," Tucker revealed. "Worked herself to the bone. Dawn till dusk, six days a week. She'd even sneak in to work on Sundays. To tell the truth, she was the hardest worker I ever knew."

Dunn stared at him.

"What?" Tucker said.

"I think that was fine of her," Fayette said. "Too many

gals these days would rather lie abed half the mornin' or sit around doing next to nothin'."

"See?" Tucker said to Dunn.

James Larn cooed to the baby and slowly rocked it back and forth. "My son will be a hard worker, just like me. I'll leave him this farm, and by then have it paid off. He'll have a better start than I did."

"Now, now," Fayette said. "We've done all right."

Dunn gazed about their cabin. He fingered the edge of the table and watched Mrs. Larn commence to ladle the soup. "I never could savvy a life like this. Tied to one place. Doing the same thing day in and day out."

"Workin' land that's yours gives you a warm feelin'," Larn said, and tapped his chest. "Right here."

"If you say so," Dunn said.

Fayette brought over a wooden bowl filled to the brim, and a large wooden spoon, and set them in front of Dunn. "Guests first. Here's yours. Now I'll get your friend's."

"Don't forget my pard outside," Dunn said.

"I'm not likely to," Fayette said. Smiling, she returned to the stove.

Dunn regarded the bowl and the spoon and placed his right hand on his hip. "I reckon we should get to it."

"Somethin' wrong with the soup?" James Larn asked.

"It smells good," Dunn said, "but I'd rather get this over with and then eat. I can relax better not havin' it to do after."

"Not havin' what to do?" the farmer asked.

"This," Dunn said. He pulled his Remington and cocked it while pointing it at Larn's face.

"What's this?"

"The part I like best," Dunn said.

Over at the stove, Fayette turned and gasped. "Here, now. We were nice and invited you in and now you're fixin' to rob us?"

"Who said anything about just rob?" Dunn said, and shot James Larn between the eyes.

Fayette screamed.

That was when the door opened and in strode Lute. He had his revolver out, and without saying a word, he shot her.

Tucker saw the bundle in James Larn's limp hands start to fall. Lunging, he caught it before it could hit the floor. "Got you," he said, and smiled.

"Your turn," Dunn said.

Tucker's smile faded. "What?"

"I did the husband and Lute did the wife. Now it's your turn."

"You want me to kill the *baby*?"

Dunn cocked his revolver. "I don't say things twice."

Chapter 2

Sweetwater got its name from Sweetwater Creek. The old trappers called the creek that because the water was always clear and cold. Fed by runoff, it flowed in years when there was snow. And in Wyoming, winter and snow were synonymous.

Sweetwater boasted sixty-four souls. That was meager as populations went, but Sweetwater also boasted a saloon and a bank and other businesses, plus its own town marshal.

Fred Hitch was getting on in years. His hair was gray, his mustache salt-and-pepper, the lines in his face were too many to count. He had a gut that came from liking to eat more than he liked to get out and about. He also liked that in Sweetwater there wasn't much for the marshal to do, so he got to spend most of his days at his desk doing what Fred did best: daydreaming.

Fred was in his chair with his hands folded over his belly and his chin tucked low, dozing, when the front door opened and the clatter of a passing buckboard woke him. He yawned and scratched himself and looked up. "What in tarnation? I must be dreamin'."

His visitor came over to the desk. "I see a star on your shirt, so you must be the law in this two-bit town."

"You have your nerve," Fred said. Sweetwater might be of little consequence in the grand scheme of things, but it was his town and he didn't like having it insulted. Especially by someone who didn't look to be much over twelve years old and barely an inch over five feet tall.

"I have that and more," the youngster said. "Are you the law dog or do you just take naps here?"

Fred studied the boy from head to toe and did it a second time because he couldn't believe what he saw.

His visitor was all elbows and knees, with spindly arms and legs. A wool cap, the kind sheepherders favored, covered a mop of ginger hair. Bangs fell to the boy's eyebrows. His eyes were the color of a mountain lake, his nose not much bigger than a button. His shirt and britches were store-bought and fit him poorly. Freckles decorated his cheeks and he had a cleft chin. "What are you lookin' at?" the boy demanded.

Fred was looking at two things in particular. First, a deep scar that ran from below the boy's left ear, along his jaw, almost to the cleft. A knife had done that, unless Fred missed his guess. But it was the other thing that dumfounded him the most.

The boy had enough weapons for a regiment. In addition to two Colts in holsters, he was carrying a Winchester. A bowie knife, of all things, hung from a cord around his neck. Strapped to his back in its scabbard was a saber with the hilt jutting above one shoulder. As if all that wasn't enough, a pair of derringers had been tucked under the boy's belt on either side of the buckle and stuck out over the top.

"What in the name of all that's holy are you supposed to be?" Fred asked.

"I'm me," the boy said. "Tyree Johnson. Out of Missouri. Could be you've heard of me."

"If I had I'd remember," Fred said. "No one is liable to forget a walkin' arsenal like you. How old are you anyhow?"

"Don't matter," Tyree said.

"It sure as St. Peter does," Fred said. "You're too young to be totin' all that artillery and whatnot. Your ma and pa ought to be ashamed of themselves, lettin' you go around like that."

Tyree's face clouded and his freckles seemed to darken. "My ma and pa are dead, and I'll thank you not to mention them again."

Fred Hitch rose and leaned on his desk. "I'm the marshal here, boy. You don't tell me what to do. I tell you."

Tyree Johnson set his rifle on the desk, leaned on the edge, and looked Fred in the eye. "You might want to watch the words you sling. I don't take kindly to them as puts on airs."

"Why, you little runt." To say Fred was flabbergasted was an understatement. He'd never had anyone so young talk to him so boldly. "I'll ask you again. What is with all that hardware? You playin' at being a soldier?"

"I don't play," Tyree said. "Not since my folks were done in. All of this"—and he patted a Colt and a derringer and the bowie—"is what I use in my work."

"Work?" Fred snorted. "What kind of job can you have?"

Tyree straightened and thrust out his cleft chin with the scar. "I hunt men for their bounty. Mostly bail jumpers but I'll hunt most anyone."

"The hell you say."

"The hell I do," Tyree said.

Fred shook his head in amazement. He closed his eyes and opened them again on the remote chance that the boy was a figment of his daydreams, but the boy was still there. "If this don't beat all."

"The sooner you get used to it," Tyree said, "the sooner I can do what I came here to do."

"Which is what, exactly?"

"I'm lookin' for a man who is wanted in Cheyenne," Tyree said. "I take him back, I get two thousand dollars."

Fred whistled. The town paid him seventy-five dollars a month, plus ten percent of all fines. Two thousand was more than he'd earn in two years. "I should give up marshalin' and become a bounty man."

Tyree squinted at him and shook his head. "I don't know as it would fit you. You don't look very tough."

Fred's amusement evaporated like water on a hot rock. "That'll be enough insults out of you. These antics of yours are over. You're not no bounty man. You're a boy, and boys don't bounty-hunt."

"That's what you think." Tyree pried at the buttons on his shirt, loosened several, and slipped a hand inside. The hand reappeared with a folded sheet of paper. "Read this. It'll save time."

Fred wondered if this might be some sort of joke. Maybe some of the townsmen had put the boy up to it. But come to think of it, he'd never seen the boy before, and he knew most everybody, at least by sight if not all their names. Suspicious, he unfolded the sheet and held it to the light from the window, but it was chicken scrawl. Opening the top drawer, he took out his wire-rimmed spectacles. "Need these to read," he said self-consciously.

"I knew a fella wore a pair like that," Tyree said. "He was blind as a bat when he didn't have them on."

"I'm not that old yet," Fred said.

"You look old to me."

Flustered, Fred held the paper closer. It was a letter of introduction, plainly written by an adult.

> *To Whom It May Concern,*
> *Tyree Johnson has been in my employ for over a year.*
> *He has brought back wanted men no one else could. I vouch for him despite his age and encourage you to give him all aid.*
> *Jefferson Benteen*
> *St. Louis, Missouri*

Fred read it a second time and peered over it at the boy. "St. Louis?"

"That's where I got my start. I've been to other places and now I'm workin' out of Cheyenne. I carry that letter with me to show to folks who don't believe I am what I am. Makes things easier."

"If this don't beat all. How old are you anyhow?"

"Fifteen," Tyree said. "Sixteen come next March."

"You don't look it. Not even with that scar. How did you get it anyhow?"

"My letter," Tyree said, holding out his hand. "I have a man to find."

"Not so fast." Now that Fred had a few moments to think, he was determined to learn more. "Let's say I buy your story. Let's say I believe you are what you say, those freckles aside. Who are you after and what makes you think he's in Sweetwater?"

"No, you don't," Tyree said. "I tell you, you'll bring him in yourself and take him to Cheyenne for the money."

"I'm not out to steal your wanted man from you," Fred said indignantly. The nerve of the boy, he thought. Little did the kid know that Fred's philosophy on life could be summed up in three words: easy does it. He liked things to be simple. His goal each day was to get through it without any irritation. That might seem to be a silly philosophy for a lawman to have, but he'd found that if he spent most of his time in his jail and made it a point to show up on those rare occasions when there was trouble after the troublemakers had left, his life stayed peaceful, just the way he wanted it to be.

"Says you," Tyree replied. "But I'll keep it to myself if you don't mind, and even if you do."

"You have a lot of bark on you, boy, for someone of your tender years," Fred scolded.

"The sooner you get over thinkin' of me as a boy, the better it will be for both of us." Tyree picked up the letter, carefully folded it, and slid it back under his shirt. As he did the buttons, he remarked, "I reckon I'll ask around on my own and you can go back to sleep."

"Don't prod me," Fred said. "This badge gives me the authority to do as I please, and it pleases me to keep you here until I learn all the particulars."

"I've told you all I'm going to."

"The name of the gent you're after?"

When Tyree scowled, it deepened his scar and made him look older. "I reckon you have the right. But try to cheat me and there will be hell to pay."

"You shouldn't ought to talk like that," Fred said. "Not at your age."

"How old do you have to be to say 'hell'?"

"The man's name?" Fred said.

"Tom McCarthy."

Fred smiled smugly. "We've got no one by that name in Sweetwater. Appears to me you've come all this way for nothin'."

"He wouldn't be usin' his real name," Tyree said.

"What did he do?"

"McCarthy strangled his wife and gutted the gent he caught her with," Tyree said. "The judge set bail, McCarthy raised the bond, and the next day he skipped."

"And whoever put up the bond sent you? He should be ashamed usin' someone so young."

"Don't start on that again," Tyree said. "Are you going to help me ask around or not?"

"I suppose I better," Fred said reluctantly. "This is my town." He stepped to a peg and took down his gun belt. The truth was, he'd rather stay there and nap. But it wouldn't hurt to escort the boy around and at the same time show everyone he was doing his job. Circling his waist with the belt, he proceeded to buckle it on.

"You're awful slow," Tyree said.

"You hear that creakin' in my joints?" Fred rejoined. Adjusting his hat, he strode to the door. "After you, boy."

It was early afternoon, and at that hour of the day, with the summer heat at its worst, only a few souls were abroad. A dog lay on a porch, sleeping, and a hog rooted at the side of the general store.

"Your town is as lively as a cemetery," Tyree said.

"I like it that way," Fred said. "There hasn't been a lick of trouble in months. Oh, we get a few squabbles and some pushin' and shovin' after too much liquor, but that's all. There's no killin'. No stealin'. Sweetwater is as law-abidin' as they come."

"Except for Tom McCarthy."

"He's not here, I tell you. Whoever gave you that notion was mistaken."

"So you say."

The boy headed down the street, and Fred followed. He was trying to be sociable and having it thrown in his face. He'd like nothing better than to send the boy packing. "I need to ask you something."

"Ain't that all you've been doing?"

Fred let that pass. "Why all the guns and the knife and that sword, for cryin' out loud?"

"Those I'm after take me more serious."

"You ever had to use any of that armament?"

"A few times."

Fred suspected the boy was lying. No one that age went around shootin' or knifin' folks. He saw the boy stare at a sign to the feed and grain across the street and his lips moved as if he were reading it. "I have a nephew who's about ten years older than you. Last I heard, he's practicin' dentistry down to Santa Fe. He likes a warm climate."

"It's pretty warm here," Tyree said, and started toward the feed and grain.

"You lookin' for some oats for your horse?" Fred guessed. When the boy didn't answer, he coughed and said, "Listen. I don't like what you're up to, but it's a free country. You like to go after bounty money, have at it. Seems like a dangerous way to make a livin', though. From what I hear tell, those who skip on the law don't go back willingly."

"That they don't," Tyree said. "But nothin' else I could do pays half as much."

Fred snickered. "You aimin' to get rich before your time?"

"No," Tyree said. "I'm aimin' to catch up to the sons of bitches who killed my ma and pa."

"*That's* why you do this?"

As they entered the store, a bell over the door tinkled.

"This here is owned by Hiram Bigelow," Fred informed the boy. "Salt of the earth, Hiram is."

"Is that a fact?"

They were almost to the counter when a rotund man came out of the back carrying a sack of seed. His florid face creased in a smile and he nodded at the marshal. "Fred. What brings you here this time of the day?"

"Hiram," Fred said pleasantly.

Tyree had turned to a shelf as Hiram Bigelow came out, but now he turned back and placed his right hand on his right Colt. "Tom McCarthy," he said. "I'm here to take you back to Cheyenne."

"Like hell you are," the salt of the earth said, and threw the bag of seed at them.

Chapter 3

For Fred Hitch, the day was one astonishment after another. He'd known Hiram Bigelow for the better part of a year. Ever since Hiram bought the feed and grain from Sam Goodman. He'd never have imagined Hiram was a lawbreaker. The notion of Hiram being a killer was downright laughable. And yet there he went, running off in a panic.

The seed bag was heavy. It hit Tyree Johnson on the shoulder and knocked him back a couple of steps. Clawing at a Colt, he hollered, "Stop right there, mister!"

Hiram—or Tom McCarthy—did no such thing. He continued fleeing down the hall.

"Wait!" Fred yelled, but it was useless. McCarthy didn't listen. Fred grabbed awkwardly for his own revolver and started to give chase, but Tyree suddenly grabbed him by the arm and yanked him out of the hallway. It was well the boy did, for the next moment the hall rocked to the boom of a shot and lead whizzed. "He's shootin' at us!" Fred exclaimed.

"They do that." Tyree peered warily into the hall. "There's a warehouse back there."

Fred nodded absently. He'd been into the back a few times. It was where Hiram—no, McCarthy—kept a lot of feed and seed and whatnot.

"Is there a back door?" Tyree asked.

"Of course," Fred said. "Every place has a back door." He would have liked to stand there where it was safe, but the boy broke into a sprint.

"Come on. We can't let him get away."

Fred followed reluctantly. He wouldn't mind at all if McCarthy got away. The man had never done him any harm. For that matter, McCarthy had been a model member of their community since he arrived in Sweetwater. From what the kid claimed, that business in Cheyenne had been over McCarthy catching his wife with another man. Granted, strangling her and cutting open the no-account who trifled with her was going too far, but people did things in the heat of rage they'd never do otherwise. And McCarthy never struck him as a killer.

"Hurry up," Tyree urged, dashing to a small mountain of grain bags.

Puffing, Fred joined him. No shots rang out. He considered that a good sign. Maybe McCarthy had ducked out the back door and they wouldn't have to swap lead.

The kid raised his voice. "Tom McCarthy! Throw down your six-shooter and give yourself up. All I want is to take you in."

From somewhere deeper in the maze of stacks and crates and piles came a mocking laugh. "That'll be the day, boy."

Forgetting himself, Fred said, "Hiram? What's gotten into you? Do as he wants so no one need get hurt."

"I let him take me, they'll put me on trial and I'll be hanged or sent to prison for the rest of my life."

"You don't know that," Fred said. "You could be let off. They have to prove you did the crime."

"That won't be hard," McCarthy said bitterly. "They found me standing over the bodies with the knife I used." He paused. "My best friend. And he was carrying on with my wife behind my back."

"I'm sorry for you, Hiram. I mean Tom," Fred said. "I'll come testify if you want. Say as how you never once broke the law in Sweetwater and were a credit to the town."

For a bit McCarthy didn't answer. Then he said, "That's damn decent of you, Hitch. You're not as worthless as I thought."

"I beg your pardon?" Fred said.

"Why do you think I settled here? That first day I rode in and you came over and introduced yourself, I saw right away that as a lawman, you were pitiful. You weren't ever likely to figure out the truth. So I gave you a fake name and started this store."

Fred was shocked. "You thought that poorly of me?"

"Hitch, everybody does."

"I never," Fred said. Here he thought he'd been doing a fairly fine job. So what if he didn't actually do much? There wasn't much to do.

"I won't let you take me," McCarthy vowed.

Fred glanced at the boy to ask what they should do — but the boy wasn't there. He'd crept off while they were talking. "Tyree?" he whispered.

"What's that?" McCarthy said.

Fred inched an eye past the sacks. The place was too dark to see much. There were only a couple of small windows and they were high up. "Tom, I wish you would reconsider."

A revolver thundered.

Fred drew back, thinking that McCarthy was shooting at him. But no, more shots banged, and he realized the kid and McCarthy were in a gun duel. He heard McCarthy cry out and the stamp of pounding boots. Then a rectangle of light spilled across the floor.

"He's hightailin' it," the kid shouted.

Fred moved around the sacks in time to see Tyree Johnson bolt out the rear door. "Damn him anyhow," Fred said, and went after him. The harsh flare of the sun made him squint. He looked right and left but didn't see either of them. Relieved, he was about to turn and go back through the store to the front when the kid popped out of an alley and beckoned.

"What are you waitin' for? This'll be easier if it's both of us."

Fred's idea of "easy" didn't include being shot at, but he dashed into the alley, puffing worse than before.

"You are awful out of shape," Tyree remarked, running smoothly.

"Don't worry about me," Fred said. He wouldn't admit it, but this was the most exercise he'd had in a coon's age. "Where did he get to?"

"The main street."

"He could be anywhere by now." Fred sought to discourage pursuit. "We might as well go back to my office."

"You do what you want, old man," Tyree said, running faster, "but I'm no quitter."

"Well, hell." Fred wished he didn't have to follow him. He'd never counted on something like this happening. Not in Sweetwater.

Main Street was deserted. A few faces peeked from windows, but most people had the sense not to show themselves when lead flew.

The boy was looking to the right. "I bet he's makin' for the stable. Does he keep a horse there?"

"Not that I know of," Fred said.

"He'll steal one, then," Tyree said. "But he'll want to saddle it first, and that will slow him some." Tucking low, he ran on. "Let's go."

Fred was tired of the boy giving him orders. He was the law. He was the grown man. He should be telling the kid, not the other way around.

The stable doors were wide-open, and nothing moved inside. The stable man, Chester, was nowhere to be seen.

Fred hoped McCarthy hadn't harmed Chester. Once a week he and Chester played checkers. And on occasion they'd claim a table at the saloon and pass a bottle back and forth. Chester was the closest thing to a best friend he had.

Zigzagging, Tyree Johnson reached the stable and put his back to the wall. He was careful, that boy, and knew all the tricks.

Fred tried zigzagging, but his knees didn't like it. When he reached the wall, he sagged against it and wheezed.

"Are you going to die on me?" Tyree asked.

"Ha," Fred said. He didn't think the boy was the least bit funny.

"Try to keep up." Instead of going in, Tyree ran to the corner and on around the side.

"I should have been a store clerk," Fred grumbled. He'd considered that in his younger days. But the notion of toting tin held more appeal. He used to daydream about epic shooting affrays with hordes of outlaws. But that was then, and this was now. The young often held foolish notions. The old knew better.

Fred hastened after him. He remembered the corral out back. It would be easy for McCarthy to go into the tack room and help himself to a saddle blanket, saddle, and bridle.

Tyree sprinted to the far end. He looked out, glanced over his shoulder at Fred, and grinned.

Struggling to breathe, Fred came to a halt and placed his hands on his knees.

"If you weren't carryin' so big a belly, you'd get around a lot better," Tyree whispered.

"Go to hell," Fred said.

"Shhh." Tyree looked out again. "He's tightenin' the cinch. We caught him just in time."

"You're not going to shoot him, are you?"

"Only if he makes me. He's worth more alive than dead." Tyree cocked both Colts. "Quietlike, now, and we can take him by surprise."

Fred was tired of that "we" business. But he stepped out when the kid did, and they quickly climbed the rails. McCarthy had his back to them and didn't see them. Taking deep breaths, Fred pointed his Smith & Wesson.

Tom McCarthy was just letting down the stirrup on a

chestnut. Turning, he reached for the reins. Tucked under his belt was a revolver. There was a red stain on his shirt, high on his right shoulder. The boy had winged him.

"Hold it right there," Tyree bellowed.

Fred was going to add his own command, but he wasn't given the chance.

Unlimbering his six-shooter, McCarthy barely had it out when Tyree Johnson fired.

And hit the horse.

The chestnut whinnied and reared, tearing the reins out of McCarthy's hand. It sent McCarthy stumbling, but he recovered and sprinted into the stable just as Tyree fired both Colts.

"You missed him," Fred said. He'd assumed that anyone who went around with as much armament as the kid wore would know how to shoot.

"I'm not Wild Bill Hickok," Tyree said.

"Good thing," Fred said. "He's dead."

"You stay here. I'll make sure he doesn't escape." Tyree ran into the stable.

Annoyed at the turn of events, Fred jogged after him.

The poor chestnut was whinnying and running in circles and tossing its head back and forth. As near as Fred could tell from some scarlet drops, the slug had nicked it on the chest.

There was a commotion in the stable, and a shot.

Just what Fred needed. A gun war in the middle of town. A lot of folks were bound to be upset. It wouldn't surprise him one bit if some of them complained to the mayor, who never had liked him. He could see the mayor using it as an excuse to claim it was time for a change in lawmen.

Fred couldn't have that. He needed to stop this before it went any further.

The center aisle was littered with straw, and a pitchfork had been propped against a stall. Only two of the stalls were occupied, the horses wide-eyed with fright.

McCarthy wasn't anywhere to be seen.

Tyree, though, was at the double doors, peering out the front. He looked back at Fred and gestured as if to say, "Where is he?"

Fred shook his head. How would he know? He went to call out but changed his mind. If McCarthy hadn't gone out the front, it must mean he was hiding in one of the stalls and the kid had run right past him. Ducking, Fred slipped into the first. He realized he was holding his breath and let it out.

Up at the front, Tyree shouted, "McCarthy! Quit bein' pigheaded. Give yourself up and you won't be hurt."

"Drop dead, boy."

Fred stiffened. McCarthy's shout came from a stall on the other side. Taking off his hat, he risked a peek and held his breath again when he spied McCarthy two stalls up, staring toward the front.

Fred debated what to do. If he was quick like the kid, he could rush McCarthy and maybe hit him over the head before McCarthy turned. But he wasn't quick. He was slow as could be. If he tried rushing him, McCarthy could put two or three slugs into him before he reached the stall.

Fred pointed his Smith & Wesson. It would be child's play to shoot McCarthy in the back. His finger tightened, but he couldn't bring himself to squeeze all the way. Back-shooting just wasn't in him. For that matter, shooting anyone wasn't in him. He drew back, bowed his head, and closed his eyes. What good was a lawman who couldn't shoot anybody? The answer was obvious. The lawman wasn't any good at all.

Fred had never felt so worthless. He almost decided to get out of there while he still could and let the kid handle things alone. But no. That wouldn't be right either. He was the one wearing a badge.

Opening his eyes, he stared at the Smith & Wesson. He wasn't a gun hand. He hardly ever practiced. That old saw about not being able to hit the broad side of a barn—that was him. He holstered it.

Fred knew what he had to do. His mouth went dry and he broke out in a sweat. It was plumb loco. But he couldn't see any other way. Jamming his hat back on, he took a deep breath and stepped into the aisle and over to the other stall.

McCarthy didn't hear him until he was almost on top of him. Wheeling on his heels, McCarthy pointed his Colt at Fred's head. "No, you don't! I will by God shoot you dead."

Chapter 4

Fred Hitch had never had a gun pointed at him before. Not this close. His whole body went numb. His mouth refused to work. He stared into the muzzle that would end his life and was paralyzed with fear.

"What do you think you're doing?" McCarthy said.

It broke the spell. Fred smiled and held out his hand. "I'll take that smoke wagon, if you don't mind."

McCarthy was incredulous. He glanced down at Fred's Smith & Wesson in its holster. "You damn fool."

"This has gone far enough. One of you might be hurt. Plus, there are the folks in town to think of. I'll have your gun, Hiram. Or, rather, Tom."

"Like hell you will," McCarthy said.

"What choices do you have?"

"How do you mean?"

The muzzle of McCarthy's Colt dipped, and Fred breathed a little easier. No, he wasn't a gun hand, but he could talk as good as anybody. People were always saying how he liked to talk and talk. He figured to use that instead of his revolver. "Let's say you get away. Where do you go? What do you do?"

"I go somewhere else and start over."

"Word will get out. The kid will go back to Cheyenne and tell whoever he's workin' for that you flew the coop. The marshal there will send out circulars. There'll be a lot of new interest in you. And who knows? Two thousand dollars is a lot of money. It could be the kid won't be the only one on your trail."

McCarthy scowled.

"You'd have to go clear to Alaska. Or, worse yet, maybe take a ship to some foreign country. Is that what you want?"

"No," McCarthy said grudgingly.

"Or let's say you fight it out with Tyree. The only way you'll stop that kid is to kill him, and then you'll have three murders on your hands. Could be more bounty will be added. You could find yourself worth more than Jesse James ever was."

"I doubt that," McCarthy said skeptically.

"The kid wants to take you alive. But from what I saw in the corral, he's a piss-poor shot. Maybe he'll only wound you. Or cripple you. All it takes is a piece of lead in the wrong spot and you'll have to use crutches for the rest of your days."

"Damn you," McCarthy said.

"I'm not done." Fred firmed his resolve. "I'm taking you into custody myself. You can shoot me, but add a lawman to your string and every tin star from here to Texas will be out to bury you. Wherever you go, you'll have to lie low. Changin' your name again might help for a while, but you won't be able to move about nearly as freely as you did here. Think about that a minute."

McCarthy lowered his revolver to his side and sighed. "All of this because I lost my head."

"We all do now and again," Fred said, although now that he thought about it, he couldn't recollect ever losing his so badly he'd strangle somebody.

"I loved her," McCarthy said. "I truly did. When I saw her with the friend I trusted most in this world, it was like a red-hot spike was driven through my head. I don't really remember much. When I came to my senses, I was standing there with the knife and the deed was done."

"How is it you talk so nice?" Fred asked.

"What?"

"I've always liked how you talk. You must be from back East somewhere. You never slur your words or mangle them like we do out West."

McCarthy looked bewildered. "I have the biggest decision of my life to make, and you bring that up?" A slight smile tugged at his mouth. "Fred Hitch, you're worthless, do you know that?"

"I try my best," Fred said.

Tom McCarthy stared at his six-shooter, then slowly held it out. "Here. Before I change my mind."

Fred took it and stepped back. "Kid!" he yelled. "It's over. There'll be no more shootin'."

"I'm right here," Tyree Johnson said, and glided out of the next stall. "I snuck up while you two were jawin'." He trained his Colts on McCarthy. "I'm plumb surprised he let you persuade him."

"Most folks aren't really bad at heart," Fred said. "Give them half a chance and they'll come around."

"Shows how much you know. There are bad men with hearts as hard as rock. They'll send you to hell as quick as look at you, and that's no lie. One day you'll trust the wrong person and he'll blow out your wick." To McCarthy he said, "On your feet. We'll hold you in the jail until I'm ready to head for Cheyenne."

Squatting there in despair, McCarthy looked up at the rafters and his throat bobbed. "I suppose I have it coming."

"I won't tell you twice," Tyree said.

Moving as slow as poured molasses, McCarthy stood and headed down the aisle, his posture that of a broken man.

"Poor fella," Fred said, keeping a few yards between them in case McCarthy changed his mind about giving up.

"I heard that crack about me bein' a bad shot," Tyree said.

"Well, you are. You shoot at a man and hit a horse, that's as poor as can be. Which reminds me," Fred said.

"I have to get word to the animal doc so he can tend to that horse. We're lucky to have one in a town this small. He does undertakin' on the side and makes fine coffins."

"For the animals too?"

"You can cut out the sass." Fred motioned at the boy's belt. "Are you any better with those derringers? Or are they just for decoration?"

"Ha," Tyree mimicked him from earlier.

"What about that bowie and your saber, of all things? You any good with them or do you hack away and hope you cut somethin'?"

"You can't miss with a bowie," Tyree said.

"You can if you don't know where the vitals are," Fred said. "Even I know that. Seems to me that for someone who hunts violent men for the bounty money, you're not much of a hunter."

"Keep insultin' me, you old goat."

Fred chuckled, and just like that, the tension drained out of him and he was his normal self again. For about half a block. Then people began coming out of their homes and businesses. Some of the men had rifles and shotguns. A lot of the women looked fearful. "It's all right, folks," he shouted to put them at ease. "Everything is under control."

"Oh, is it?" said a jowly man in a bowler who carried himself as if he were important.

"Mayor Crittendon," Fred said.

"What is going on here?" the mayor demanded. "Why is that ridiculous-looking child holding guns on Hiram?"

"I'll show you ridiculous," Tyree said.

"We should talk about it in my office," Fred suggested. Folks were pointing and murmuring and he didn't like being the center of attention.

"We'll discuss it here and now," Mayor Crittendon said. "Hiram is one of our leading citizens and I won't stand for him being mistreated."

"You should pick your citizens better," Tyree said.

"Your Hiram is a murderer twice over, and one of those he killed was a woman."

"The devil you say," Mayor Crittendon exclaimed, and grabbed McCarthy by the arm. "What is this non-sense? Tell me it's not true."

McCarthy bleakly nodded. "I'm afraid so, Horace."

"My word," the mayor said, and jerked back as if he were touching a snake. "And you contributed to my cam-paign."

"Go away," Tyree said. "We have to get him to the jail."

Mayor Crittendon sniffed. "Who are you to be telling me what to do? I'm the mayor of Sweetwater. What are you? You're certainly not a lawman, as young as you are. Why, you're barely out of diapers, yet you're a walking armory."

"Diapers, is it?" Tyree growled, and raised a Colt as if to bash the mayor on his bowler.

"Don't you dare," Fred said, moving between them. "I'll have to arrest you for assault."

Glaring at Crittendon, Tyree pushed McCarthy and they walked on, the people in the street parting to make way.

"Who *is* that boy?" Mayor Crittendon said.

Fred told him. About the bounty money, about the chase and the capture, finishing with "That reminds me. Can you find Sam and let him know one of the horses got shot?"

"How did that happen?"

"It stepped in the way of a bullet," Fred fibbed.

"Tell Sam yourself. I'm not your errand boy. I have important duties to attend to."

Fred should have known better. Their mayor never did anything he could get others to do for him. As for those "important duties," they generally consisted in the mayor indulging in frequent glasses of rum at the saloon with his constituents.

"Have you considered what will happen if word of this gets out?"

"I thought you had duties to do," Fred said.

"Answer the question."

Fred had been too busy trying not to be shot to consider much of anything. "Which word are you talkin' about? That we arrested a murderer?"

"Honestly, Hitch," Mayor Crittendon said in mild disgust. "Obviously it hasn't occurred to you that Sweetwater will become the laughingstock of the territory."

"What's to laugh at?" Fred asked in confusion.

"Do you mean *besides* the fact that we've had a notorious killer living among us and we had no idea?"

"How were we to know?" Fred said. "He didn't use his real name."

"Which you never caught on to. A good lawman would have. A good lawman would have sensed that something about Hiram was amiss and done some digging into his background."

Fred stopped and rounded on Crittendon. "Now, you just hold on. You're not layin' this on me. Hiram—I mean McCarthy—acted as decent as could be. He even had you fooled."

"Not really," Crittendon said. "I've long had my suspicions about him."

Fred almost bashed the mayor's bowler himself. "That's a lie. You and him were friends. He's been to your house many a time."

"I couldn't let him suspect that I suspected."

Fred bit off some cusswords. He'd forgotten how oily Crittendon could be, or most any politician, for that matter. They were forever scheming, forever manipulating. Their knack for talking out both ends of their mouths was a wonderment. "Claim what you want, but everyone knows better."

"We're getting off track," Crittendon said. "The issue isn't me. The issue is how to keep Sweetwater from being sullied by scandal."

"A good sullying might be good for us."

"Be serious. It's your civic duty to do all in your power to prevent that from happening."

"And how do you suggest I do that, exactly?" Fred demanded. "Not let anyone leave town from now until kingdom come?"

"Spare me your attempts at humor," Mayor Crittendon said. "I propose that we hold a town meeting and advise everyone to keep quiet about it. They're not to mention it in letters, or talk about it when strangers are in town."

"Make a mountain out of a molehill, why don't you?" Fred said.

"In my judgment you fail to appreciate the stigma this could bring down on our heads," Crittendon criticized. "In fact, your handling of this whole affair has been less than exemplary. You allowed that child to accost Hiram in his place of business. You let a revolver fight spill into our streets."

Fred was trying to remember what *accost* meant. He couldn't recollect ever hearing it before. "No one was hurt."

"You're forgetting the poor horse." Mayor Crittendon smoothed his jacket and ran a finger along his pencil-thin mustache. "No, Marshal Hitch. You have performed poorly all around. It wouldn't surprise me if the good people of Sweetwater regard you in a whole new light after this. There might even be talk of replacing you with someone more competent."

It took a lot to rile Fred, but he was riled now. Clenching a fist, he started to raise it so he could shake it in the mayor's face but caught himself in time. "Are you threatenin' me?"

"Perish the notion," Crittendon said. "I'm only offering my opinion on how events might develop."

"Two can play at that," Fred said.

The mayor smirked. "What can you possibly do?"

"I lose this badge," Fred said, tapping it, "I'll ride clear to Cheyenne and tell the *Cheyenne Leader* everything that happened. Care to bet they won't be interested? Care to bet the story isn't in their next edition?"

"You'd go to the newspaper?" Crittendon said in horror.

"I will if you don't leave it be. Let me handle this. That kid will likely leave in the mornin' and it will all be over."

Mayor Crittendon's face twitched a few times, as if he were about to have a fit. Instead he said, "Very well, Marshal Hitch. We'll do it your way. And may I say that I have underestimated you? I took you for a pushover, with no more spine than a bowl of pudding. But you've surprised me. You have more mettle than I'd imagined." Crittendon touched his bowler and walked off after the townsfolk, who had followed Tyree and McCarthy.

"Well, now," Fred said, and grinned. "Ain't I somethin'?"

Chapter 5

Everyone had left: the mayor, the townsfolk, even the kid. Except for Tom McCarthy, seated forlornly on the bunk in his cell, Marshal Hitch had his office to himself.

"Finally," Fred muttered as he bent to open the bottom desk drawer. He moved some papers, took out his silver flask, and opened it. A glance at the window showed no one was looking in. He raised the flask to his lips, swallowed happily, and sat back. The pleasant sensation that spread through his body made him smile. Propping his boots on the desk, he held the flask in his lap where no one could see it.

Fred was aware that there were whispers about his drinking. He liked his Monongahela, no doubt about that. He wasn't supposed to treat himself while he was working, but after the ordeal he'd just been through, he deserved a few nips.

McCarthy didn't notice. His face was in his hands, and his shoulders were slumped in misery.

Fred didn't blame him. The man was in for sheer hell. And all because he lost his head.

Taking another swallow, Fred coughed. One thing he could pride himself on was that he rarely lost his. He'd been that way since he was little. Other kids teased him and tried to make him mad, and it seldom worked. He had an easygoing nature, his mother used to say. *Too* easygoing, she'd often complained. He never let anything get to him. Not deep down the way most folks did.

Fred drank and sighed with contentment.

Chester, over at the stable, once asked him why he drank so much if it wasn't to dull whatever problems plagued him. The answer was simple. Fred *liked* to. For him liquor wasn't a crutch. It was an enjoyable pastime. Some people liked to read. Some knit. Some played checkers. He drank.

"How about letting me have a nip?"

Fred almost jumped.

"Just a couple of swallows," McCarthy said. "I could really use it."

Fred could see that. The man looked as forlorn as a human being could look. "Why not?" Rising, he went over and extended the flask between the bars. "So long as you don't tell your friend the mayor."

"Crittendon is a jackass."

"For that you can have an extra swallow," Fred said with a grin.

McCarthy took a tentative sip and grimaced. After a couple more, he passed the flask back. "I'm grateful."

"I'm sorry, Tom," Fred said. "I've always liked you."

"Same here. You're about the nicest lawman I ever ran across. You don't put on airs. You don't boss people around."

"My mother used to say that I was too nice for my own good," Fred revealed. "The mayor thinks the same. He called me a weak Nancy once when I refused to arrest a couple of cowpokes who broke a mirror at the saloon. I made them pay for the mirror and told them to go sober up, but that wasn't enough for him."

"You should have been a parson."

"To do that you have to be good at rememberin' things so you can quote the Bible in your sermons. I can barely recollect what I ate the day before."

McCarthy gave a slight smile. "You're all right, Hitch.

Don't let that jackass get to you. Go on being as you are. There aren't enough nice people in this world."

"I've always thought that," Fred agreed.

"If I had your disposition," McCarthy continued, "I wouldn't be standing here. I wouldn't have lost my temper when I caught my wife and my friend in our bed. I wouldn't have done what I did."

"Sometimes we can't help what we do. It just comes over us."

"What a damn decent thing to say," McCarthy said. "But there's no excusing what I did. It was wrong. Had I to do it over again . . ." He shrugged.

Fred tried to lighten his mood by saying, "I bet you never expected some boy to come after you."

"Not in a million years," McCarthy said. "If anything, I figured it would be a U.S. Marshal or a deputy from Cheyenne. I murdered two people, after all. It surprised me considerably that no one ever showed up until now."

"I wonder how the boy found you."

McCarthy gripped the bars and placed his forehead on them. "I believe I know. I made the mistake of writing a letter to my sister. Confided where I was and the name I was using, and told her I'd be happy as could be if she paid me a visit someday. The boy must have found out from her."

"Would she betray you like that?"

McCarthy grew thoughtful. "She was good friends with my wife. I thought we were closer, but it could be I was mistaken."

"Well . . . ," Fred began, and got no further. Boots clomped outside and the front door was flung open. He moved his arm behind his leg to hide the flask as he turned.

A man who worked at the general store was in the doorway, breathless from running. "Tully the bartender sent me," he said. "You have to come quick."

"What's going on?"

"It's that kid with all the hardware. He's threatening to shoot somebody."

"Go back and tell Sully I'll be right there."

The man nodded and ran off.

Going to his desk, Fred replaced the flask in the drawer. He hurried out and over to the saloon and heard the kid before he reached the batwings.

". . . by golly have one. And don't you call me no kid again, you peckerwood. I'm as much a man as you."

Fred pushed on in.

Tyree Johnson had both hands on the bar and was glaring at the bartender. "Give me a damn bottle."

"I will not," Tully said. He wore an apron and had skin that was the color of old parchment. "You're too young. I'm not supposed to serve young'uns."

"You'll serve me."

Fred advanced, saying, "What's going on here?"

"I want a drink and this cantankerous buzzard won't give me one," Tyree growled.

"The town council says I'm not to serve no kids," Sully said. "You know that, Fred."

"He's right," Fred said to Tyree.

"I'm not no kid," Tyree practically yelled. "And after the day I've had, I should be allowed. One measly drink is all I want."

Fred thought of his flask. "Give him one."

"You sure?" Tully said. "The mayor won't like it."

All the more reason, Fred almost said. "Give him one on my say-so. But only one and no more."

"I'm obliged, Marshal," Tyree said.

"How long have you been drinkin', boy?" Fred asked. He'd started sneaking drinks from the family cupboard when he was eight or nine.

"I hardly ever do," Tyree said. "I just wanted one today, is all." Leaning an elbow on the bar, he said, "How's my bounty money doing?"

"He's in misery."

"He should be, killin' his wife and his friend like he done. It would serve him right if they stretch his neck."

"You have a lot of bark on you for someone your age," Fred observed.

Tyree touched his scar and said, seemingly to himself, "I have cause to be."

Curious, Fred said, "How did you get that, if you don't' mind my askin'?"

"I don't rightly know."

"How can you not? That's one big scar."

"I don't need to be reminded, thank you very much," Tyree said resentfully. Tully placed a glass in front of him and he grabbed it, spilling a little as he raised it to his mouth.

"You're sure tetchy," Fred said.

"You would be too, were you me." Tyree moved toward a table, ignoring the stares of the other customers.

Fred went with him.

Hooking a chair with the toe of his boot, Tyree pulled it out and sat. "Why are you followin' me?"

"Thought we might talk some."

"You thought wrong."

Fred pulled out another chair anyway. "What else do you have to do? You're not leavin' until mornin', right?"

"About noon," Tyree said. "I aim to sleep in. Haven't had a wink in two days. Rode hard to get here so I can get back to Cheyenne that much sooner."

"What's your rush?"

Tyree didn't answer.

"You're a strange one, son," Fred said. He chose *son* instead of *boy* in order not to anger him.

"Don't ever call me that."

"See? Tetchy," Fred said.

"I'm no one's son. I lost my folks when I was in the cradle. Been on my own ever since."

"That explains a lot," Fred said, and changed the subject by asking, "Doesn't that saber poke you in the back when you sit in a chair?"

"It's in a scabbard."

"Why tote it around? What with those pistols and those derringers and that bowie, you hardly need it."

"It was my grandpa's," Tyree said, "or so I was told. The bowie was my pa's. The guns are just mine."

Fred began to see the kid in a new light; Tyree had a sentimental streak. "I have a watch that was my pa's."

"Good for you."

"You can quit bein' prickly," Fred said. "I'm the only friend you've got here."

"Is that what you are?" Tyree said. "It makes you the only friend I've got anywhere. Not that I need one."

Fred forgot himself and said, "A boy your age should have lots of friends."

"There you go with that boy business again."

"Sorry," Fred said. "Habit."

"I don't have time for friends," Tyree said. "I work every day. Sundays too. When most folks are in church, I'm huntin' wanted men down."

"Everybody needs a day off."

"Not me," Tyree said. "Not so long as they're out there, somewhere. I'll find them, sooner or later."

"Who?"

Instead of answering, Tyree nodded at the batwings. "Ain't that your mayor moseyin' on in?"

Fred shifted. Sure enough, Crittendon had entered and was coming toward them. The last thing he needed was another argument with His Majesty. "What can I do for you, Horace?"

Without being asked, Crittendon pulled out the last chair. "I've been looking for you. Stopped at the jail and tried to talk to Hiram. . . . Sorry, McCarthy . . . but he clammed up on me."

"And here you are," Fred said.

Crittendon smiled at Tyree. "How's our bounty man?"

"I'd tell you to go to hell, but you called me a man," Tyree said. "Most are too dumb to do that." He gave Fred a pointed stare.

"Anyone who does what you do, that's what he is, a man," Mayor Crittendon said.

"You hear that?" Tyree said to Fred.

"He's a politician. He always says what he thinks people want to hear," Fred enlightened him.

"No need for insults," the mayor said. He removed his bowler, placed it on the table, and ran his fingers through his stringy hair. "Now, then. I've been giving it some thought and I've come up with an idea."

"Givin' what some thought?" Fred asked.

"What were we discussing earlier? How Sweetwater will be a laughingstock when people hear about McCarthy pulling the wool over our eyes all this time."

"I doubt anyone will care," Fred said.

"*I* care," Crittendon said. "So does the council. We got together at my house and talked it over. That's when I had my inspiration."

"I can't wait to hear it."

Crittendon turned to Tyree. "If you don't mind my asking, when do you plan to leave with your prisoner?"

"Like I told your law dog, about noon or so. My horse can use the rest, and I'm tuckered out too."

"That's fine," Crittendon said. "It gives our marshal plenty of time to get ready."

Fred didn't like the sound of that. "For what?"

Mayor Crittendon bared his teeth like a cat about to devour a canary. "To go with him, of course."

Both Fred and Tyree said, "What?" at the same moment.

"We want you to go along, Marshal Hitch, to make sure McCarthy gets to Cheyenne to stand trial," Mayor Crittendon said. "It will show everyone we take our law here in Sweetwater seriously, and that if someone hoodwinks us, we do all in our power to see that justice is served."

To Fred it was preposterous. "Cheyenne is over three hundred miles."

"It's not the distance; it's the message we'll send to

lawbreakers," Crittendon said. "It's sure to be mentioned in the newspaper, and you're fond of newspapers, as I recall."

"Consarn you, Horace," Fred said.

"Refuse, and we'll remove you from office for dereliction of duty." Crittendon smiled and held out his hand. "And if that's the case, you might as well give me your badge here and now."

Fred was appalled. A journey to Cheyenne was no picnic. The country was rugged, and there were hostiles and outlaws and who knew what else? Without thinking he said, "I haven't been out of Sweetwater in years."

"Then the trip will do you good," Crittendon said, and laughed. "What do you say?"

What could Fred say except "Son of a bitch"?

Chapter 6

The wilds south of Sweetwater were as picturesque as they were dangerous. Browned by the heat of summer, the high grass of the valleys rippled in the wind.

Higher up, ranks of pines and scattered oaks covered ever steeper slopes. Near the summits, firs and aspens were common.

The region teemed with wildlife. Antelope bounded off in incredible leaps, deer sniffed and bolted. Elk stayed in the deep thickets except in early morning and at dusk, when they came out to graze. In the autumn, when the males were in rut, noisy battles were fought over harems a Turkish sultan would envy.

Or so Marshal Fred Hitch had heard. He wasn't keen on the outdoors himself. Give him his office and his flask and he was content. But now here he was, trailing behind Tom McCarthy and Tyree Johnson, on their way to Cheyenne.

Fred was fit to be tied. He disagreed with the mayor and the council. His going wouldn't prove a thing. It certainly wouldn't improve the town's reputation, no matter what Horace Crittendon claimed.

Fred suspected there was more to it. Crittendon was as shady a character as the year was long. Fred wouldn't put it past him to have concocted the feeble reason for him to go in the hope that he might never make it back. After all, Fred had threatened to go to the newspapers.

"If I make it back . . . ," Fred said, and imagined himself pistol-whipping Crittendon. But who was he kidding? "Damn me and my nice nature anyhow."

"What was that?" Tyree called from up ahead.

"I was talkin' to myself," Fred admitted.

"I hear tell that old folks do that a lot."

Fred pressed his lips together to keep from remarking about kids who were too big for their britches.

A pair of red hawks wheeled high on the air currents. The male uttered a piercing cry and the female answered.

Fred rubbed a kink in his neck. He wasn't one of those who admired animals on general principle. Some folks would look at those hawks and think how grand they were, soaring so nobly in the sky. All he saw were hawks.

Tom McCarthy sat his saddle like a man going to the gallows. He hadn't objected when the kid tied his wrists. The man seemed to have given up on life. He didn't care about anything.

Fred cared. About breathing anyway. And there were plenty of things in the wilds that could do them in.

Rumor had it some young Cheyennes or Arapahos were on the warpath. Fred couldn't recollect which. A few outlaw gangs plagued the territory too. And then there were grizzlies and buffalo and cougars and wolves, to say nothing of rattlers, which loved the hot weather.

Sweetwater wasn't three hours behind them, and Fred missed his office more than anything.

Unconsciously Fred placed his hand on his Smith & Wesson. Not that it would do him much good, as poor a shot as he was. A Winchester jutted from his saddle scabbard, but he wasn't much better with that. Guns never interested him much, not even when he was young. Whenever his friends wanted to go hunting, he'd always made excuses to bow out.

Fred's interest in the law didn't stem from any childish hankering for gunplay.

He liked helping folks, was all. Being a lawman was one of the few jobs he could do that let him lend a helping hand when an occasion called for it. He wasn't smart enough to be a doctor, and was squeamish about blood besides. And as he'd told the kid, his poor memory would make him a poor pastor.

Fred almost wished he was back East somewhere, where being a lawman was easier. There weren't any hostiles to worry about, and few outlaws. Gangs like the James brothers and the Youngers were few and far between. A lawman could live out his days without ever having to resort to violence. Fred liked that. He'd tried his best to do the same and until the kid showed up, had succeeded.

It was Tyree who called a halt when the sun perched on the western horizon, blazing the sky with vivid streaks.

Fred stripped his bay and gathered wood for the fire. Tyree got it going using a fire steel and flint like what the old trappers used. And it was Tyree who filled the coffeepot and put coffee on to brew.

"What do you plan to eat?" Fred asked. It had occurred to him that they hadn't brought a packhorse. He had some grub in a saddlebag, but it wouldn't last the whole trip.

"Tonight it will be beans," Tyree said. "Tomorrow maybe I'll shoot a rabbit or somethin' else."

"Beans will do," Fred said, although he wasn't all that fond of them. He had a cousin who could eat beans three meals a day for the rest of his life. Fred couldn't think of any food he liked that much. Well, except whiskey. But whiskey wasn't really a food.

McCarthy hadn't said a word since they left Sweetwater. He sat at the fire as he'd sat his horse, miserable as could be.

It upset Fred just looking at him. "How about you?" he said to draw McCarthy out of himself. "You ready for some beans?"

"He better be because that's what we're havin'," Tyree

said. He had a can of Brick Oven Baked Beans and was prying at it with an opener.

"You must be awful hungry," Fred said to McCarthy. The man hadn't eaten a thing at the jail.

McCarthy just sat there.

"Pay him no mind," Tyree said, working the opener. "I've seen this before. Some of them when they're caught stop eatin' and talkin' and pretty near everything else."

"They give up on life," Fred said.

"It's their own fault. I wouldn't be after them if they hadn't done somethin' stupid like your friend here."

"Haven't you ever done anything stupid?" Fred asked. "I know I have."

"I can't think of anything, no."

"How about shootin' that chestnut? I wouldn't call that an act of brilliance," Fred remarked.

"It was an accident. Accidents ain't stupid. They just happen." Tyree bent the lid and sniffed the beans. "What are some of the stupid things you've done?"

"Letting Crittendon talk me into this was the latest."

"He didn't give you much choice. I was surprised that you let him run roughshod over you. You're the marshal. You should have had more say in what you do or don't do."

"You'll find when you get older that there are a lot of things you have to do that you don't want to."

"Not me," Tyree said. "I live as I please. If I was the law and your mayor got uppity with me, I'd tell him to go to hell and I'd find me a job marshalin' somewhere else."

"I guess I like Sweetwater too much to risk havin' to give up my badge," Fred said.

"You like makin' excuses—that's for sure," Tyree said. "If you ask me, you could do with more gumption."

Fred was about to say that Tyree was a kid and what did kids know?—but the boy was right. He wasn't a coward, but he was short on grit when it came to standing up for himself.

"I learned younger than most that a body has to look out for himself because no one else will," Tyree said as he spooned the beans into a pot. "It's sink or swim and that's no lie."

"That's sort of harsh," Fred said.

"Did you have a ma and a pa growin' up?"

"Most do."

"Not me. No sisters, nor no brothers neither. No cousins or kin came to help me out. It was me and only me."

Fred tried to imagine what it must have been like to have no one to depend on. To be totally alone. "There must have been somebody. Who raised you?"

"I was in an orphanage until I was ten," Tyree said, stirring the beans. "You ever been to one?"

"Can't say as I have, no."

"Wretched places," Tyree said. "There's hardly ever enough food. The clothes are hand-me-downs, the blankets so thin, in the winter you shiver all night long. The man who ran the one I was at had a hickory stick he loved to use. Switched me once for not makin' my bed right. Thirty times, he hit me. I counted each and every one."

"My word."

"That's all right," Tyree said, and grinned at a memory. "I got back at him the night I snuck off. I stuck a cat in his room while he was sleepin'."

"A cat?"

"He was allergic, they call it. Put him near a cat and he couldn't hardly breathe. Once one got in the orphanage; we didn't see him for a week. The cook said he'd swelled up somethin' awful and kept chokin' and coughin'."

"You shouldn't have."

"When someone has made your life a livin' hell, you give him some hell back."

"What did you do once you were out?"

"I wound up in St. Louis and lived on the streets. Fell

in with some pickpockets. Got to where I could lift a purse without the person knowin' it was lifted. I was there about a year and a half when the police shot a couple of my friends. The police there take a dim view of those who help themselves to others' money."

"It's their job to protect folks."

"There you go again," Tyree said. "Anyway, I went to look for my pa's brother. He'd sent me a letter once at the orphanage. Just a couple of lines sayin' how sorry he was about my pa and my ma. He never came to see me, though. Would you believe he lived in a fancy house? And was well-to-do? I asked him right out why he didn't adopt me and he claimed it was because he'd never been married."

"It's usually married couples who adopt," Fred said. "I think it's a rule."

"If you ask me, he was makin' an excuse, like you do. But he dug out my pa's bowie and my grandpa's saber and gave them to me. Out of guilt, I suspect."

"Thank you for lettin' me know all this," Fred said. He felt he was beginning to understand the boy better.

"Don't know why I am," Tyree said. "Except there's nothin' else to do. I don't have cards or dice with me."

"I'm not a gamblin' man."

"I'm plumb shocked."

"So, how'd you start huntin' men for bounty money?"

"It was my uncle's doing. I told him I was lookin' for work and he took me to Mr. Benteen."

"Hold on," Fred said, doing the arithmetic in his head. "That would have been when you were twelve?"

"Slightly over. Mr. Benteen laughed at my uncle and me and said we were crazy, but my uncle asked him to give me a chance and Benteen owed him a favor." Tyree gestured at McCarthy. "And here I am."

"You ever think of doing somethin' else?"

"No."

"There are safer professions."

"The one I have is fine."

"You could clerk or cowboy or do any of a hundred things."

"No, I said," Tyree snapped. "This suits me down to my socks, and serves a purpose besides."

"Which is?"

"None of your damn business."

Fred pretended to be interested in the blossoming stars. The boy was fickle. Friendly one minute, not friendly the next. It promised to be a long ride if they couldn't get along better.

Off in the distance a coyote yipped.

"That reminds me," Tyree said. "We'd best be on our guard against wolves. I saw some fresh sign earlier."

"The only wolf attack in these parts I ever heard about was when they went after a rancher's bull once." Fred was convinced the bull initiated the ruckus when it attacked the wolves as they crossed the pasture where it was kept.

Tom McCarthy broke his long silence by looking up and saying, "You should be more worried about the Arapahos who left the reservation. They killed and scalped a man over in the Wind River country."

"You know that for a fact?" Fred said.

"Remember that cavalry patrol that passed through Sweetwater a week ago? A sergeant told me about it."

"Injuns don't worry me none," Tyree said.

"They should," Fred said. "We've taken their country from them and they resent it. Can't say as I blame them."

"Now you're excusin' killin' and scalpin' by a pack of redskins?" Tyree shook his head. "What will you do if you're jumped by a grizzly? Say you understand why it's eatin' you while it's eatin' you?"

"That's just silly," Fred said.

One of the horses nickered, and a few moments later all three were staring into the night with their ears pricked.

"Somethin' is out there." Tyree stated the obvious.

A deep, rumbling growl came out of the dark. Then, from a different spot, came another.

Fred leaped to his feet and yanked his Colt. Not that it would do much good. "You had to mention wolves, consarn you."

"I did, and here they come," Tyree said.

Chapter 7

The mere notion of a wolf pack hurtling out of the night at them sent a spike of cold down Marshal Hitch's spine.

Back when he was younger than Tyree, his father had made him go on a hunting trip. His first, and his last. He could barely hold the big rifle his father used, but his father insisted he try to down a deer. He hadn't wanted to. He liked deer. Deer came around their place a lot, and he'd liked how the young ones gamboled and frolicked.

Fortunately for him, or perhaps not so fortunately, their hunt had been brought to an early end by a grisly incident he'd never forget.

It involved a mountain man, one of the old breed who'd refused to change his ways when beaver hats went out of style. He lived alone high in the mountains, and one day he stepped out of his cabin to go to a nearby spring for water. A grizzly had had the same idea. It'd taken one look and charged. The mountain man had left his Hawken inside and tried to reach it, but the griz brought him down and set to eating him—while he was still alive.

The grizzly dined its full and wandered off.

Shortly after, one from their hunting party came upon the mountain man and hollered so as to bring the rest. When Fred and his father got there, a hunter was on his hands and knees, retching. The others looked sickly.

Fred's father had gone over, so Fred tagged along. It never occurred to any of the men to stop him. The next he knew, he was standing next to what was left of the mountain man.

The memory was seared into his brain.

Incredibly, the man had still been alive. How that could have been when most of the man's innards were missing was a mystery. The grizzly had eaten him out, leaving a blood-filled cavity. Not only that, but the bear had ripped off an arm and crushed a knee.

The horror of it had almost crushed Fred. Bile had risen in his throat and he came close to pitching to his hands and knees as the other hunter had. Somehow he'd stayed upright as the men talked about how terrible it was and one of them tried to get the mountain man to say whether there was anything they could do for him.

"I just want to die," the man had gurgled.

No one wanted to shoot him, though.

"It's a shame," Fred's father had remarked.

Another hunter said something that had stuck with Fred too. "This is what a wild animal can do to you. It's why we'll all be a lot better off when there are a lot fewer of them."

The men completely forgot about Fred until his father, taking a step away, bumped into him and exclaimed, "Oh my word. My son."

They whisked him off, but the harm had been done. To this day, the mention of a wild-animal attack caused his heart to leap into his throat.

Now, out in the dark, several shapes appeared, slung low to the ground. Three pairs of eyes glowed in the firelight like demons from the pit.

Tyree whipped out his Colts. "If they come any closer, I'll shoot."

"No," Fred said. "You'll only make them mad." A wounded animal was far more dangerous.

Tom McCarthy startled Fred by laughing and saying the strangest thing. "If they attack, I'll let them kill me."

The largest of the wolves slunk closer, its entire head appearing out of the dark, but not the body. It lent to the illusion the head was detached and floating in the air.

"One more step, you mangy beast," Tyree said. "My pistols will bring you down. You and your friends."

"Don't shoot," Fred said quietly. "They don't often attack unless they're given cause."

"If they do they might go for our horses."

There was that possibility, Fred admitted. And their horses were picketed and would be easy prey.

"Simpletons," McCarthy said. "I am being taken to my execution by simpletons."

"What do you know?" Tyree said.

"This," McCarthy said, and stood. Waving his bound arms, he hollered at the top of his lungs, "Go bother someone else, damn you! Scat! You hear me? Leave us be!"

Fred braced for a charge.

With a loud growl, the large wolf pawed the ground, then wheeled and loped away, its long tail trailing. The other wolves did likewise, vanishing like four-legged ghosts, with no more sound than real spirits.

"See?" McCarthy said, sitting back down. "That's all it took."

"You had no way of knowin' that would work," Tyree said. "You could have gotten us killed."

"I'm going to die anyway," McCarthy said. Closing his eyes, he lapsed into the same sorrowful state as before.

Tyree shoved his Colts into his holsters, hunkered, and picked up the big spoon he stirred with. "If you don't want to tag along, you don't have to."

Still staring after the wolves, Fred said, "Are you talkin' to me?"

"He's right about one of us bein' a simpleton. You have no business bein' here." Tyree stirred, took a taste, and said, "Sometimes they heat up slow."

Fred moved to where he could sit and watch the direction the wolves had gone. They might decide to come back. "What was that about me not taggin' along?"

"Ain't it plain? You don't want to go to Cheyenne. You reckon it's a waste of your time. So why bother?"

"The mayor and the council want me to."

"Who says you have to go all the way? Stay here. Camp out. Or go to a friend's and stay with them for a couple of weeks. Then report back that you helped me deliver McCarthy."

Fred became suspicious of the youngster's motive. "Why are you tryin' to get rid of me all of a sudden?"

"I'm tryin' to do you a favor."

"Well, that's decent of you, but I'd better see this through," Fred said. He added, "As much as I don't want to."

"See? You shouldn't let those others boss you around. Are you the marshal or a sissy boy?"

"Now, see here," Fred said.

Tyree busied himself with the beans. He would stir and taste and wait, then stir and taste and wait some more.

Fred was content to hold his hands to the fire and warm himself. He couldn't remember the last time he had spent a night outdoors. It might have been that elk hunt in the mountains. He never went hunting after that. His father was disappointed. He said Fred was breaking the family tradition. Fred's father hunted and his father before him and his father before him. "And now there's you," his father had said, crestfallen.

Fred refused to change his mind. Shooting an animal never appealed to him. Oh, he'd do it if the critter was trying to tear him to pieces or eat him. But otherwise, it was let bygones be bygones, whether two-legged or four.

A shooting star blazed the heavens. Fred watched for more, but there were none. When he looked at the boy to see if the beans were ready, the boy was looking at him.

"What?"

"Why are you so nice to folks? I saw how you were in town. You had good cause to be mean, but you weren't.

You were always nice. I figured maybe you were yellow, but you didn't spook when those wolves paid us a visit."

"I was plenty spooked inside me," Fred assured him.

"You're a puzzlement," Tyree said.

Fred decided to enlighten him. "It's not in my nature to be mean to folks. Oh, I can get mad now and then. But usually I do to others as I'd like them to do to me."

"Where'd you pick up a peculiar notion like that?"

"It's in the Bible."

"Ain't that the one that says we shouldn't kill?"

"It is."

Tyree snorted. "Whoever wrote it never lived west of the Mississippi."

The baked beans were finally hot enough to suit him. The boy spooned some out for each of them and sat eating his slowly, chewing each mouthful so long Fred thought it was comical. As for him, he practically gulped his food. Baked beans had never tasted so good. He attributed that fact to going most of the day without food or drink. Which he would remedy later.

McCarthy barely touched his meal. He'd fallen back into his deep depression. Fred mentioned that he needed to keep his strength up, and McCarthy replied, "Whatever for?"

After their meal they turned in. It was sort of pleasant for Fred, lying there with his blanket to his chin, the stars sparkling overhead and the creatures of the night serenading the stars with their cries and hoots and howls.

Fred waited until he was sure Tyree and McCarthy were asleep before he slipped his flask from his saddlebags. He'd brought two full bottles besides. He could go without his comforts if he had to but not without his Monongahela. Taking a sip, he smiled and said, "Ahhh."

Life was good, for the moment. But he mustn't fool himself into thinking this was how it would be the whole way. The wilderness was treacherous. About the time a man let down his guard, he'd find himself in peril for his life.

Folks were always saying that was bound to change. A new century was a decade off. The railroad was spreading over the West, making travel safer. New inventions were making life easier. Not long ago the newspaper crowed about how Cheyenne had electric lights and then prattled on about how one day everyone would have electric lights in their homes, as well as other marvels.

It sounded too good to be true, and Fred had learned long ago that usually meant it was. All those marvels wouldn't come free. People would have to earn more to keep up, meaning they'd have to work longer hours, which to Fred's way of thinking put them in thrall to their purse. Money became their master, and he disliked having anyone or anything lord it over him.

Listen to me, Fred reflected with a wry grin. *Thinking I'm halfway smart.*

His grandpa had always said a man should know his limits, and Fred knew his. His mind worked slower than some. He often had to chew on an idea like a dog worrying a bone before he could make up his mind what to do.

He liked his life to be easy and would do whatever he had to in order to make it stay that way. Sometimes he compared himself to a prairie dog that liked to lie at the entrance to its den and watch the world go by, wanting no part of it.

Fred chuckled and drank. The kid would brand him as silly, but he didn't care. He was what he was.

The kid. Fred glanced over at Tyree Johnson, who let out little snores. Now, there was someone who hadn't had it easy. His parents murdered when he was an infant. Raised in a hellhole of an orphanage. And here he was, making his living by going after hard cases who were as likely to do him in as agree to be taken back to face justice.

No, sir, that kind of life wasn't for Fred.

He felt sorry for Tyree. From the sound of things, the boy never had anyone treat him halfway decent. That uncle had proven next to worthless. Tyree needed someone to take him under a wing and show him that life wasn't always as cruel as Tyree's had been. Show him there was goodness in the world if a person looked for it.

One of Fred's few regrets was that he'd never had any kids of his own. But to have kids you needed a wife, and Fred was about as attractive to the opposite sex as, say, sour milk. He'd tried a few times in his younger days to strike up an acquaintance with females, but they never showed any interest. One lady told him flat out that he bored her. That his conversation was dull. That he'd never amount to much because he had no ambition. She was the last one he tried to woo.

He didn't need the humiliation.

But Fred would have liked a kid. A boy more than a girl. He was so bad at getting along with females that he'd probably be bad at raising a daughter. But a boy, now. He'd been one once, so he should be able to raise one.

McCarthy put an end to Fred's musing by rolling over and muttering in his sleep, something about stabbing someone.

There was another sad case. A moment of rage, and his life was forever changed.

Yet another reason Fred was glad he was so even-tempered. Rage never got a man anywhere except the gallows.

Fred's eyelids were growing heavy. Capping his flask, he replaced it in the saddlebag and made himself comfortable. Gradually he felt himself slipping into welcome slumber.

Then a scream pierced the wilds, far off, a shriek of pure terror.

Fred sat bolt upright. His skin prickling, he glanced at the others, but neither had heard it. He was sure it was a human who screamed and not an animal.

He waited in tense expectation for the scream to be repeated, but the night had gone deathly quiet. The scream had silenced the other cries. Even the animals knew death when they heard it.

Uneasy, Fred settled back down. He held the blanket close and sought to drift off, but his nerves were on edge. When a horse thumped a hoof he sat up again, but it was nothing.

"Damn Crittendon anyhow."

He shouldn't cuss, Fred told himself. It was one habit he hadn't gotten into, largely because of his mother. She'd washed his mouth out with soap more than a few times to discourage him. That, and her observation that folks cussed because they were immature.

Tyree cursed a lot, Fred had noticed. He'd like to break him of it, but the boy wasn't his responsibility. They'd only be together as far as Cheyenne and then they'd get on with their individual lives. Which suited Fred fine. He could get back to his marshaling and his office and the peace and quiet he loved.

Now if only he could get to sleep.

Chapter 8

Two days went by. Two days of long hours in the saddle and baked beans for supper. The steep slopes and heavy timber made for slow going.

Midway through the next morning, they descended a ridge and came on a stream. Tyree called a halt to let their horses rest.

Fred liked that the boy was considerate toward his animal. It showed Tyree wasn't as heartless as he pretended to be.

Dismounting, Fred put a hand on the small of his back. He was sore from all the riding. Once this trip was over, if he never sat a horse again, it would be fine by him. He led his bay to a spot where the bank leveled off. He was about to step down but drew up short.

There were footprints in the soft earth at the water's edge.

"Look at these," Fred said.

Tyree came over and squatted. He traced the outline of a print with a finger, and scowled. "Injuns."

"You're sure?" Fred wasn't much of a tracker. And these prints didn't show much detail.

"Do you see a heel mark?" Tyree said. "No, you don't. The soles are flat, and that means redskins."

Putting his hand on his Colt, Fred scanned the shadowed forest.

"Relax," Tyree said. "These were made a day or so ago or better. The Injuns are long gone by now."

"You hope," Fred said.

"You're one of those pessimists, aren't you?" Tyree said.

"No."

"Like hell you're not. A fella told me about them once. He said that pessimists always look at the bad side of things. They always expect the worst. I kind of like that word, so it stuck in my head."

"I like to think of myself as practical."

"You're somethin'," Tyree said, and grinned.

Tom McCarthy had knelt to cup a hand in the stream. He hadn't spoken since the other night, but now he laughed and said, "So it's Indians now? That figures. Life is out to get me."

"How?" Fred absently asked.

"The way my luck is going, these Indians will turn out to be hostiles," McCarthy said. "A tomahawk is as good as a rope, after all."

"It could be a huntin' party of tame ones," Tyree said.

"You know better," McCarthy said. "We keep going, we're bound to run into them. Mark my words, boy."

Fred worried that McCarthy was right. The whole rest of the day he was a bundle of nerves.

A small valley offered haven for the night. They camped in a grove of oaks. Tyree got a fire going and put on the inevitable beans.

Fred stripped their horses and picketed them. He looked forward to a quiet meal and a good night's sleep. Dusk was falling, the shadows lengthening, and as he turned to go to the fire he spotted an orange glow at the other end of the valley. "Look yonder," he exclaimed in alarm.

Tyree was busy spooning beans. "At what?"

"Another fire."

The boy came over. "I'll be damned," he said. "You have good eyes. They're in some pines, it appears."

"Who?" Fred said.

They looked at each other.

"We have to find out," Tyree said. "One of us had to go have a look-see. Since I have to stay with McCarthy, you're elected."

The last thing Fred wanted was to go sneaking around in the dark. "I can stay with him."

"He's my prisoner, not yours. Go slow and you should be fine. It could be white men for all we know."

"Sure," Fred said, but he didn't believe it and neither, he suspected, did the boy.

Tyree moved to their fire and began stamping it out. "If we can see theirs, maybe they can see ours."

Taking his Winchester from the saddle scabbard, Fred licked his dry lips and headed out.

"Don't get killed," Tyree said.

Fred could have done without the warning. At the edge of the oaks he hunkered and went on doubled over. The grass wasn't high enough to hide him, but in the growing darkness he'd be hard to see. Rather than go straight across, he made for the woods bordering the valley floor. Once in the trees, he wasn't quite so tense.

Stars were out, but they did little to relieve the mantle of black. Fred kept bumping into things. A bush here, a tree there, a boulder now and again. He took to groping with a hand to feel his way.

It took forever to reach the other end of the valley.

Fred lost sight of the fire. Whoever they were, they were well hid. It was pure luck he'd spotted it the first time.

An open space of twenty feet or so separated the stand of pines from the forest proper. Fred hesitated, then sucked in a breath and darted across. He was enormously pleased when nothing happened.

The scent of the pines in his nostrils, Fred crept forward, a human snail. The slightest sound might give him away. He heard muffled voices. A little farther, and it was obvious they weren't speaking English.

Flattening, Fred crawled. When he came to a log he removed his hat and rose high enough to peer over. Apprehension flooded through him.

The fire was small. A rabbit was on a spit, being roasted. In a circle around it were seven young warriors, their faces painted for war. Most wore buckskins and a few had feathers in their hair. Beyond the fire were their mounts.

It was their faces that filled Fred with fear. Their faces had paint on them. He was looking at an Arapaho war party.

Fred had never been this close to hostiles. If they spotted him, he was as good as dead. But they were at least sixty feet away and intent on whatever they were talking about.

He noted how young they were. Not much older than Tyree. Yet here they were, hunting for whites to kill.

Fred looked for guns. They had knives and tomahawks and bows and one had a lance. Not a single firearm, which was small comfort. From what Fred had heard, a skilled warrior could unleash four or five arrows as quick as thought and hit what he aimed at.

He debated what to do. He had his Winchester and his Colt, more than enough bullets to drop them where they were, provided he didn't miss a single shot. Which was about as likely as him walking on water.

Fred started to lower his head, and froze.

One of their horses was staring right at the log.

Fred's mouth went dry. The animal must have seen him. He dreaded it would whinny and give him away.

A warrior with stripes on his face reached behind him and held up something for the others to admire.

It was a fresh scalp, the flesh the hair was attached to still pink.

Fred remembered the scream from a few nights ago, and shivered. He yearned to get out of there, but the horse hadn't stopped staring. He held himself still, refusing to even blink. The young warriors were passing the scalp around and fingering it as a trapper might a prime pelt.

Without warning a warrior rose and came toward the trees. He was armed with a bow. Exceptionally long whangs hung from his buckskins and swayed with every stride. Like the others', his hair had been parted in the middle and hung in long braids on either side of his head, down past his shoulders.

Fred braced for the worst. He figured the warrior had seen him and was coming to investigate. But no. The man came to a stop about ten feet away and hitched his long shirt up.

Fred didn't look. That sort of thing should be done in private.

The horse had lost interest and was nipping at grass.

Fred got out of there. Jamming his hat on, he crawled until he was clear of the pines, then rose and started up the valley. He wasn't worried about being seen. The night was so dark he could barely make out his hand at arm's length.

A twig crunched under Fred's foot, and he stopped. Indians had keen ears. But a minute went by and then another, and there was no outcry.

Figuring he must have been born under a lucky star, Fred continued on.

He looked back often, but the warriors weren't following.

He made so much noise that Tyree was on his feet with a revolver cocked when he got to their camp.

"Well?" the boy asked. "Friendly or not."

"Not," Fred said. "Unless you call liftin' scalps the height of brotherhood."

"No redskin will ever lift mine," Tyree said. "I'll blow my brains out first."

"Let's hope it doesn't come to that. I'm fond of what few brains I have, and don't care to be parted from them."

McCarthy didn't show any interest whatsoever. He had made a teepee of his hands and was resting his chin on them.

"How many?" Tyree wanted to know.

Fred told him.

"That's all?" Tyree grinned. "Between your pistol and my pair, we can fill them full of lead before they can so much as blink."

"I doubt that very much," Fred said. "I can't shoot that fast and I doubt you can either."

"What would you do?"

"Sneak off while we can."

"Turn tail?" Tyree shook his head. "I've never shown yellow my whole life. We'll cat-foot on over there and blow them to Hades."

"Count me out." Fred wouldn't push his luck a second time. "We should go up the mountain and lie low until they move on.

"I can't do it by my lonesome," Tyree said. "Not one against seven, I can't."

"Then quit your foolish talk of wipin' them out and come with me. Or have you forgot that horse you shot?"

"Why do you keep bringin' that—" Tyree began, and stopped. "Hell in a basket. Where did he get to?"

Tom McCarthy was gone.

"Weren't you watchin' him?" Fred said.

"He was right there a minute ago." Tyree commenced to rove in a circle. "He can't have gotten far."

"Maybe he's answerin' nature's call," Fred said.

"With those hostiles nearby?"

Fred failed to see how the Arapahos would keep a man from his bodily functions, but he kept quiet about it and moved in the other direction. "He has to be here somewhere."

"Unless he skedaddled."

"Without his horse?" Fred said. No one in their right mind would risk being stranded afoot in the wilds. Unless they were well armed and could live off the land, it was the same as a death sentence.

"McCarthy!" Tyree whispered. "Where in hell are you?"

"Tom?" Fred whispered. "Say something."

The silence mocked them.

Fred didn't know what made him turn and gaze off toward the other end of the valley. Maybe it was a hunch. Maybe it was instinct. He glimpsed a short figure moving into the grass, and bleated, "No."

"What?" Tyree said.

"He's headin' for the Injuns," Fred said, and ran in pursuit. What McCarthy hoped to accomplish was a mystery. With his wrists bound and no weapons, McCarthy couldn't defend himself. He'd be taken alive and tortured, and whatever was left of him left for the vultures.

"He won't get far," Tyree said, jogging at Fred's side.

McCarthy showed no sign of stopping and was almost out of sight. He didn't respond when Fred whispered his name.

Fred increased his pace.

"Faster or we'll lose him," Tyree urged.

Fred was doing the best he could. All that sitting at a desk had turned what few muscles he had to mush. His legs weren't half as strong as they used to be, and his stamina was laughable. But he kept running.

Tom McCarthy disappeared. One moment his silhouette was vaguely visible, and the next he wasn't there.

Fred stopped in case it was some kind of trick.

Tyree stopped too and looked at him. "What are you stoppin' for? Is somethin' the matter?"

Fred pointed at the empty air where McCarthy had been, and squatted. "He's gone to ground. Maybe he aims to jump us."

Hunkering beside him, Tyree said, "If this don't beat all. Him comin' out here, where those Injuns are likely to spot him. If he's not careful, he won't have to worry about bein' hanged."

Insight washed over Fred like a rain shower of cold water. "That's it! It must be. You've hit the nail on the head."

"I have?"

"You saw how McCarthy has been. He's given up on life. He doesn't care what happens to him. But hangin' is an awful, horrible way to die, so he's chosen another he thinks is better."

"You're sayin' he wants those hostiles to kill him?" Tyree said in amazement. "The damn jackass. They might carve on him before they do him in, and that's worse than just havin' his neck stretched."

"That's not the worst of it," Fred said. "If he goes waltzin' into their camp, they'll know there must be other white men around and come lookin' for us."

"Oh, hell," Tyree said.

Chapter 9

Marshal Fred Hitch and Tyree Johnson flew to overtake Tom McCarthy before he reached the pines. They had covered almost the entire distance before Tyree pointed and exclaimed between puffs of breath, "There!"

Fred tried to fun faster, but his body refused. He kept forgetting he was fifty years old.

Tyree pulled ahead. The boy had some extra steam in his engine and poured it on in a desperate attempt to stop their prisoner.

As for Tom McCarthy, he was moving woodenly, his gaze on the pines. He must have heard them coming up behind him, but he didn't turn.

Fred was worried about the Arapahos hearing. Much closer, and they would. He was under no illusions about the result. Two against seven was no better than one against seven when he was one of the two.

Tyree was really flying. His saber was smacking his back and that bowie flapped about his neck, but neither slowed him. He launched himself into the air, his arms spread wide, and slammed into McCarthy low in the back. Both of them went down in a jumble. Fortunately McCarthy didn't cry out. Before either could gain their feet, Fred was there. He grabbed one of McCarthy's arms while clamping a hand over his mouth, and together Tyree and he hauled McCarthy up and spirited him away.

McCarthy didn't resist. He didn't try to shout or make any noise whatsoever. He was limp and dazed and had lost all spirit.

"You damn fool," Tyree hissed in his ear. "You almost got us killed."

Fred watched the pines, but no warriors appeared. He had never been so relieved in his life.

"We're not stickin' around," Tyree said after they had gone more than half the way. "We'll walk our horses until we're far enough to be safe."

As tired as Fred was, he didn't object.

"As for you," Tyree said, giving McCarthy a shake, "I'm going to tie your legs too from here on out. You're not walkin' off on me again." He looked at Fred. "This is what I get for going easy on him on your account."

"Mine?"

"Usually I truss them up so they can't hardly twitch, but I didn't with him because you were along and I figured you'd raise a fuss, you bein' so nice and all."

"That was considerate of you," Fred said.

"It was stupid. I've never been considerate of anyone before. Why should I start with you?"

"It's never wrong to try to do right by people," Fred said.

"It is if it gets you killed."

Fred had no rebuttal to that. He concentrated on his breathing. His lungs were straining from his exertions.

"This is the last time I let a law dog accompany me." Tyree wouldn't let it drop. "I should have told that mayor of yours to go to hell. Him and his bossy ways. If you make it back to that two-bit town, punch him in the mouth for me."

"That would be a first," Fred said. "I've never hit anybody."

"How can that be? What kind of lawman are you?"

"The kind who likes to resolves spats peacefully," Fred said. "The kind who doesn't like violence."

"Damn, you're peculiar. It's a good thing you tote tin

in a town like Sweetwater. In Cheyenne or Denver you wouldn't last six months."

Fred considered that an exaggeration but held his peace.

Tyree had more to say. "If there's one thing I've learned, it's that you have to be hard to get ahead in life. You go too easy and others will eat you alive."

"That's not true," Fred spoke up. "Look at me. I've been the law in Sweetwater for a long time and never had to draw my pistol. People aren't as vicious as you make them out to be."

"Some are. You've just been lucky you ain't met any yet except that mayor of yours."

"Horace Crittendon isn't vicious," Fred scoffed.

"Oh? He sent you along, didn't he? Probably hopin' somethin' would happen to you and you wouldn't make it back. If that's not vicious, I don't know what is."

Since Fred had harbored the same suspicion, he couldn't very well disagree.

"There are different kinds of vicious. Some use their fists or a gun. Some, like your mayor, use their wits and words. You ought to know that, a man with as many gray hairs as you have."

"How did you become so wise?" Fred asked, partly in jest.

Tyree took him seriously. "When you're on your own, you learn fast. You have to, or folks take advantage of you. That orphanage taught me it's everybody for himself, and everyone else be damned."

Fred was appalled. The boy's outlook on life was terrible. "A man should stand on his own two feet, yes, but he doesn't have to be ugly about it."

"Ugly?" Tyree said, and gave a little laugh.

"You know what I mean. He doesn't have to be meantempered all the time. He doesn't have to cuss. He can show some respect for others, and offer a helpin' hand when one is needed."

"Is that your, what do they call it, philosophy on life?"

"I suppose it is," Fred said. He'd never really thought about it before.

"Sad," Tyree said.

On that note they fell silent until they were at their camp. Tyree was true to his word and bound McCarthy's ankles. McCarthy just lay there and let him. Fred had to help get McCarthy belly-down over his saddle. Then they were under way, Tyree leading McCarthy's mount as well as his own.

Fred had never been so tired. He couldn't stop yawning and wished he was under his blankets. He thought about what the boy had said about him being too nice for his own good, and he refused to accept that. If everybody went through life with Tyree's attitude, the world would be an awful place. It would be dog-eat-dog, with the weakest always suffering. No one with a sense of right and wrong could abide that.

Pretty soon he had to forget about the problem of being too nice and focus on climbing. Here in the timber it was black as pitch. He was forever stumbling. His horse moved quieter than he did. Once he ran into a low limb that gouged his cheek. Later he tripped and fell to a knee, hitting it on a rock. He had to clamp his jaw to keep from crying out.

Tyree did better. He made a lot less noise. Twice he told Fred to pick up the pace, that he didn't want to be at it all night.

They reached the crest of a ridge and started down the other side.

Fred's legs were ready to give out. He moved as woodenly as McCarthy had done. His attention perked when he heard a grunt that he was sure was a bear. Either Tyree didn't hear it or he didn't care, because he continued on. Fred envisioned a grizzly rushing out at them, which lent his legs new energy.

At long last they came to a shelf and Tyree stopped. "Here will do. There's grass for the animals."

"Thank the Lord," Fred said.

"We'll leave the saddles on in case we have to get away quick."

That was fine by Fred. He helped the boy with McCarthy, then untied his bedroll and turned in. He half expected to lie there awhile, too overwrought to sleep, but he was out practically the moment he closed his eyes. He slept so soundly that he was slow to rouse when someone began shaking him.

"Wake up, consarn you. The sun is up and the day is wastin'."

Blinking in the sunlight, Fred rose sluggishly and went through the motions of putting his bedroll on the bay. "I could use some coffee." A pot or two, at least.

"Not this close to that valley," Tyree said. "The wind is blowin' their way, and the smell would bring them lickety-split."

"You think of everything, don't you?"

"I try."

Fred was amazed by the youth's confidence. At that age, he hadn't had half as much. He was almost twenty before he mustered enough to fulfill his dream of helping people by becoming a law officer.

They got under way.

Fred was stiff and sore in places he couldn't recollect ever being sore before. He was hungry and thirsty, but Tyree refused to eat until they had put more distance between them and the war party.

A couple of hours of hard travel brought them within sight of a broad vista of lowland that swept to the south for as far as the eye could see.

"Finally the prairie," Tyree said. "Ranchin' country. We can make good time from here on out."

Fred was all for that. "I'd like to stop and eat once we're in the open."

"In the middle of the day?"

"I'm not as young as you," Fred said. "My body isn't as durable. I go without food, I can't function."

"Old people sure are a nuisance. Can't it wait until

suppertime? Eat some jerky if you have to. I have plenty."

McCarthy, who hadn't uttered a peep since they caught him, stared fixedly at the grassland. "Cheyenne," he said.

"Is a ways off yet," Tyree said. "We're not halfway there."

"Cheyenne," McCarthy said again.

"What about it? They'll throw you behind bars and put you on trial and that will be that."

"Cheyenne."

Tyree shifted in his saddle. "What's the matter with him, law dog? Why's he keep sayin' that?"

"His mind is going," Fred suspected.

"I never had one like him before," Tyree said. "Usually they're mad at bein' caught and stay mad until I turn 'em over. Now and then a weak sister will cry, and I always laugh at that."

"You would cry too if you were in their boots."

"Not in a million years. I'd blow out my own wick if I was that worthless."

"Everyone feels miserable now and then."

"So what? They don't have to blubber about it. You and your excuses. There's no end to them."

Fred figured his companion was indulging in more posturing. "You don't have to act tough all the time."

"Says the gent who's never hit anyone or shot anyone."

By noon the last of the timber was behind them. To Fred's delight, Tyree only went a short distance onto the plain and announced they'd rest their horses for half an hour or so. Gratefully climbing down, he stepped over to McCarthy. "Give me a hand. He must be in pain from bein' on his belly so long."

"Serves him right for his stunt last night."

"Please," Fred said. "I'm askin' you."

Tyree sighed. "You try a person's patience, do you know that? But if it will keep you from pesterin' me . . ."

McCarthy was a limp sack. He stirred as they set him on his back, and gazed to the south. "Cheyenne," he said.

Stepping back, Tyree shook his head. "I'm stuck with a do-good and a crazy man. Days like this, I wonder why I do this."

"Why do you?" Fred asked.

Tyree looked as if he were sucking on a lemon. "None of your business. And don't bring it up again."

"We've been saddle pals for days now. I should think you'd be friendlier," Fred remarked.

"You thought wrong."

Tyree moved off to be by himself, leaving Fred to guard their prisoner. All the riding they'd been doing, Fred didn't care to sit. He walked in a circle, flexing his legs and wishing he were anywhere but there.

"Cheyenne," McCarthy said.

"I heard you the first four times," Fred said.

"It's not every day a man knows when and where he will meet his Maker," McCarthy said quietly.

Fred glanced down. Some measure of sanity had returned to McCarthy's eyes. "You're back among us."

"I never left."

"You could have fooled me."

McCarthy actually grinned. "The shock caught up to me."

"After all this time?"

"Before it was like a nightmare. It didn't seem real. Now it does, and the shock was almost more than I can bear. I don't want to die, Marshal. I would have been happy to live out my days in Sweetwater."

"Can't blame you there," Fred said. "I'm fond of the town myself." Fond of the people. Fond of the slow pace of life. Fond of just about everything.

"I've always liked you, Fred. It's a shame you have to be a party to this. I'd hate for any harm to come to you on my account."

"And I've always liked you. If you want, I'll be a character witness at your trial," Fred offered.

McCarthy stared out across the prairie. He coughed lightly a few times and said, "That kid is wrong. About life and about you. You're a decent human being. Don't pay him no mind from here on out."

"I want to help him. He can amount to something if he lives long enough."

"You want to help everybody." McCarthy turned his head toward the mountains and his smile faded. "Just when I was almost my old self again."

"I beg your pardon?"

"Maybe I was wrong. Maybe I won't die in Cheyenne. Maybe it will be sooner."

McCarthy bobbed his chin.

Fred turned, and his blood stopped pumping.

High up on the last mountain, silhouetted against the blue sky, were seven riders in buckskins—the Arapaho war party.

Chapter 10

They rode and they rode, at a trot for a while and then slower to give their animals a breather, and then at a trot again. Racing for their lives across an undulating sea of grass while behind them seven specks stayed glued on their dust.

Marshal Fred Hitch had a hunch the warriors were matching their pace, never falling behind, never gaining. Eventually his bay and the other horses would succumb to exhaustion and the war party would close in.

Tyree did a lot of swearing. Every time he looked back, he cursed. He was setting their pace and now he slowed yet again and patted his lathered mount. "You're doing fine, fella."

On his belly over his saddle, Tom McCarthy flopped and jounced, yet not once did he complain. He looked back now and then too, and each time he laughed.

Now, as Fred slowed the bay to a plodding walk, he asked, "What do you find so funny?"

"Life," McCarthy said.

"Loco bastard," Tyree muttered.

"Don't you see it? Either of you?" McCarthy glanced at the war party and laughed some more. "There I was, petrified at the notion of being hanged, and all that worry was for nothing. My end won't be a strangulation jig at the end of a hemp noose. It will be an arrow through my neck or a lance through my chest or a tomahawk will cut deep, and then I'll have my hair lifted."

"You call that an improvement over hangin'?" Tyree said.

"You're missing the point, youngster."

"Don't call me that."

"My point is that all my fretting was pointless. I might as well have spared myself the misery."

"We'll have plenty of that if those redskins catch up to us."

"Maybe not," Fred said. He had been doing a lot of thinking as they rode and he had come to a decision. He might not be a scrapper like the kid, but he refused to have his wick snuffed without putting up a fight.

"Are you going to ask those redskins, pretty please, to spare us?" Tyree joked. "Good luck with that."

"No," Fred said, "I propose we make a stand."

"Where'd this sudden gumption come from?"

"Hear me out," Fred said. "We find a spot we can defend. All three of us, not just you and me. That'll even the odds some."

"You want me to cut my prisoner loose and give him a gun?"

"The more guns, the better. We're none of us marksmen. You proved that when you shot that horse."

"Aren't you ever going to forget that?" Tyree regarded McCarthy, while gnawing on his bottom lip. "I don't know. He might turn his gun on me and make a break. It's what I would do if I was in his boots."

"What if he gives his word not to?"

"When you were little were you kicked by a mule?" Tyree said. "Only you would take the word of a murderer who would do anything to keep from being hanged."

"Think about it." Fred reined his bay alongside McCarthy's animal. "You will, won't you? Promise not to shoot either of us?"

"Do you know what you're asking? If I help you, and

we beat those Indians off, you'll still take me on to Cheyenne to meet my end, won't you?"

"That's the deal."

"How about if I help you and if we live, you let me go?"

"That's not up to me."

"No," Tyree said. "It's not. And you're worth two thousand dollars to me, McCarthy. So forget your pipe dream. I'm not cuttin' you free and damn sure not givin' you a smoke wagon."

Fred hoped the kid would change his mind. For now, they had more hard riding to do. Overhead, the summer sun climbed. He sweated so much his shirt was plastered to his skin and he continually mopped his brow with his sleeve.

With each mile the mountains shrank in size until finally they were no longer visible. Here and there a bluff reared, and dry washes were common. Antelope fled at their approach, and once a gray wolf bolted out of a gully and loped off in a blur of hair and tail.

When Fred spied several large animals in the distance, he called out a warning. "There are some buffalo yonder."

Tyree barely gave them a look. He was more concerned with what was behind them.

"We shouldn't get too close," Fred cautioned. He remembered an incident from years ago when a party of surveyors strayed too near a herd. A bull took exception and gored one of the surveyors. Opened the man from crotch to sternum, and broke half his ribs besides.

"They're half a mile off yet," Tyree said.

Fred shucked his Winchester from its scabbard anyway. It had been so long since he used it he couldn't recall if it was loaded and worked the lever to see if a cartridge fed into the chamber. It was and it did.

The next time they slowed, Tom McCarthy raised his head and shoulders to say, "I've given it a lot of thought. It wouldn't be right to let you two tangle with those hostiles by yourselves. I'll help, and I give you my word I won't back-shoot either of you and run off the first chance I get."

"You call that a promise?" Tyree said.

"What more do you want?"

"I don't want anything. That includes your help. I don't trust you, mister, any further than I can toss one of those buffs." Tyree rose in the stirrups and cocked his head. "Well, look at that. No humps but plenty of horns. I stand corrected."

Wondering what he was on about, Fred rose in the stirrups too. He didn't see any humps either, and realized what that meant. "Cattle, by heaven. We must be near a ranch."

"Don't get excited," Tyree said. "This is open range. The nearest ranch house might be days away."

"You don't know that," Fred said. "Look for smoke from a chimney. Or horse tracks that could lead us to the ranch house."

"You're clutchin' at straws."

Fred would grasp at anything that might save them. "If there are cattle, there must be water." Their horses could use a drink. They'd last longer refreshed.

"I could drink a gallon," Tyree said. "I'm hot enough to bake alive."

So was Fred, but he was more concerned about their mounts. The horses were plodding along with their heads hung low. McCarthy's wheezed every now and again.

Fred prayed the Arapahos' animals were in the same shape.

"I could use a thick steak too," Tyree mentioned.

The cattle were growing fat on the lush grass. Come the next roundup, most would be shipped East, where beef was at a premium. The U.S. population had been growing like a swarm of locusts since the Civil War, and all those people needed something to eat. Fortunes were being made in the cattle industry.

Fred had never hankered after great wealth himself.

It seemed pointless to devote himself to something he couldn't take with him beyond the grave. A fancy home, a carriage to cart him around, what was the point? Some would call his lack of ambition a character flaw. He called it sensible.

"I'm hurting," McCarthy said.

Fred looked at him. "What?"

"I said I'm hurting. My gut feels as if I've been stomped on. I can't take much more of this."

"I don't blame you." Fred doubted he'd have lasted half as long.

Tyree overheard, and said, "A little pain won't kill you. Quit your bellyachin'." He chuckled at that.

"All I ask is that you untie my legs so I can sit the saddle."

"No."

"We'd make better time," Fred argued for McCarthy's sake. "And if his hands are still tied, what can he do?"

"Ride off and leave us," Tyree said, "and I'm not takin' the chance."

Fred had always prided himself on being a reasonable man, but the kid was so pigheaded it tried his patience. He reckoned it was about time he stood up for himself. Reining over, he snatched the reins from Tyree's hands and brought the bay and the sorrel to a stop.

"What the hell?" Tyree said, drawing sharp rein. "What did you do that for?"

"I've put up with a lot from you, but no longer," Fred said. Alighting, he gripped McCarthy by the shoulders and pulled, thinking to slowly slide him off. He'd forgotten how heavy McCarthy was. Fred tried to brace him, but McCarthy slipped from his grasp and thudded to earth, his shoulders bearing the brunt.

"You trying to break my neck?"

"Sorry." Fred helped McCarthy to sit up, then held his hand out to Tyree. "Let me borrow that bowie."

"Who do you think you are? I just told you I don't want him cut free and you want to do it anyway?"

"You see this?" Fred said, tapping his badge. "Like it or not, I'm the law. He might be your prisoner, but he's mine as well, and I have a say in how we treat him. I'm cuttin' his legs loose so he can ride."

"Not with my bowie you're not."

"You're being petty."

"You bet your britches I am," Tyree declared. "You've picked a piss-poor time to show some grit."

Fred snapped his fingers. "The bowie. I mean it." He was bluffing. He wouldn't do anything if the kid refused.

Tyree looked fit to bust a blood vessel. "I knew you comin' along was a bad idea." With an oath, he slid the cord over his head and tossed the bowie at Fred's feet. "You want it, there it is."

"I'm obliged."

"Go to hell."

Sliding the big knife from its leather sheath, Fred cut the rope around McCarthy's ankles. He could have untied him, but the knots wouldn't come undone easily and they didn't have time to spare. Gripping McCarthy's arm, he hauled him to his feet. "There you go."

"I'll need a boost up."

"Sure."

Tyree made a sound of disgust. "Hug him, why don't you? Are you this friendly to every murderer you meet?"

"He's the first," Fred said. Gripping McCarthy's arm, he steadied him as McCarthy hooked a boot in the stirrup. With a grunt and a push, Fred hoisted him onto the saddle.

"You're a good man, Marshal Hitch," McCarthy said.

"He's a jackass," Tyree said.

"Enough of your guff." Fred went over and held the bowie up for him to take. "I'll take full responsibility for what he does from here on out."

"You will?" McCarthy said.

"You deserve fair treatment and I aim to see that you get it," Fred replied. It felt good to assert himself. He should have done it sooner.

Tyree wasn't interested in them anymore. He was gazing at their pursuers. "They've seen that we've stopped."

Judging by the dust they were raising, the warriors were coming on fast. They must want to end the chase.

Quickly forking leather, Fred assumed the lead. "We won't stop again until dark." Once night fell, they should be able to slip off undetected.

"Should we call you General Hitch now?" Tyree said.

"Grow up," Fred said.

For over an hour they pushed hard. Fred flattered himself that they were increasing their lead, but it could be a trick of his eyes. They weren't as sharp as they once were.

The countryside became more open. They encountered more cattle but saw no sign of any cowhands. That wasn't unusual. Some ranches encompassed hundreds of square miles. A whole week could go by without a puncher drifting through.

McCarthy's mount was wheezing again, and every so often it would stagger but right itself. It did so now, and he firmed his hold on the reins and said, "Whoa there."

"Just what we need," Tyree said.

"Do you ever look at the bright side of things?" Fred asked.

"When there is one."

Fred checked on the Arapahos. They were closer. No doubt about it. He could see their buckskins as plain as anything. "We need to pick a spot to make our stand."

"There you go again, General," Tyree said.

Fred ignored him. "A gully, a ravine, anything will do." A bluff would be ideal to defend if they could climb to the top, only there weren't any in sight.

"Do you hear that?" McCarthy asked suddenly.

"Tyree complainin' all the time?" Fred said.

"No. Listen." McCarthy drew rein.

Fred followed suit. All he heard was the horse wheezing. "What is it I'm supposed to be listenin' to?"

"You don't hear anything . . . unusual?"

"I do," Tyree said.

Presently Fred heard it too, a fluttering sound he couldn't identify. It reminded him of air being forced from a blacksmith's bellows, only quietlike. He gigged the bay and had only gone a dozen feet when he came on a hollow that he'd never have suspected was there.

And in the middle of the hollow was the last thing he would have expected to find.

Chapter 11

It was a man.

Sound asleep.

The sleeper had used his saddle for a pillow and was curled on his side, his blanket pulled as high as his ear. The fluttering sound came from underneath, and was him snoring. A shock of black hair was all that poked out. His hat and a coiled rope were next to him, and a rifle butt stuck from the saddle scabbard. Near him on the other side, a palomino was tied to a picket pin.

"Don't this beat all?" Tyree said. "It's not even nighttime."

"We have to wake him," Fred said.

"We don't have the time to waste. Let's go around and leave him to his dreams." Tyree raised his reins.

"We leave him there, the Arapahos will find him. And you know what they'll do."

Tyree nodded. "It will delay them so we can get away."

"You could do that?" Fred was appalled. "Let someone be killed and scalped to save your own skin?"

"He's nothin' to me."

"You are worse off than I thought," Fred said. To do that to a fellow human being was incomprehensible. "I'm wakin' him up and warnin' him." Clucking to the bay, he rode into the hollow.

McCarthy came with him, but Tyree sat there muttering. Glancing back at the Arapahos, he said, "You'd better make this quick."

Fred intended to. Dismounting, he stepped up, bent, and nudged the man's shoulder. "Mister?"

The man went on snoring.

"Mister?" Fred said again, and shook him harder. "You need to wake up. You're in danger."

The snorting stopped and a deep voice said, "What?"

"Mister, consarn it all. Hostiles are after us." Fred shook him harder yet. "Wake up or you're liable to lose your hair."

The edge of the blanket inched down and a blue eye peered out. "Go away. Can't you see I'm sleepin'?"

"Don't your ears work? Didn't you hear me?" Fred touched his badge. "I'm Marshal Hitch out of Sweetwater. We're takin' a prisoner to Cheyenne and an Arapaho war party is after us. They'll find you here if you don't get your ass up and light a shuck with the rest of us."

Another blue eye appeared. "Is that all?" he said with a slight drawl.

"There are seven of them and they mean business." Fred tried to impress his peril upon him.

"I can mean business too." The man rolled onto his back and the blanket fell away. He was bronzed from the sun, and had a square jaw that made Fred think of an anvil. Yawning, he ran a hand through his black mane and squinted at the sky. "Well, hell. I've slept half the day away."

"If you don't get on your damn feet," Tyree said impatiently, "you'll be sleepin' forever."

The man squinted at him. "You shouldn't ought to mouth off like that, boy. Not to me, you shouldn't."

"I'm plumb scared," Tyree said.

"Who are you?" Fred asked. "What are you doing here?"

"I'm Aces Connor," the man said. "And in case you ain't heard, they call this 'sleepin'.'"

"By golly, I've seen you before," Tom McCarthy broke

in. "You're a cowpoke. You ride for the Circle H. You were with Miles Horrell when he paid my store a visit. I remember you helping to load the grain."

"Used to be I rode for the Circle H," Aces Connor said. "Not anymore. I'm ridin' the grub lines these days, lookin' for work."

Fred was annoyed that the cowboy still hadn't gotten up. "Those Arapahos will be here soon."

"Well, hell," Aces said again. He slowly sat up and rubbed his square jaw. Picking up his hat, he smoothed his hair and jammed the hat on. "Folks sure can be a nuisance."

"Do you mean them or us?" Tyree said.

"If the boot fits, boy," Aces said. He flipped the blanket off and stood, revealing that he had slept with his boots on. His clothes showed a lot of wear but were clean. Strapped around his waist was a gun belt with a nickel-plated, ivory-handled Colt in the holster. The likeness of a rattlesnake had been carved into each grip, and the revolver was engraved with curlicues.

Tyree whistled in appreciation. "That there is some pistol."

Fred thought so too. In his experience it was rare for a cowboy to wear a revolver like that. Most went for the plain variety. Ivory handles and nickel plating added a lot to the cost, and few cowpokes indulged in such extravagance. They'd rather spend their hard-earned money on the best saddle they could find, or the best-quality hat.

This particular cowboy favored a brown hat with a round crown and a narrow brim. He hadn't put it on as most did, on top of his head, but jammed it onto the back of his so that it was tilted with the front brim slanted up. Somehow it stuck there as he stood and stretched and did more yawning.

"Take your sweet time, why don't you?" Tyree said.

Aces Connor looked him up and down and smiled. "What are you supposed to be, boy? A walkin' arsenal?"

"Stop callin' me boy, you damn cow nurse. I hunt men for the bounty on their heads."

"Well, good for you."

Fred was growing increasingly impatient. "Those Arapahos I was tellin' you about? They'll be here any minute."

"First things first," Aces said. Still smiling, he walked over to Tyree's mount, looked up at him, and before Tyree could guess his intent, he seized Tyree by the front of his shirt and threw him bodily to the dirt. "That'll learn you to watch your mouth."

For all of ten seconds Tyree was too stunned to do more than lie there. Then, swearing, he came up off the ground, clawing for both Colts.

Aces Connor was quicker. His hand flicked, and the ivory-handled Colt was leveled at Tyree's belly.

Tyree froze. "Whoa . . ."

"Don't you ever try me, boy," Aces said. "You get this one time because we're not acquainted, but if you ever try to pull on me again, I'll gun you where you stand. You hear me?"

Tyree couldn't take his wide eyes off that ivory-handled Colt.

"Answer me."

"I hear you," Tyree said.

Aces twirled his Colt into his holster and turned his back to Tyree with no more concern than if Tyree were a kitten.

"Those Arapahos," Fred said again.

"You and your darn Injuns," Aces said. Moving to his saddle, he shucked the rifle, a Winchester.

Fred was familiar with the model. It was a Browning 1886, with the finest wood stock money could buy, and a target sight attached. Like the cowboy's Colt, it cost more than the regular model.

Aces bent over his saddle, rummaged in a saddlebag, and took out a box of .45-90 cartridges. One by one, he fed seven in, then jacked the lever to feed a cartridge into the chamber. "Where are these varmints of yours?"

Fred pointed to the north.

Aces ambled toward the top of the hollow.

"What does he think he's doing?" Tyree said. He seemed to have forgotten the indignity of being dumped from his saddle and outdrawn.

Shrugging, Fred went with the cowboy. After a short hesitation, so did Tyree. McCarthy had stayed on his horse, but he was curious too, and clambering down, he joined them.

Aces Connor stood in plain view of the approaching warriors. By now they weren't more than a couple of hundred yards out. At the sight of him, they stopped. One brandished a lance over his head and yelled in the Arapaho tongue.

"They'll charge us any moment," Fred said.

"Not if Sassy can help it," Aces said, and patted his Winchester.

"You gave your rifle a name?"

"If it was good enough for Davy Crockett to do, it's good enough for me." Aces raised the target sight, adjusted it, and pressed the Winchester to his shoulder.

"Kill them," Tyree said gleefully. "Shoot every one of the savages."

"What would I want to do that for?" Aces said. "Now hush, infant. If I'm off by a whisker, I'll splatter his brains."

Out on the prairie, the warrior with the lance appeared to be working the others into a frenzy. He pumped his lance and was shouting and pointing.

Aces Connor took a deep breath and held himself still. His trigger finger slowly curled.

The Winchester Browning boomed like thunder.

Fred saw an incredible thing. The warrior who was working the others up had an eagle feather in his hair, and at the shot, the feather flipped into the air, then fluttered to earth. It awed him as much as it did the Arapahos. They looked at the feather and then at Aces as he worked the lever and prepared to shoot again.

"Damnation!" Tyree exclaimed.

Aces raised his cheek from the rifle and shouted something, but not in English. He took aim once more and said, to himself apparently, "I hope they don't push it."

To Fred's astonishment, the warriors reined around, jabbed their heels, and departed at a gallop, several twisting their heads as if they feared being shot in the back.

"Drop some of them!" Tyree urged.

"No."

The Arapahos didn't slow until they were a quarter of a mile away. Soon only the dust they raised was visible.

"I'll be switched," Fred said. "You drove them off as slick as anything."

Aces had lowered his Winchester. "No one wants to die." Turning, he started back down.

"What did you say to them?" Fred wanted to know.

"Run or die."

"In their own tongue?" Fred marveled. "Where in creation did you pick up Arapaho?"

"Mr. Horrell used to give the tame ones some cows now and then," Aces said. "Mostly to help them get through the winter. He's a fine Christian gent, and always doing good by folks."

"That doesn't explain you speakin' their tongue."

"I only knew a handful of words," Aces said. "Some of the warriors like to gamble, and we'd throw dice or play cards."

"That was some shootin'," Tyree said. "If it had been me, I'd have gunned every last one of the red vermin."

"They're people, boy, like you and me."

"The hell you say."

On reaching his saddle, Aces shoved the Winchester into the scabbard and squatted to roll up his blankets. "Where are you gents headed, if you don't mind my askin'?"

"Cheyenne," Fred said.

"Hmm," Aces said, and went on rolling.

Intensely curious, Fred asked, only partly in jest, "Are

you sure you're a cowboy and not a gun hand? I never saw anyone draw as fast as you, and you're no slouch with that Winchester."

"Everyone was somethin' else before he became what he is," Aces replied.

"Huh?" Tyree said.

"I've been nursemaidin' cows going on ten years now," Aces informed them. "I was with Mr. Horrell for the last five, but he had to fire me a couple of months ago and I've been lookin' for work since."

"Why did he have to, if you don't mind *my* askin'?" Fred said.

"I shot somebody," Aces said, "and Mr. Horrell has a rule about not havin' shootists on his payroll."

"Who did you shoot?"

Aces looked at him. "You ask a lot of questions."

"It's the badge," Fred said.

"Sure it is." Aces picked up his saddle blanket in both hands and shook it. "I was in a card game over to Casper and the tinhorn who was dealin' slipped a card from the bottom of the deck. I told him to reshuffle and deal again, but he went for a hideout and I shot him dead."

"So you shot in self-defense," Fred said. "It doesn't seem fair that your boss fired you over that one killin'."

"There were three."

"You shot the other cardplayers?"

"No. About six months before that I'd shot a rustler. Caught him in the act of using a runnin' iron to change the Circle H brand and told him to throw up his hands. He did, but he had his six-shooter in one and I had to perforate his brainpan."

"What about the third?"

Aces was moving to his palomino. "A year or so before that I shot a drummer who'd stopped at the ranch to sell ladies' corsets to Horrell's missus. While all the hands were stuffin' their faces with chuck at the cookhouse, the drummer snuck into the bunkhouse and was helpin' himself to our plunder. I told him to throw up his hands and he drew a belly gun. I shot him in the arm, thinkin' to spare him, but the arm became infected and he died anyway."

"You don't have much luck with people throwin' up their hands," Fred observed wryly.

"I surely don't." Aces draped the saddle blanket over the palomino and smoothed it. "As soon as I'm saddled we can head for Cheyenne like you want."

"We?" Fred said.

"I'm going with you."

Chapter 12

Ohio was a good place to grow up.

The land was fertile, crops thrived, and Donald Connor did well by his wife, Martha, and their four sons and two daughters. He did so well that he got it into his head that he'd do even better if they moved west of the Mississippi River, where the land was a lot cheaper. Instead of the two hundred acres he had, they could have thousands.

Don had a plan. He'd homestead, add more land as his finances allowed, and in a few years he and his wife would be sitting pretty. He worked it all out on paper and showed it to her.

Martha didn't want to leave the home she loved, but she was willing to give the West a try. If her husband said they could do it, they could. He was the brains of the family. After all, he'd had schooling up to the sixth grade and she had only gone as far as the fourth.

They sold their farm, loaded their possessions onto a Conestoga, and set out.

Martha fretted about the dangers, but everyone assured her that the Indians were mostly peaccable and outlaws were few and they'd do fine. It wasn't like in the old days when half the tribes were on the warpath and banks and trains were being robbed right and left.

The days of the famous gangs like the James brothers and the Youngers were long over.

Don picked Kansas for their new home. He'd heard that the earth was as rich as Ohio earth and crops would grow with a minimum of tending. He'd been told the land was flat as a plate and easy to plow. That the summers were mild and the winters saw less snow than most Eastern states.

As it turned out, everything he'd been told by people who had never been there was wrong.

For starters, the land was a lot drier. Where Ohio received over thirty inches of rainfall a year, most parts of Kansas were lucky to see fifteen to twenty, and most of that came in the form of afternoon thunderstorms that didn't do crops a lot of good. Considerable irrigating was called for to make a large farm prosper.

As for the claim that the ground was easy to plow, Don found that it was so hard-packed and hid so many rocks that plowing was a Herculean effort.

And then there were the winters. Bitterly cold winds howled out of the arctic north, and the temperature plummeted to ten degrees. That same wind made it seem like fifty below. As for the snow, two to three feet wasn't uncommon, with drifts of six to eight.

Within a year of their move the family was barely getting by. They were so destitute that Don did something Martha resented for the rest of her days. He sold their oldest son as an indentured servant to a man who ran a freighting outfit.

The custom was well established. In the early days of the Colonies and for a long while after, a lot of immigrants came to America as indentures. It was popular with the poor because it enabled them to come to the land of opportunity, and after working as an indenture for a set number of years, they were given their freedom and could do as they pleased.

In recent years the practice had been on the decline, but it was still done now and then.

Don met the freighter in Salina. Over drinks at a saloon, Don shared his tale of woe. It was the freighter who suggested he'd be willing to take on the oldest boy as an indentured servant for, say, a hundred dollars. The boy would have to work for ten years to pay the debt off and then would be set free.

So it was that young James Connor, who had just turned twelve, found himself doing a man's work under the always critical eye of a taskmaster who seemed to delight in taking a switch to him for any excuse whatsoever.

Young Jim had been in shock. That his own pa had done this to him crushed him. He cried a lot those first weeks, and if the freighter caught him, he was switched until he bled. After a few times of that, Jim made sure not to be caught.

He grew to hate being indentured, and to hate the freighter even more. The man worked him to the bone from dawn until well past dusk, seven days a week, month in and month out.

The only real rest Jim had was when the freighter let him handle a team. He was a top driver by the time he turned fifteen.

They freighted all over. His master, as the freighter called himself, liked to boast that they'd haul freight anywhere, and that they did: from Missouri to New Mexico, from Texas to Montana.

By his sixteenth year Jim had put on weight and muscle. So much so his boss stopped using the switch. But the freighter still treated him as if he were less than the mud that clung to their boots when it rained.

One day Jim made bold to ask if there was anything he could do to get out of being indentured early. Sure, the freighter laughed, give him the hundred dollars, plus interest. How much interest? Jim asked. Another hundred should do, was the freighter's reply.

Two hundred dollars. To Jim it was a fortune. He had no money of his own, and no need for any. His clothes and his food were provided by the freighter.

Acquiring the two hundred became Jim's dream. His

obsession. He would somehow get his hands on it and be free to live his life as he pleased. The mere notion was a tonic for his spirit.

The "how" eluded him.

Then one day they were in Kansas City. The freighter had gone off to see a man about a job. Jim was left to watch the wagons and happened to notice several black men rolling dice in an alley. He drifted over to watch, and the oldest of the men asked him if he wanted to sit in. Jim said thanks, but he didn't have anything to bet with. The black man asked why not and Jim told him about being indentured.

Jim would never forget the look that came over that man, or what he said.

"They even do it to their own."

To Jim's astonishment, the black man peeled a bill from his hand and held it out. "What's this?" he'd said.

"Your first step on the road to freedom," the man said, and wagged the bill. "Five dollars. Take it. It's yours."

Jim had protested, saying it wouldn't be right, but the black man pressed the bill into his hand and made him take it. Even more astonishing, the man then prevailed on his two friends to contribute.

That night Jim lay under a wagon, where he usually slept, and fingered the godsend he'd been given. Each of the others had given him three, for a total of eleven. He felt rich, as if all the money in the world had been dropped in his lap. It intensified his yearning to be free.

All he needed was another one hundred and eighty-nine dollars.

Obtaining it became all he thought about.

It was why he took the risk he did.

Jim sat in on a card game.

They were in Denver. The freighter had gone to visit a sporting house, informing Jim he'd be gone all night and to stay with the wagons, which were parked in a freight yard. Other freighters were there, and their loud voices and laughter drew Jim to a poker game. He watched for over an hour, torn between fear of losing all he had and his desire to add to his Freedom Purse, as he called it. When one of the players left, the others asked if anyone wanted to take his place.

Jim offered to.

It was a friendly game and they were playing for small stakes. Nickels and dimes and quarters. The most a player could raise was a dollar.

Jim lost fifteen cents and then twenty more and was tempted to quit, but his next hand was three of a kind and he won twenty-five. Lady Luck liked him and he ended up winning more hands than he lost so that by midnight, when the game broke up, he was six dollars and forty cents richer.

Jim had found a new passion. From then on, he played poker every chance he got. He had to do it behind the freighter's back, but that just added spice to his pleasure.

He grew better fast. He learned to read the other players, to tell when they had a good hand and when they were bluffing. He learned to bluff himself, to turn his expression to stone and not give his hand away.

In Kansas City he was first called Aces. During a late-night game he won three big hands in a row, all with three aces. The odds against that happening were astronomical. One of the other players started calling him Aces as a friendly joke, and the rest took it up. He liked the nickname.

From then on he called himself Aces Connor.

By the end of his seventeenth year Aces had one hundred and eighty-seven dollars and sixteen cents in his Freedom Purse. All he needed was twelve dollars and eighty-four cents.

He won it in Wichita. The moment he had the full two hundred, he bowed out and made for the saloon where he knew the freighter to be.

His master was at the bar, a bottle of whiskey half-gone. He glowered when Aces strode up and growled,

"What in hell are you doing here? You're supposed to be with the wagons."

"Two hundred dollars, you said."

"What?"

Aces pulled the Freedom Purse from his pocket and smacked it down in front of the freighter. "Two hundred dollars it is."

"What?" the freighter repeated himself.

"For my freedom. There's your money. I want out of the contract you talked my father into signing."

The freighter had struggled to collect his wits. He blinked in confusion and opened the purse. All that money cleared his head right quick. Mumbling, he counted the bills and coins. "I don't believe it."

"So, are we square?" Aces had said.

"Not so fast," the freighter said. "Where did you get this? I don't pay you a cent. Did you steal it?"

Aces told him about the poker games.

"So you've been sneaking away when you were supposed to be working?" the freighter said. "I should take a switch to you for that."

"Try," Aces said.

The freighter was bigger, although not by much. He gauged the width of Aces's shoulders and the breadth of Aces's chest, and frowned. "You're past that age. But I can punish you in other ways."

Aces jabbed the purse angrily. "You have the two hundred. What more do you want?"

"You're supposed to be mine for another five years yet," the freighter said. "This ain't hardly enough."

"It's how much you told me."

"I wasn't thinking," the freighter said. "I didn't take you seriously. I said whatever popped into my head."

"You son of a bitch."

"Don't talk to me like that," the freighter warned. "You're still mine to do with as I damn well please, and it pleases me to let you know that it will take four hundred to buy out your contract." He shook the purse. "Twice as much as you have here."

"You greedy bastard."

"Keep this up and I'll have you thrown behind bars. I'm within my rights. I can't help it if you were stupid enough to think two hundred would do."

Aces hit him. He'd never struck another human being, but he unleashed an uppercut to the jaw with all his rage-driven strength behind it and knocked the freighter down. Cursing, the freighter stood and Aces punched him again, full in the face. It sent the freighter crashing onto a table, and the table upended, landing on top of him. Aces moved in, set to pound the freighter into the floor.

Only the freighter wasn't moving. Blood flowed from a deep gash on his forehead, and he didn't appear to be breathing.

In a sudden panic, Aces fled. He was sure he'd killed him. Sure that the law would be after him and he'd be put on trial and thrown behind bars.

Aces would be damned if he'd let that happen. He didn't have any money and he didn't have a horse, but he knew of another freighter who was leaving for Texas in the morning, and he asked the man if he could go along. The man was a driver short and happy to have him.

Only later did Aces learn he needn't have run off. His "master" wasn't dead. The bartender splashed water on his face and the freighter got up, grabbed the purse, and staggered out. He never pressed charges. Never sent anyone to bring Aces back.

Texas was a lot to Aces's liking. The folks there kept to themselves and didn't badger others with a lot of questions. He worked as a store clerk in Dallas long enough to buy new clothes and save twenty dollars so he could sit in on a poker game.

From then on, it was poker and only poker. He became a gambler. He wore a wide-brimmed black hat and a black frock coat, and carried a pair of pistols in the pockets. Dallas, Houston, San Antonio, wherever there was a high-stakes game, that was where you'd find him.

Aces might have gone on gambling forever if he hadn't run into a young woman one day while he was strolling about to stretch his legs. Her name was Susie. She was his age, the daughter of a rancher, and the most beautiful female he had ever set eyes on. One look, and he was smitten. He struck up a conversation. Susie was warm and friendly and had the most perfect teeth in all creation.

She made it a point to mention that she came into town once a week with her mother, and Aces made it a point to be on the lookout for her when she did. They'd walk and talk, and at night he'd dream of her.

Aces imagined Susie as his wife. Imagined having a home and kids. Imagined living as he had lived before his father betrayed him. To test the waters he remarked to Susie how nice that would be. Susie said she'd like nothing better and her mother wouldn't mind, but her pa would never let her marry a gambler.

Aces was mulling over how he could change her father's mind when the matter was taken out of his hands.

He killed somebody.

Chapter 13

It started over cards.

Aces had learned all the tricks that cheaters used. Marked cards. Dealing from the bottom. Sleeve rigs. He had to. Not so he could use them himself, but to make sure no one cheated him.

He thought of gambling as an honorable profession. Certainly luck was a factor, but so was skill. Cheating destroyed the luck element and made a mockery of the skills needed to be a consistent winner.

Whenever Aces caught someone cheating, it was like a slap to the face. He took it personal. He pistol-whipped a cheater once. Another, he busted the man's nose with the flat of his hand.

He had a reputation for fair play and he stuck to it like a medieval knight to his standard.

Then one day he was invited to sit in on a high-stakes game involving several wealthy ranchers. It was an annual affair. He'd been invited once before and had a fine time. That he came away from the table over four thousand dollars to the better had a lot to do with it.

Little did he know at the time but one of the ranchers resented it. The man was named Sparks. He was a poor loser but clever enough to hide the fact. Since a lot of that four thousand had been his, he conspired to get even.

There they were, Aces and five of the biggest ranch-men in all of Texas. They'd been at the game for hours. The room was thick with cigar smoke. The smell of liquor, the clatter of chips, the quiet slap of cards when they were placed down—the pulse of play was friendly and reserved.

Then Aces saw Sparks dip two fingers into a sleeve. Not up under it, as was normally done when a cheater used a wrist rig, but *into* the underside of the sleeve itself.

And wouldn't you know it? Sparks flourished four kings to win the largest pot of the night.

As Sparks grinned and reached for the chips, Aces had lowered his right arm to his side, close to his pocket with its special leather lining for his pistol.

"I shouldn't think you'd need to, a man with as much as you have," he'd remarked with an edge to his voice.

Sparks went still, his hand half across the table. "What do you mean by that, Mr. Connor?"

"The size of your ranch, you have more money than you know what to do with. Why cheat?"

The other ranchers shot sharp glances at Sparks. They all knew Aces, knew he believed in fair play and was as honest as the year was long. It was part of the reason he'd been invited to sit in.

"I don't know what in hell you're talking about," Sparks replied, "and I resent your accusation."

"Resent it all you want," Aces said. "But you are a no-account cheat and out of this game."

"Like hell I am."

"I'll have a look at that left sleeve of yours."

"Like hell you will." Spark slid his arm close to his vest.

"You've taken advantage of your friends. They trusted you to play fair. As have I. If you won't tell us why, we'll at least know how."

"You so much as touch me and I'll shoot you," Sparks said.

The rancher who had organized the game said, "Sparks, please. We're all gentlemen here."

"He isn't," Sparks snarled, with a nod at Aces.

"What have I ever done that you'd say that?" Aces asked.

"You don't have to do anything. You're a gambler. You put on airs of respectability but prey on the misfortunes of others for your livelihood. You're despicable, each and every one of you."

"I never knew you felt that way."

"I'm not the only one. That filly everybody knows you're sweet on? Her pa is a friend of mine. He told me flat out once he'd never let a gambler marry his daughter, not from now until kingdom come."

"Keep her out of this."

Sparks had sneered and said, "What's the matter? Don't you like hearing the truth?"

"The issue is you cheatin'," Aces had said. "Show us that sleeve."

"Go to hell."

"Then I'll take a look myself."

Aces had started to rise. Sparks, with an oath, reached under his jacket and drew an Open Top Pocket pistol. He pointed it, but Aces had his own Colt out and up. Aces fired as Sparks went to shoot. The slug smashed Sparks against the back of his chair, but he gamely tried to take aim. Aces fired again. The chair tilted and Sparks heaved out of it, screeching like an enraged bobcat. He got off a wild shot, putting a hole in the forehead of the player on Aces's right. Aces shot Sparks in the face.

Everyone said the shooting was justified. That slit in Sparks sleeve held a queen and an ace. The sheriff refused to prosecute, despite the outrage from Sparks's kin.

Aces should have been happy. His reputation wasn't tarnished. He could have gone on gambling the rest of his days, but he lost his enthusiasm for the game. Part of it was that the cards turned cold. Not just for a game or two. All the time. It was as if he'd been jinxed.

The cards weren't to blame for the final blow to his

gambling days. He'd continued to see Susie until one day her mother came to their rendezvous instead and informed him that the father, who appeared to be the last person in Texas to find out about their secret romance, had become incensed and prohibited Susie from seeing him.

No daughter of his would marry a worthless tinhorn.

Rumor had it that a relative of Sparks had whispered their secret into the father's ear to get back at Aces.

Aces was heartbroken. He lost all enthusiasm for cards and the saloon life. Even the taste of whiskey went flat in his mouth. He kept on playing, but he lost every cent he'd socked away.

Six months after his heart was crushed, Aces was busted and drifting. He got rid of his gambler's duds. There was no sense in dressing as one when he wasn't.

There he was, twenty years old, with no life to speak of. He had no prospects whatsoever.

Then he ran into a rancher he'd played cards with a few times. The man took pity on him and offered him a job as a cowhand. Just until he was back on his feet, the rancher said.

With nothing else to do and about ten cents to his name, Aces figured he might as well. He would eat regular and have a roof over his head when he was at the bunkhouse.

He could ride and he could rope, so it wasn't as if he was worthless at it. He got better at the roping and learned as much about cows as he'd learned about cards, and something unexpected happened.

Aces found that he liked it. He liked being a cowboy. Liked being outdoors, liked working cattle, liked the company of other cowhands. He soon became a top hand and was well respected by his brothers in the profession.

He was also more than a little feared.

Aces discovered that a shooting marked a man for life. Everywhere he went, people whispered and pointed.

He wasn't just Aces Connor, cowboy. He was Aces Connor, gun shark. Aces Connor, shootist. In his own eyes he was no such thing, but what he thought didn't matter. He was whispered about, and pointed at.

Aces had a brainstorm. To escape his past, he left Texas and drifted as far as Wyoming before he found a job that suited him, working for Mr. Horrell. The whispering and the pointing stopped.

For years he didn't shoot anybody. Then came that cardsharp and the rustler and the drummer, and Mr. Horrell, as decent a man as ever drew breath, had had enough and let him go. It was nothing personal, Horrell said. He just couldn't have a man-killer on his payroll. It gave a ranch a bad reputation.

Now here Aces was, riding south with an old lawman, a kid with an attitude, and a poor soul bound for the gallows. It was the day after he drove off the Arapahos and they had been riding for most of the morning when Marshal Hitch brought his bay alongside the palomino.

"Mind if we talk?"

"So long as it's not about those men I shot."

"It's about why you're taggin' along. Cheyenne is a far piece and we're all strangers to you."

"What else do I have to do?" Aces said, not without bitterness. "No one in these parts will hire me."

"Man-killers aren't all that popular, I'm afraid," Fred said.

"Yet folks gab about them no end."

The marshal shrugged. "That's human nature, I reckon. Most people live humdrum lives. They go day in and day out with no excitement whatsoever. So when they hear about someone like you, it makes you special."

"Special, my backside," Aces said.

"It's like back in ancient times. You ever hear of a place called Troy? Or a warrior called Achilles? Or how about Robin Hood? There was a book written about him not long ago."

"Now you're bein' ridiculous."

"It's the same thing, I tell you. Folks look up to those who do things they couldn't do. Brave things. Excitin' things."

"There's nothin' excitin' about shootin' somebody."

"There is to those who never have," Fred insisted. "Shootists become heroes of sorts, whether they're on the right side of the law or the wrong side. Look at Billy the Kid. Or Wild Bill Hickok. Or John Wesley Hardin. Hell, I could name twenty more."

Aces didn't say anything. He hadn't ever thought of it that way.

"Like it or not, you've sort of become a hero to some. Take Tyree. I can tell he looks up to you."

Aces had noticed the boy giving him peculiar looks. "What's the kid's story anyhow?"

"His folks died when he was in the crib and he grew up in an orphanage. That's all he's been willin' to tell me."

"He seems a little young to be going after bounty money," Aces observed. Especially since most of those who had bounties on their heads wouldn't hesitate to do in whoever was after them.

"There's more to him than meets the eye," Fred observed. "I don't have him entirely figured out yet, but I'm workin' on it."

Aces put the kid from his mind. It was none of his affair. Then that night, as they sat around the campfire drinking coffee and not saying much, he caught the boy giving him that peculiar look again. "Cut it out."

"Cut what out?" Tyree replied, sounding surprised.

"You know damn well. I won't be gawked at, thank you very much." Aces had had his fill of that.

"You've shot three men," Tyree said.

"Four, but who's countin'?" Aces frowned and rested his elbows on his knees. "Shootin' a man isn't anything special. Sometimes it has to be done. You do it and get on with your life and hope others will forget, but they don't."

"You know you can squeeze the trigger when you have to. That's somethin'."

"How so?"

"What if you had it to do but didn't know if you could?" Tyree said. "I shot at McCarthy there—"

"And hit a horse," Fred interjected.

Tyree glared at him, then said to Aces, "But he's the only one I've ever shot at, so I can't say as how I'll be when I have to do it again."

"Why is that so important to you?" Aces asked.

"It just is," Tyree said sullenly.

Aces sipped coffee and pondered. He hadn't lost his knack for reading people, and he read something here. "Tell me," he said. "How'd you get that scar?"

"I've had it since I was in diapers. And the how is none of your business."

"You were a baby?" Fred said.

"Let it be," Tyree said to him.

Aces refused to. "I was just askin'."

"And I'm just tellin' you it's not anything I'll talk about, now or ever. So let it be."

"It looks like someone cut you." Aces had seen more than a few knife wounds. Some were downright ugly, like this one.

"Who would cut a baby like that?" Fred said.

"Someone who wanted the baby dead," Aces said.

Tyree set down his tin cup so hard his coffee spilled. Heaving upright, he spat out, "You will not pry into my past, you hear me? You're nuisances, the both of you." Wheeling, he stormed off.

"Where does he think he's going?" Fred said. "We're in the middle of nowhere."

Tom McCarthy, who had been disconsolate all day and refused to say much, now stirred. "You hurt the boy's feelings. What do you expect?"

"He's sure a puzzlement," Fred said.

"Not if you can add two and two," McCarthy said. "He's already told us his parents were murdered when he was a baby."

"So?" Fred said.

"So whoever murdered them tried to kill him and cut him like that."

"That's terrible," Fred said.

"Worse things have happened."

"I can't think of anything worse than hurting a baby," Fred said.

"Instead of badgering the kid, you should try to help him."

"You can't help someone who doesn't want to be helped."

"You can try," McCarthy said.

They fell silent.

As for Aces, he drank more coffee and did more pondering. And a seed took root and sprouted.

Chapter 14

Aces waited a couple of days for the kid to simmer down.

They had stopped for the night. Aces and the marshal gathered firewood and the kid kindled the fire.

Earlier in the day, Aces had dropped an antelope with his Browning. "Time to carve this critter up," he announced. The kid gave him the opening he needed by drawing the bowie that hung from a sheath hung around his neck.

"Here. You can use this. It's as sharp as can be."

Aces took it and tested the claim by lightly running a finger over the edge. A thin line of blood welled. "Nice honin' job."

"I like a sharp knife," Tyree said. "What good is a dull one?"

Aces chuckled. "About as good as an empty six-shooter." He was glad when the kid laughed. Now all he had to do was figure out how to get at what he wanted to know without offending him. Rolling the antelope over, he inserted the tip of the bowie and set to work. He didn't like the stink of the guts and the internal juices, and held his breath at the worst of it.

"I've been wantin' to ask you a question," Tyree said.

Aces smothered a smile. "I'll swap you," he said.

"Swap how?"

"A question for a question. You get to ask me one and I get to ask you one and we both have to answer true."

"I never had anybody ask me to do that before," Tyree said. He didn't sound the least bit suspicious.

"Ask yours," Aces said as he cut.

"Why weren't you scared of those Arapahos? You acted as if they were no more bother than some flies that needed shooin'. You just told them to get and shot that feather and they skedaddled."

"Did they scare you some?"

"I wasn't lookin' forward to takin' an arrow," Tyree said, hedging. "Until we ran into you, that was how I'd reckoned it would go. So how come they didn't worry you even a little bit?"

"I suppose I didn't give myself time to be worried. I did what needed doing and that was it." Aces peeled part of the hide from the underbelly. "It's the same with the shootin' scrapes I've been in. It always happens fast. You don't have much time to think. You just shoot. It's over before you can get scared."

"I wonder if it can be that easy."

"I never said it was that," Aces said. "For me, the hard part is always after the shootin'. When I look back and think how I could have done things different."

"But those times you told us about," Tyree said, "you had no choice. It was you or them."

"That's what lets me sleep at night. I have a conscience, and it bothers me on occasion."

"I might have one of those," Tyree said. "I get bothered sometimes by this bounty business I do."

"Then why do it?"

"I need the practice trackin' men down," Tyree said. "And I hate outlaws worse than anything."

Aces let a minute go by. His next slash caused some of the intestines to ooze out and he helped them along using the flat of the bowie as a scoop. "My turn. And remember. You gave your word to answer."

"I reckon I know what you're fixin' to ask," Tyree said, and touched his scar. "You want to know about this."

"It would please me considerable," Aces said. He saw that Marshal Hitch was listening but pretending not to, and McCarthy had raised his head.

Tyree grimaced as if he were in pain. "You have to promise not to say a word to anybody. I can't have word gettin' around that I'm after them."

Aces nodded. "You have it."

"I reckon I can trust you." Squatting, Tyree folded his forearms across his knees. "The vermin who murdered my folks gave me this scar. I reckon they aimed to slit my throat, but in the dark they botched it."

"And it's them you're huntin'."

"Figured that out, did you?" Tyree gave a grin, but it faded. "I'm from Missouri. That's where the orphanage was. When I got out of that place, I asked around. Found a couple of people who could tell me how my folks died. It was outlaws, they said. So I went to the sheriff, but he was new and he told me to look up the man who had the sheriffin' job before him. I found the old sheriff, sure enough, and he said he was happy to see me grown. He remembered the killin's as if it was yesterday. Especially what they'd done to me."

"No one forgets a baby bein' hurt," Fred said.

Tyree didn't seem to hear him. "The sheriff tried his best to find who did it. He said there were tracks of three riders. He gathered up a posse and they spent ten whole days combin' the countryside, but the killers got clean away. The sheriff must have seen how unhappy I was at that news, because he patted my arm and said it wasn't entirely hopeless."

"If you don't know who you're after, how will you find them?" Aces asked.

"That's the thing. A year or so after my folks were killed, the sheriff arrested a man for stealin' someone's poke. The man he caught offered to give the sheriff some information if the sheriff would see to it the judge went easy on him. The sheriff wasn't interested until the man told him he knew who had killed that farmer and his wife and cut their baby."

Caught up in the boy's story, Aces leaned toward him. So did Marshal Hitch. McCarthy just looked sad.

"It had stuck in the sheriff's craw that he never caught those who were to blame, so he agreed. The thief told him there were three, which the sheriff already knew. And that one of them was called Tucker."

"Did the sheriff say how the thief knew that?" Marshal Hitch asked.

Tyree nodded. "The thief claimed he had a friend who knew Tucker, and that Tucker had parted company with the other two over the murders, and gone West. The thief had the notion that Tucker was powerful afraid of them."

"Tucker," Fred said. "I think I met a Tucker once. He was older than me, though, and repaired shoes and boots for a livin'."

"That wouldn't be the one I'm after," Tyree said.

Aces went back to skinning the antelope. He didn't want to discourage the boy, but the marshal had no such compunctions.

"Ever hear of lookin' for a needle in a haystack?" Fred said. "That's what' you're tryin' to do."

"Don't care," Tyree said.

"You have any idea how vast the West is? From the Mississippi River to the Pacific Ocean, and from Canada clear to Mexico? You could live a thousand years and not cover a tenth of it."

"I'm not givin' up."

"I admire your grit. I truly do. But you're throwin' your life away for what? Revenge?"

"It's my life to throw," Tyree said.

"I grant you that," the marshal said. "But it's been, what, fifteen years? You were a baby when it happened. You never knew your folks. It's not as if you have memories of them."

"Be real careful," Tyree said.

"I just hate to see you waste your life. Put it behind you and get on with livin' and doin' something with yourself."

"I can't."

"Why in blazes not?"

"You don't understand," Tyrce said. "It's not whether I did or didn't know them. It's that they were my ma and my pa. I owe it to them. I don't know how else to explain it except to say that if I stopped huntin' their killers, I'd betray the feelin's I have for them, even though I never knew them. And when you betray somebody, that's the worst thing you can do."

The word *betray* knifed into Aces like the bowie into the antelope. He'd been betrayed, not once but twice. The first time it was his father, selling him into indentured servitude. The second time it was Susie, who could have stood up to her pa and married him but didn't.

"You can't betray someone you didn't know," Fred said.

"I knew you wouldn't savvy."

Aces made up his mind. "I do."

"You do?

"More than that, I don't think you can do it alone. Like the marshal says, the West is a mighty big place. You can use help and I'm offerin' mine."

"You are?" Fred Hitch said.

"I am, if Mr. Johnson here will let me."

"It's Larn," Tyree said. "I tell everybody it's Johnson so the killers won't know I'm after them. They might have known who my ma and pa were. My real name is Tyree Larn."

"That's smart," Aces complimented him. "Real smart."

"Do you really want to help me?"

"Wouldn't have said I did if I didn't."

"Good. It'll make this next easier. I was wonderin' how I could ask it of you."

Aces waited.

"I never saw anyone draw as fast as you can. I'd be obliged if you'd teach me. I've practiced some on my own, but back in Sweetwater I shot a horse by mistake, and you don't do that unless you can stand improvement."

"I've been tellin' you that all along," Fred said.

Aces was slow to answer. Lending the boy a hand was one thing. Teaching him to be a better killer was another, and that was what teaching him to shoot amounted to.

"Well?" Tyree said. "I'm imposin', I know, and I never imposed on anybody before. I'll pay you once I have some money, if that's what it takes."

"Whoever heard of payin' to learn to shoot?" Fred threw in.

"Will you at least think about it?" Tyree asked.

"I will," Aces said.

That night when he turned in, Aces's thoughts drifted to Susie and his dream of a family and kids. He thought about his pa, and his years with the freighter. And he knew what he was going to say.

Dawn broke crisp and cool, but that would change as soon as the sun rose high enough. They ate antelope for breakfast, washed it down with coffee, and were under way.

Aces didn't keep the kid in suspense. He fell in besides him, smiled, and announced, "I'll do it."

Tyree lit up like a candle. "When do we start?" he asked excitedly.

"When we stop for the night."

The kid wore a grin the entire day. He'd glance at Aces and the grin would widen. Once he took to whistling to himself.

"I've never seen that boy so happy," Marshal Hitch said at one point. "I hope you know what you're doing."

"He has no one," Aces said.

"Is that why? I took pity on him too, but turnin' him into a gun hand isn't doing him any favors."

"It's for when he finds them, if he does," Aces said. The chances were slim, and nothing might ever come of it.

"Who's to say he stops there?"

"You think that poorly of him?"

"He's fifteen. And before you say anything, yes, some his age are married with jobs and all that. They're responsible. Mature." Fred gazed at Tyree. "He seems responsible enough, doing what he does. But I wouldn't say he's all that mature. He has a lot to learn."

"Could be I can teach him."

"Ah," Fred said.

Aces wondered what that was supposed to mean. He didn't change his mind, though. He was Tyree's age once. With no one to look up to, no one to teach him how to be a man, he'd done all right by himself. With him to lend advice, Tyree would do even better.

That evening it began. They were camped in cottonwoods. Aces broke a branch into long sticks and pushed each stick a thumb's length into the ground. "These will be our targets."

"If you say so," Tyree said skeptically.

They moved back about ten steps. Aces flexed his fingers a few times to limber them, then drew and shot from the hip. The top half of a stick went flying end over end, and he twirled the Colt into his holster.

"Land of Goshen," Fred exclaimed.

Tyree's grin about split his face. "That was some shootin'. How long does it take to get that good?"

"Depends on the shooter," Aces said. "On how quick he is and if he has the eye for it and how much he wants it."

"I want it more than anything."

"Then give it a try."

Rather sheepishly, Tyree drew his right Colt, took aim, and missed. He cocked the Colt, fired again, and did the same. "See?"

"You're just startin'," Aces said. "Before I'm done, if you have the knack, you'll be able to do what I just did nine times out of ten."

"I can't wait."

Chapter 15

Tyree Larn took to the instruction like a duck to water. He was eager to please, and practiced his draw every time they stopped. He practiced shooting too, although not as much.

"I only have half a box of cartridges," Tyree mentioned. "I don't usually carry a lot with me."

Aces knew that neck of the country well, and had an idea. "Sutter's Stump is only half a day away. We can swing by and get you some."

"Never heard of it," Tyree said.

"I have," Marshal Hitch said, and asked Aces, "Are you sure you want to stop there? The stories I've heard . . ." He didn't finish.

"We'll get in and out quick," Aces said.

"Is it a town?" Tyree asked.

"Not exactly," Aces said. Some folks would call it a blight. Originally a trading post built by a man named Sutter—the *Stump* part came from a giant tree stump next to the post—it had changed hands a few years back. The new owner converted part of it to a saloon and built shacks out back for fallen doves to ply their trade. His name was Bascomb. Rumor had it he was a bad man from Texas who'd helped himself to a bank's assets, fled north, and invested those assets in the trading post.

Aces had stopped there a few times. The liquor was

watered down, the doves weren't the cream of the female crop, and a lot of hard cases hung about, not doing much of anything except drinking and playing cards and sizing up anyone who stopped by. He had never been bothered, but he'd heard of others who had. Whispers of men being robbed. Whispers of a few who had gone missing.

Aces wasn't worried. He was more than a fair hand with a pistol. And the lawman was along. Even Bascomb would think twice about trying to rob or harm a tin star. The law dog fraternity took a dim view of that.

Tyree was excited. The kid had a new air about him. He wasn't as angry all the time, and he smiled more often.

They weren't more than an hour out of Sutter's Stump when the palomino acquired a second shadow.

"I hope you know what's you're doing," Fred said. "I've heard only bad things about Sutter's."

"In and out," Aces said.

"We had someone from Sweetwater go to Cheyenne last year. He never came back. I sent inquiries and found out he might have stopped at Sutter's on his way back. Probably for a drink or to dally with a whore, or both."

"We'll watch ourselves."

"You have more confidence than I do," Fred said. "As gun wise as you are, I don't blame you. Me, I like to be more cautious."

"A man gets into the habit of runnin' from trouble," Aces said, "people start to call him yellow."

"It's not runnin' so much as avoidin'," Fred said. "Why ask for it if you don't have to?"

"I've never lived my life with my head in the ground," Aces said.

"There's where we differ," Fred said. "I stuck mine in a hole a long time ago and kept it there. The kid is right. I could never be a lawman in a place like Cheyenne or Denver. Too much happens. There would be no hiding from it."

"You're not as worthless as you make yourself out to be."

Fred blinked in surprise. "What a kind thing to say. But you don't know much about me. Most of my nourishment comes from a flask. And as a shooter, I'm pitiful."

"I could give you lessons the same as Tyree."

"No, thank you. I'm too old to become a gun hand. All I want is to get McCarthy to Cheyenne and go back to my comfortable office and my flask."

"Folks like what they like," Aces said. Some people refused to change bad habits no matter what. They were content with their lot in life, and the world be damned.

That had never been his outlook. Maybe it had to do with being thrown on his own so young. On being forced to sink or swim. He'd seen a lot of folks flounder and go under, usually because of bad choices in their life. He tried to avoid bad choices. The code he lived by helped, things he wouldn't do no matter what. For instance, he never broke a law except when it was necessary. The same with killing.

Aces was no do-good, though. His helping Tyree had more to do with memories of his own childhood, and how different his life might have been if his pa hadn't set him adrift on the sea of life and severed the rope of caring that connected a son to his father.

Sutter's Stump hadn't changed since his last visit. The combination saloon and trading post was made of logs. The shacks for the doves had been built out back a sensible distance from the outhouses.

Over a dozen horses were at the hitch rail, and a buckboard was parked nearby. From inside came an oath and the clink of a glass.

"Stay close to me," Aces advised Tyree. "This place isn't for greenhorns."

"Ain't that the truth?" Fred Hitch said. He rubbed his hand over his badge, to wipe away the dust, and gripped McCarthy's arm. "You stay close to me, Tom. No talkin' unless I say so."

"What do I care?" McCarthy said. He was constantly sullen, and more than a little testy.

His spurs jingling, Aces pushed on the batwings. As was to be expected, every pair of eyes in the place was fixed on the newcomers. Hooking his thumb in his gun belt close to his ivory-handled Colt, Aces ambled over to the bar.

At a table several cold-faced men were playing cards. They appraised Aces and his companions like wolves sizing up prey.

Aces gave them a cold-eyed stare in return.

A few drinkers were at the bar. One wore a bowler and had a carrying case such as drummers used.

Bascomb was known for doing his own bartending. It wasn't that he was fond of serving drinks, Aces suspected. It was so he could do some sizing up of his own.

A big, burly man, the cutthroat always had his sleeves rolled up, and at the moment had a towel over his shoulder. He came down the bar like a bear leaving its cave and placed his hairy hands on the counter. "Aces Connor," he rumbled. "It's been a spell."

"You remember me," Aces said. "I'm flattered."

Bascomb's smile held no warmth. "I never forget a gun hand. Fact is, I like to learn all I can about them."

"So you'll know who to steal from and who to let be?"

"That's what I like about you," Bascomb said, his tone suggesting he didn't like it at all. "Your sense of humor." He regarded the others. "And look at this. You're keepin' company with a lawman these days."

"Marshal Hitch out of Sweetwater," Fred introduced himself. "Helpin' to take a prisoner to Cheyenne."

"You don't say," Bascomb said. "And who's the boy?"

"Don't call me that," Tyree said.

"You don't even shave yet," Bascomb said. "I'll call you what I damn well please."

Tyree colored and might have taken exception, but Aces glanced at him and gave a slight shake of his head.

"So he's your pup?" Bascomb said.

"He's a friend," Aces said. "And so is the marshal. It might do to keep that in mind."

"How about you?" Bascomb asked Tom McCarthy. "Are you one of this cowpoke's friends too?"

McCarthy was showing an unusual interest in things. He had been gazing about the saloon and across the way at the shelves of drug goods and other items for sale and trade. "I hardly know the man."

"So you're not, then?"

McCarthy held up his bound wrists. "You see this? He's helping to get me hanged. What do you think?

"Do tell," Bascomb said.

"I'd like a drink," Fred said. "Whiskey will do."

"How about you, boy?" Bascomb said to Tyree. "Are you man enough for some Monongahela?"

"None for him," Aces said. "All he wants is a box of cartridges."

Bascomb motioned toward the shelves. "Go on over. You've been here before. You know where they are. Caleb will wait on you."

Aces started over, saying, "Come with me" to Tyree.

Behind them Marshal Hitch said, "I've heard you have doves, but I don't see any ladies about."

"I have three, but it's early yet," Bascomb said. "They'll be in toward sundown. I can rustle one up, though, if you'd like a poke."

"I'd like that whiskey more than anything."

Aces frowned. He'd hoped Hitch would stay on his guard.

The cartridges were in a glass case where rifles, revolvers, and shotguns were on display. All were trade-ins being sold for twice what a new gun was worth. The cartridges cost more too, but Aces figured the extra dollar and a half was worth it for the boy's sake.

Caleb was the opposite of what you'd expect a clerk to be. A hulking mountain of bone and muscle, he had carrot-hued hair and an expression as dull as an ox's. He wore an apron that barely fit and never spoke unless spoken to. Word was that he had come north from Texas with Bascomb and practically worshipped him.

As Aces was paying for the box, Tyree said, "I don't like that Bascomb. He looks at me strange."

Caleb heard, and his dull eyes glittered. "Don't be talkin' about Ira that way."

Tyree seemed startled. "Well, he does."

"How about I stomp you?" Caleb said.

"What did I do?"

Aces placed his hand on his Colt. "There won't be any stompin' today, if you don't mind, and even if you do."

Caleb glanced at Aces's holster and showed he wasn't as dumb as he appeared to be. "I know about you, mister. You're a shooter. Mr. Bascomb says to be careful around shooters."

"Does he, now?" Aces nudged Tyree. "Let's go." As they moved off he lowered his voice and said, "That was careless, provokin' him."

"How was I to know he'd take offense?"

"He works here, doesn't he? That should have told you right there that he and Bascomb must be friends."

Aces came to the saloon and stopped.

Over at the bar, Marshal Hitch was leaning on an elbow while drinking and talking to one of the cold-eyed men from the table. The lawman's back was to Tom Mc-Carthy, who had his head bent close to Bascomb's. The two appeared to be whispering.

Aces strode over. His spurs gave him away, and Bascomb moved away from McCarthy, wiping at the bar with his towel.

McCarthy smiled.

"What were you talkin' to him about?" Aces asked.

"Oh, this and that," McCarthy said. "A fine gentleman, Mr. Bascomb. The world could do with more like him."

Aces didn't like the sound of that. He didn't like that

Marshal Hitch was being friendly with one of the curly wolves either. He tapped the lawman's shoulder. "We're ready to light a shuck."

"What's your rush, mister?" the wolf said. He was tall and lean with pockmarked cheeks and wore a Remington butt-forward on his left hip. "The law dog and me are just gettin' acquainted."

"We're leavin'," Aces said to Hitch.

"Sure," Fred said. "Give me a minute." He took another sip. "I'm going to have my flask filled."

Aces could have kicked him. "Make it quick."

"You're awful bossy," the wolf said.

"What's it to you?"

The wolf grinned. "Bascomb there tells me you're a quick-draw artist. I find that interestin'. I jerk a pistol pretty slick myself. Could be you've heard of me." He paused. "Puck Tovey, from the Staked Plain country."

In fact, Aces had. Tovey was a notorious man-killer who had terrorized the borderlands for a dozen years or better. "You're a mite off your range."

"That I am," Puck said. "The Texas Rangers had it in for me. With them, you shoot one and they put a whole company on your trail."

Aces suddenly recollected something else. Puck Tovey was different from most shootists in that whereas those with any common sense avoided tangling with other leather slappers of note, Puck Tovey was noted for seeking them out and prodding them into going for their six-guns. Tovey was a shark who liked to kill other sharks.

"So, how many has it been for you?" Puck asked.

Aces didn't need to ask what he meant. "None of your business."

"How about I make it mine?"

Aces saw where this was leading. A feeling came over him, the sort of feeling a man had when he stood on the brink of a precipice and was about to go over. The other wolves had risen from their table. A glance at the mirror showed Bascomb had stopped wiping the bar and stood with one hand under it.

Aces couldn't count on Tyree or Hitch for help. The boy was fondling the box of cartridges as if they were a Christmas gift, and the lawman had his mouth glued to his glass.

"Didn't you hear me?" Puck Tovey asked.

Aces set himself. "I heard an ass break wind."

Chapter 16

Puck Tovey was sure of himself. He straightened and took a step back, saying, "Well, now. It's been a coon's age since anyone was dumb enough to insult me."

"Maybe you're just too dumb to notice." Aces took a step too, away from the bar. Out of the corner of his eye he saw that Tyree had caught on that trouble was brewing and had lowered his right hand to his Colt.

As for Marshal Hitch, he drained the last of his glass, sighed, and set the glass down. "That was nice. I could use another."

Puck Tovey gave him a look of amusement. "You might want to move, law dog, or you're liable to take lead."

"Must be Mr. Connor is right about you," Fred said. "Shootin' a lawman isn't very smart."

"I've done it before," Puck told him.

"Shootin' a lawman whose brother is a federal marshal and whose uncle is a federal judge is even dumber."

"The hell you say."

"I just did."

This was the first Aces had heard about Hitch's brother and uncle. Then again, there hadn't been cause for Hitch to mention it.

Acting as if he didn't have a care in the world, Fred stretched and said, "Shoot me and there will be a federal warrant for your arrest. Every federal marshal in the territory will be after you. They might not be as formidable as the Texas Rangers, but do you really want that?"

Puck was studying the lawman. "What did you say your last name was? Hitch? I never heard of any federal marshal with that handle."

"Met them all, have you?"

"How do I know you're tellin' the truth? You could be makin' it up to save your hides."

Reaching for the bottle, Fred began to refill his glass. "Oh, I doubt Mr. Connor's hide needs savin'." He stopped pouring and set the bottle down. "I've seen him draw, and you don't have a chance in hell of beatin' him."

"Is that a fact?"

"Especially if he has help," Fred said.

"What kind of help can you be, you old goat? You don't look to me to be no gun hand."

"I'm the kind who thinks instead of shoots," Fred said, and threw the whiskey in his glass into Puck Tovey's face.

Backpedaling and blinking, Tovey stabbed for his Remington.

Acres drew and shot the Texan in the head. Pivoting, he caught Bascomb in the act of bringing a shotgun from under the bar. He fanned two swift shots, just below the sternum. Jolted onto his heels, Bascomb dropped the scattergun and looked down at himself in shock.

"Hell no," he said, and melted.

Aces was already swiveling to train his Colt on Tovey's pards. Everything had happened so quickly that they were frozen in surprise. Not one had gone for his six-shooter. Now one started to but stopped at the click of Aces's Colt. "If you're hankerin' to die, try,"

Tyree had a six-shooter out but hadn't fired. He seemed as awed as the rest.

Of them all, only Tom McCarthy showed disappointment. "Well, hell. Bascomb said he would set me free for five hundred dollars."

"Your idea or his?" Aces said without taking his eyes off the others.

"I might have mentioned it first," McCarthy said.

Fred grabbed hold of McCarthy's wrists. "The hell you say! That's what I get for turnin' my back to you. From here on, you're not to talk to anybody unless I say you can."

"I'm a walking dead man," McCarthy said. "I'll do whatever I have to in order to keep that from happening."

"We're leavin'," Aces announced. "I'll go last." So he could cover them as they backed out.

Fred grabbed the bottle. "This goes with us. I figure I'm entitled."

"Bring a case if you want," Aces said.

"Would that I could," Fred said with a laugh. Pulling McCarthy after him, he made for the batwings.

"Look out!" Tyree cried.

Caleb was lumbering out of the store with his big fists balled. "You shot Ira!" he shouted at Aces.

Aces trained his Colt on him. "I don't want to have to shoot you too." Two in under a minute was more than enough.

Caleb was so mad his entire frame shook. "He was my friend and you killed him. You'll answer for it, you hear?"

"Let it go," Aces cautioned.

Seldom had anyone looked at Aces with such intense hatred. For a few moments Aces thought Caleb would rush him. Aces reached the batwings and pushed outside. Once Tyree and the marshal were in their saddles, he darted around the hitch rail and forked leather.

Worried they might be shot as they rode off, Aces bawled, "Ride!" and used his spurs.

But no one appeared. No one fired at them.

Tyree let out a whoop and Aces almost did the same. They'd made it out in one piece. By nightfall they'd be so far from Sutter's Stump he reckoned that no one stood a prayer of catching them.

Only after they'd gone a mile did Aces slow.

Scanning their back trail, Tyree chuckled. "That was fun. We should do it again sometime."

"We were lucky," Fred said. "Of course, that business about my brother and my uncle helped some."

"Was that true or not?" Aces asked.

"Not," Fred said, and laughed.

"Mighty quick thinkin'," Aces said. "So was throwin' your drink in Tovey's eyes. You might have saved our hash."

"I'm happy to be useful," Fred said.

Tyree still held the box of cartridges. "I'm happy that I can practice all I want to now."

"That's all you care about?" Fred said.

"It's what we went there for," Tyree replied. Turning, he chuckled at Aces. "When word of what you did gets out, you'll be downright famous. Folks will point at you and stare."

"I've had enough of that, but thank you," Aces said. Adding to his tally was the last thing he wanted. All the ranchers in the territory would hear of it. Finding work would be harder than ever.

"I don't see why you're so upset," Tyree said. "If it was me, when we get to Cheyenne I'd celebrate."

"You worry me some," Aces said. "You truly do."

"Why? I haven't even shot anybody yet."

"You shot a horse," Fred said.

Tyree jaw muscles twitched. "I swear, you would make a great biddy hen. You should have been born a girl."

Tom McCarthy had been listening and now he snorted in disgust. "Hypocrites. You go around killing and talking about killing, yet you insist on turning me over to the law for doing the same thing you do."

"You're loco," Fred said. "A shootin' affray isn't the same as muderin' your missus and her lover."

"What do you know?" McCarthy said. He was clearly in a mood for an argument, but Fred didn't take the bait.

That evening, Aces gave Tyree another lesson. He explained that it was important not to lose one's head in a fight. "A clear head gives you an edge on a man who is mad or drunk."

Tyree was more interested in bettering his draw. He had a tendency to grab at his pistols instead of drawing them. Aces showed him how to do it with a smooth down-and-up motion.

"No wasted movement. That's the key."

Tyree was an eager pupil. He practiced drawing both his right and his left hands, singly and together, until they were ready to crawl under their blankets.

As Aces was sinking back on his, the boy came over, beaming.

"I think I have it."

"Show me."

Wagging his arms to loosen them, Tyree drew. "What do you think?" he asked anxiously.

"Keep at it and you'll be able to hold your own against most anybody," Aces said. He'd like to see the boy be faster, but it was important to encourage him.

"It's the three who killed my ma and pa I want in my sights," Tyree said. "If only I can find them."

"When you do, remember what I told you about keepin' your head."

"That might be hard to do," Tyree admitted. He began to spread out his bedroll, pausing to say, "I can't tell you how much this means to me. No one has ever helped me like you're doing."

It had been a long day and Aces was looking forward to catching some sleep. But just when he was on the verge of drifting off, Marshal Hitch came over.

"Did you hear anything?"

"For instance?" Aces said.

"While you were givin' the boy his lesson, I thought I heard hooves." Fred pointed back the way they'd come. "A couple of horses, or more."

"Why didn't you say somethin'?"

"I heard it and then I didn't. It could have been my ears playin' tricks on me."

Aces stared into darkness. "We'll take turns keepin' watch," he proposed. "Better safe than sorry."

"Fine by me," Fred said. "I'll go first, if you don't object."

"Stay awake," Aces cautioned.

"You can count on me."

Aces hoped so. He folded his hands on his chest and waited, but sleep eluded him. He tossed and turned and finally succumbed, but he couldn't have been asleep more than an hour when Marshal Hitch shook his shoulder to wake him.

"Your turn, shootist."

"I'm a cowpoke and don't you forget it," Aces said irritably. "The shootin' just happens."

"A lot," Fred said.

Sitting up, Aces riffled his hair and put his hat on and tried to get his brain to work. Fortunately, half a pot of coffee was being kept warm on a flat rock by the fire. He filled his tin cup and gratefully drank.

Tyree was snoring. Somewhere out on the prairie a wolf howled.

Aces had always liked to listen to wolves, to their high, throaty cries and their lonesome laments. At times a wolf could sound happy and at other times so inexpressibly sad that it plucked at a man's soul. Some nights, packs would sing in chorus together, and he would lie there and thrill to the beauty of it.

Aces finished his coffee and stood. He needed to stretch his legs and clear his head. Stepping around the fire, he went over to the horses. The palomino, the bay, and the sorrel were dozing. He went out farther, to where the glow of the firelight met the black of night.

He saw nothing; he heard nothing other than the wolves.

Aces admired the stars awhile, then returned.

Tyree was muttering in his sleep and moving his arms and legs as if he were running.

Aces wondered if the boy was dreaming about the men who murdered his folks. What a burden that would be, carrying a thing like that around in your head for the rest of your life.

Aces refilled his cup. He was about to take a swallow when he heard a faint metallic clink. Not a click, as a gun hammer would make, but a slightly louder, sharper sound. He didn't know what to make of it. It reminded him of a pickax striking a rock, but who would be using a pickax in the middle of the prairie in the dead of night?

He hoped it would be repeated, but it wasn't.

But someone, or something, was out there.

Aces set his cup down. The coffee could wait. He went back to the horses and stood between the palomino and the bay, his hand on his Colt.

The minutes dragged and the fire burned low, the flames crackling softly. Now and again a piece of fire-wood popped. Smoke rose in gray ribbons.

Aces figured he must be mistaken. Whoever or what-ever was prowling around out there should have shown by now. He had started to come out from between the horses when he heard the clink again, closer this time.

His palomino raised its head and pricked its ears. It was staring to the north, the way they had come.

Aces debated waking the others.

Suddenly the bay and the sorrel both looked up. The sorrel nickered lightly and stomped a front hoof.

Figures moved just beyond the firelight. It was hard for Aces to tell, but there appeared to be four or five. They were spread out like soldiers in a skirmish line.

Aces let them come closer so he'd have targets to shoot. Faces took form, pale against the dark. One was a lot higher than the rest.

Aces placed his hand on his Colt. Whoever they were, they must intend to shoot his friends in their sleep.

The big one crept forward. For his size, he was as silent as an Apache. Metal glinted in his hand. He was carrying a long-handled ax.

Aces had seen enough. He was about to step into the open when a gun barrel was jammed against his spine.

Chapter 17

It was rare for Aces to be taken so completely by surprise. He froze, his hand still on his Colt.

"Not so much as a twitch," the man behind him growled. "You do, and I blow you in half."

Aces's hand was yanked away and his Colt was snatched from his holster. Whoever was behind him grabbed him by the back of his shirt and shoved from between the horses.

"Walk toward the fire and keep your hands where I can see them."

Aces looked over his shoulder. His captor was one of the men who had been playing cards with Puck Tovey. Grizzled and thick-lipped, he wore a buckskin shirt and britches and a floppy hat. "Never had anyone sneak up on me like that."

"I'm good at sneakin'," the man said. "I was a scout once." He jabbed Aces with an old Maynard buffalo gun.

Marshal Hitch and Tyree were sound asleep, the boy on his back with his blanket to his chin and his hat half-down over his eyes.

"Your pards are in for a surprise," the scout said.

The silhouettes in the dark emerged.

Caleb was the large one. He had a revolver around his waist but was carrying an ax. The other two were from the card game.

Smirking, Caleb glowered down at Aces. "Didn't

reckon on seein' us again, did you?" He spoke quietly so as not to wake the marshal and the boy.

"We watched our back trail but saw no sign of you," Aces admitted. Truth was, Caleb had been cleverer than he figured.

"You killed my friend," Caleb said, and held the ax head under Aces's nose. "The best partner I ever had."

"He was about to back-shoot me."

"You should have let him." Caleb wagged the ax. "You see this? I aim to chop you into bits and pieces for what you done."

"I thought you were here to chop firewood," Aces said.

"Funny man," Caleb said, and slammed the flat of the ax head against Aces's temple.

Pain exploded, and Aces lost his hat. He sank to a knee, the world spinning, and felt a drop of blood trickle down his cheek.

"I'm going to enjoy choppin' you up," Caleb said quietly. He turned and regarded Hitch and Tyree. "Them too."

"Let's get on with it," the scout said.

"What's your hurry, Kline?" Caleb said. "We've got them right where we want them."

"Do you?" Tyree Larn said, and sat up. His blanket fell away, revealing a cocked Colt in each hand, pointed at Caleb's broad chest. "Drop that ax and have your pards drop their rifles or I'll put holes in you."

Caleb showed no alarm whatsoever. Sneering, he said, "Listen to you, boy. If'n you shoot me, Kline and these others will blow out the cowboy's wick and do the same to you and that no-account tin star."

"Maybe they will and maybe they won't," Tyree said. "But you won't be around to see it."

Aces wished the boy had come out from under the blanket with his pistols blazing. Any moment, Kline or one of the others might take it into his head to shoot him.

"I've been shot before," Caleb said. "It don't worry me none."

Aces saw that Kline had tucked his ivory-handled Colt under a wide leather belt the old scout wore. It was within easy reach, provided he had a distraction.

"Shows how few brains you have," Tyree said.

Caleb's bushy eyebrows met over his eyes. "All my life folks have been callin' me dumb. It riles me something fierce."

"For the last time, you ugly-as-hell giant, drop the damn ax."

Caleb looked at it, and smiled. "That's not going to happen, boy. What *will* happen is this. You'll shoot me, but it won't bother me none, and then my friends will shoot you and I'll take this ax to the gun hand."

"You take a lot for granted, mister." Tyree glanced at Aces as he said it, and Aces gave a slight nod. "There ain't none of us bulletproof."

"It's you who should drop those pistols," Caleb said.

"To make it easier for you to kill me?" Tyree laughed. "You must reckon I'm as dumb as you."

"There you go again," Caleb said. "Someone shoot this brat so we can get on with the killin'."

"You first," Tyree said, and fired both Colts.

Caleb was jolted back by the twin slugs tearing through his body. One burst out his back, high on his shoulder, spraying drops of blood.

At the twin blasts, Aces sidestepped and spun. He counted on Kline having turned his head toward Tyree and Caleb. It bought him the split second he needed to yank his Colt from under Kline's belt, cock it as he raised it, and shoot the old scout in the face. Whirling, he fanned shots at the others. Tyree was shooting at them too. The boy must have figured that Caleb would fall, but Caleb didn't. Instead the giant roared like an enraged grizzly and hurled his bulk at Tyree, raising the ax on high. There was another shot, just one, and Caleb's head snapped back and he buckled to sprawl in a heap next to the fire.

Both Aces and Tyree looked over at Marshal Hitch.

The lawman had risen on an elbow, his revolver poking from under his blanket. He seemed as surprised as they were. "For Pete's sake. I've killed somebody."

"I'm damn glad you did," Tyree said.

Aces went from body to body, making sure.

"It happened so quick," Tyree said. "Just like you said it would. I didn't hardly have time to think."

"I've never killed anybody before," Fred said, staring aghast at Caleb's sprawled form.

"It's about time you did, you bein' the law and all," Tyree said. "If you're that weak sister about it, hand in your tin star and become a chicken farmer."

"Who is the man here and who is the boy?" Fred said.

"Cluck, cluck," Tyree said.

Satisfied their enemies were dead, Aces commenced to reload. "You did fine, Tyree. Right fine."

The boy grinned and held out his Colts. "I did, didn't I? I did just like you told me and kept my head and shot that big one."

"You put slugs into two of them," Aces said.

"I did, didn't I?" Tyree said once more, proud of his accomplishment. "It shows I can do it when I find those who murdered my ma and my pa."

"That you can," Aces said.

"How can you be so happy over killing someone?" Fred said. "It will eat at me the rest of my days."

"You are the most peculiar law dog I ever met," Tyree said. "You're always nice to folks. You don't like to shoot anybody. I reckon you must cry at a hangin'."

"They don't please me none, no."

"If chickens aren't to your likin', how about raisin' hogs?"

"Cut it out," Fred said. "This is serious."

"What makes you think I wasn't?" Tyree pushed his blankets off and stood. Nudging Caleb with a toe, he laughed. "I did it. I actually did it."

"You don't have to keep crowin' about it," Fred said.

"Sure I do," Tyree said. "I'm not a weeper like you."

"Aren't you forgettin' something?" Aces asked him.

Tyree tore his gaze from Caleb. "Like what?"

"What's the first thing you're to do after you shoot?"

"Reload," Tyree said. Replacing his left Colt in its holster, he slipped a cartridge from a belt loop. "Sorry. I got excited."

Aces grinned. "So I noticed."

Marshal Hitch rose, his features downcast. "I'd be obliged if neither of you mentions my part in this to anyone."

"You don't want us to brag on you shootin' that Caleb?" Tyree said.

"I surely don't."

"See what I mean about him bein' peculiar?" Tyree said to Aces. "You ever met a lawman like him?"

"I surely haven't." Aces mimicked the boy.

"Have your fun, both of you," Fred said. "But it would please me mightily if we stopped talkin' about it."

"I have one last question for you," Tyree said.

Fred sighed. "Let me hear it."

"Where the hell is our bail jumper?"

Aces turned. He'd forgotten about Tom McCarthy in all the excitement. McCarthy's blanket had been flung aside, and he was gone.

"How in the world?" Fred exclaimed. "I tied his hands and feet, both."

Aces went over and squatted. A jagged rock and pieces of rope explained things. "He must have sawed himself free before Caleb and those others showed up."

"Then took advantage and ran off while we were busy with them," Fred said.

"He won't get far on foot," Tyree declared.

Struck by a thought, Aces straightened. "He might get farther than you think. Caleb and his friends left their horses out there somewhere."

"Oh, hell," Fred said. "We can't go runnin' off in the dark. We have no idea which way he went."

"I'll catch him tomorrow, wait and see," Tyree said confidently. "I did it once. I can do it again. There hasn't been a bounty yet who escaped me."

"We'd best get some sleep," Aces said. If McCarthy did get hold of a horse, it promised to be a long day.

"What about the bodies?" Fred said.

"Buzzards get hungry too," Aces said.

"That's not right."

"It would take all night to bury them and we'd be worthless in the mornin'. Is that what you want?"

"I suppose not," Fred said. "What's one more thing I never thought I'd do? I make it back to Sweetwater, I'm never leavin' again. This world is too rough for my tastes."

"Strangest lawman ever born," Tyree said.

Aces found sleep elusive, and he wasn't the only one. He'd been lying there for about fifteen minutes when Tyree let out a long sigh.

"Are you awake, Aces?"

"Afraid so."

"I can't fall asleep for the life of me. I'm too wrought up. It feels as if my blood is racin' through my body."

"That can happen your first time."

"I'd like it to happen every time," Tyree said. "It's a good feelin'. All warm and tingly."

"I never felt the tingly part," Aces said.

"I feel like I'm on top of the world. Like I've proven somethin' to myself that most folks don't ever get to."

"You shot somebody. That's all."

"Two somebodies," Tyree said, and chuckled.

Aces was a little disturbed by how happy the boy was about it. "Listen, Tyree. You're young yet, so it's natural you're het up. But there's no glory in shootin' someone. Even when they deserve it."

"It's glorious to me," Tyree said.

"That will wear off. When you're my age you'll see things more clearly."

"I'm not your age. I'm me."

Aces rolled over to face him. "Don't let it go to your

head. You start struttin' around like you're the toughest hombre who ever lived, and you won't last long. The loud ones, the proud ones, never do."

"I'd never go that far."

"Keep a sensible head and you'll live to a ripe old age, like Hitch yonder."

"I heard that," the marshal said grumpily. "And I'm not ripe yet, I'll have you know."

"You could have fooled me," Tyree said, "the notions you have."

Aces wasn't done trying to make things clear. "Keep your shootin' to yourself. Don't get drunk and boast. Don't prod when there's no call. Don't scare folks for the fun of it."

"What do you think I am?" Tyree said.

"It happens," Aces said. "Puck Tovey thought he was the cock of the walk and look at what it got him. There's always someone faster. Someone smarter. Live by the gun and your name is on a bullet. You just never know when or who will pull the trigger that does you in."

"I like how you put that," Fred said. "Heed him, boy."

"I do everything he says, don't I?" Tyree said. "I've never looked up to anybody as much as I look up to him."

Aces was flattered.

"Truth is, I never had anyone to look up to before. No one's ever taken the time to teach me anything."

"Life can be cruel," Fred said, "but it can be good too. It's up to us, with the decisions we make. Puck Tovey made his decision to be a bad man a long time ago, and look at where it got him."

"You are a mother hen," Tyree said. "I'm not going to be like Puck Tovey. I'm going to be like Aces. I won't ever shoot anyone unless they deserve it."

"What?" Aces said.

"Like you did with that rustler and that tinhorn. They deserved it, didn't they? There are always some who do."

"Happy now, Aces?" Fred said.

"Don't you be pickin' on him," Tyree said. "Thanks to Aces, from this day on, I'm not Tyree Larn, a nobody. I'm Tyree Larn, gun hand."

"God help us," the marshal said.

Chapter 18

Tyree's last comments bothered Aces. They bothered him considerably. But he put them from his mind for the time being to concentrate on catching Tom McCarthy.

At daybreak the three of them were in the saddle. They left the bodies, although Marshal Hitch once again objected. They did bundle all the rifles in a blanket and tie it to the lawman's bay. They also collected all the six-guns and put them in saddlebags. Leaving bodies to rot was one thing. Wasting good guns was another. Aces went through the pockets of the deceased and came up with fifty-four dollars in bills and coins. Aces and Tyree split the money.

They headed north at a trot. Tyree was eager to overtake McCarthy quickly, but that wasn't going to happen.

The hulking Caleb and his friends had left their mounts in a dry wash about two hundred yards out. McCarthy had found them and helped himself to two of the horses. The others were still there, ground-hitched.

"Why'd he take two animals?" Tyree wondered. "Is he usin' the second as a packhorse?"

"He'll ride the first into the ground to get as far ahead of us as he can," Aces reckoned, "then switch to the second animal."

"He probably rode all night," Marshal Hitch said. "He could be to Sutter's Stump soon."

"Hell in a basket," Tyree said.

"We'll take the extra horses with us," Aces said. "Use them when our own get tired."

They rode hard. Tyree's sorrel played out first and he switched to a pinto. Hitch's bay lasted another hour and a half, and then he had to switch to a chestnut.

The palomino had more stamina. It was tired but gamely held to the pace Aces set.

Night was falling when they came within sight of Sutter's. Lamplight bathed the windows with a rosy glow. Half a dozen animals were at the long hitch rail out front.

Aces dismounted, looped the reins off, and started toward the batwings but drew up short.

A crudely fashioned casket, made of oak, had been propped against the front of the building. The top was off, and in the casket, his arms folded across the chest, were the mortal remains of the former owner.

"Bascomb, by heaven," Fred exclaimed.

"Why haven't they planted him?" Tyree wondered.

"The novelty of it."

"The what?"

Fred stepped to the casket. "It's not every day we get to see a dead person. They put him out here to give themselves somethin' to talk about."

"That's silly," Tyree said.

"No, son. It's human nature. In some towns, if a famous person dies, the undertaker props the coffin outside his establishment and charges folks for the privilege of gawkin' at the dear departed."

"I'd never pay to see somebody dead," Tyree said. "Hell, I wouldn't pay to see somebody alive even if they were famous. What's famous anyhow but folks talkin' about a person a lot?"

"Some folks like that. They think that being famous is all that matters in life."

"Seems senseless to me. All that fame ends up in the same place," Tyree said, and nodded at the coffin.

"Are you two done?" Aces asked.

"Would you want to be famous?" Tyree said.

"No."

"Wild Bill Hickok was, and folks still talk about him. So maybe I was wrong and being famous is good for you."

"A hundred years from now no one will remember who he was," Aces said. "And he's long past carin' already."

"How do you know?" Fred said. "If there's a hereafter, he might hear what folks say and take some comfort in that."

Aces stared at him.

"What?" Fred said.

Aces pushed on the batwings. Two men were at a corner table, drinking. A stocky man with curly russet hair was tending bar. No one appeared to be in the store section.

"Well, look who it is," the russet-haired man said when they reached the bar. "You've got some nerve."

"I beg your pardon?" Marshal Hitch said.

"You heard me," the bartender said. "You killed Mr. Bascomb and now you must have killed Caleb and those who went with him or the three of you wouldn't be standin' there."

"We defended ourselves," Fred said. "A man has that right."

Aces was more interested in finding McCarthy. "Our prisoner got away. Have you seen him?"

"I sure ain't," the barkeep said.

"And you wouldn't tell us if you had," Aces said.

"I didn't say that."

"You didn't have to," Aces said. "Your face said it for you."

"Where is he?" Tyree demanded. "Is he still here or did he fan the breeze?"

"Go to hell, kid."

"After you," Tyree said, and drawing a Colt, he leaned across the bar and struck the bartender across the jaw with the barrel.

Crying out in pain, the man stepped back.

"I'll do that again if you don't tell us," Tyree said.

Clutching his chin, the bartender became as red as a beet. "You damn kid. You had no call to do that."

"Where's McCarthy?"

The two men at the corner table began to rise, but Aces swung toward them, his hand poised over his ivory-handled Colt. "Stay where you are, gents. This is none of your affair."

Fred tapped his badge at them. "And the law is involved. So behave."

"Where's McCarthy?" Tyree asked the barkeep a second time.

The bartender hissed like a kicked snake. "I have half a mind to come around there and stomp you into the floor."

"If you can stomp with lead in you, you're welcome to try." Tyree smiled, pointed his Colt, and cocked it. "The days when someone can take a fist or boot to me are over. I'll shoot you like I did your dumb-as-a-stump friend."

"*You* shot Caleb?"

"Let's say I helped. Now, where's Tom McCarthy? Is he here or not? And keep in mind that if you lie to us, we'll come back, and the next time I'll march in shootin'. Do yourself a favor and don't be as dumb as Caleb."

"Do you a favor is more like it," the bartender said. "But yes, he was here. Rode in hours ago with an extra horse. Had himself a couple of drinks, filled a canteen, and lit out again. I expect by now he's clear to Montana."

"Not likely," Fred said. "We'll catch him soon." He beckoned to Aces and Tyree and turned to go.

"Hold on," Aces said. Something in the bartender's manner rang false.

"What's the matter?" Tyree asked.

"We don't take his word for it. You check the back rooms. Marshal Hitch can check the shacks and the out-house."

"Why me?" Fred said.

"You stay and watch these three, then," Aces said, and marched on out. The temperature had dropped and the cool of night was a welcome relief from the blistering heat.

The three shacks were as crudely built as the coffin. Only the first and the third showed light. The middle one was dark.

Aces debated marching on in and decided not to. The doves might be with customers in a state of undress. Not that he'd mind seeing a naked lady. He had only ever been with a dove once, more out of curiosity than any-thing. Some men claimed they couldn't go without. He wasn't one of them.

Careful not to stand in front of the door, Aces knocked. A voice hollered that she would be right there. When the door opened he was ready to draw.

"Well, who are you and what do you want?" the dove demanded, looking him up and down. She had to weigh three hundred pounds and had more canyons in her face than Arizona. "Did Frank send you? I told him I was layin' off tonight on account of Bascomb bein' blown to hell and back."

"I'm lookin' for someone," Aces said. "Short fella with extra pounds, goes by the handle of McCarthy?"

"What do you have against extra pounds?"

"His pounds have nothin' to do with it." Aces set her straight. "He's a lawbreaker. Murdered his missus and skipped bail."

"Killed his wife, you say?" The dove was horrified.

"Strangled her with his own hands. And knifed her lover besides." Aces tried to see past her, but she blocked his view.

"If she was sneaking around behind his back, she had it comin'."

"No one has strangulation comin'. Now, is he in here or not?"

"Not. But you can look anyway. I'm Tilly, by the way. Maybe I'll change my mind and let you have a poke. You're easy on the eyes."

"No, thanks," Aces said. "Findin' McCarthy is more important."

"Nothin' is more important than pokes."

Aces got out of there. She was wasting his time. He went past the second shack with its dark window to the third. Again he knocked. This time the door was opened by a broomstick of a gal in a red dress that had been painted on. She had red rouge on her cheeks and cherry red lips and a red barrette in her red hair.

"Well, lookee here," she said, and smiled.

"Who might you be?" Aces asked.

"Folks call me Red."

"What was I thinkin'?"

"Sorry?"

Aces told her about McCarthy and asked if she had seen him, and Red answered that she hadn't, that she'd been in her shack since some "low-down stinkin' son of a bitch shot Mr. Bascomb."

"Mr. Bascomb was fixin' to shoot that son of a bitch in the back."

"Good for him," Red said. "When you've got to kill somebody, you can't be fussy 'bout whether it's their front or their backside."

"I'll try to remember that." Aces thanked her and left. He was almost to the back door to the saloon when he remembered Bascomb telling Marshal Hitch that there were three doves. There had been no sign of the third in the saloon. Which made him wonder about that dark shack. Pivoting on a bootheel, he stalked back and pounded on the door. It could be she was in there asleep.

He forgot to stand to one side as he had done at the other shacks. Which was why he nearly lost an eye when a gun boomed and a slug tore through the door and buzzed past his head. Throwing himself against the wall, he slicked his Colt. "McCarthy? Is that you?"

There was no answer.

"I'll take you alive if you'll throw out that six-shooter and come out with your hands where I can see them," Aces offered.

"Go to hell!" Tom McCarthy hollered.

"Well, now," Aces said.

"I have a dove in here," McCarthy yelled. "And I'm holdin' a pistol to her pretty head."

"He is, mister, he is!" a woman squealed. "Help me."

Aces heard a slap and McCarthy snarled at her to shut up. "Give up while you can, Tom. I won't ask again."

"You have it backward. You and the others light a shuck or I blow out her wick, so help me."

"She's nothin' to me," Aces said.

"Her death will be on your conscience."

"That's funny, comin' from you."

"Quit bandying words," McCarthy yelled. "I'll count to ten and if you're still out there, she goes to meet her Maker." He didn't wait but started right in. "One!"

Aces swore. McCarthy had him over a barrel. He wouldn't let an innocent woman die if he could help it. "All right!" he shouted. "I'm backin' off." And he did, retreating to the rear door of the saloon. He thought he glimpsed a face in the darkened shack window but couldn't be sure. As he was about to reach for the latch, the door opened.

"What's going on out here? What's all the shoutin'?" Tyree asked.

Aces told him about McCarthy. "That barkeep was lyin'. Either McCarthy paid him or promised to pay him or the barkeep hates us for shootin' his boss."

"Some people will hate for any old reason, won't they?" Tyree said.

Slipping inside, Aces closed the door nearly all the way.

"What's your plan?"

"We wait for him to make a break. If he's got the woman, we hold off until he lets her go."

"He might take her with him," Tyree said. "What then?"

"Let's cross that . . . ," Aces began, and stopped.

The shack door had opened. A terrified young woman was pushed out and stood quaking. McCarthy had hold of her hair and was crouched so only his head showed above her shoulder.

"There they are," Aces said.

"We should rush him," Tyree proposed. "One of us is bound to drop him before he drops us."

"Listen to you," Aces said. "You shoot a couple of men and you think you're Hickok. And you're forgettin' the woman. She might take a slug."

"She's nothin' to me." Tyree echoed Aces's very words.

"I tried that bluff and it didn't work."

"Who says I'm bluffin'?"

Aces tore his eye from the crack. "You're startin' to worry me. Learnin' to shoot is only part of being gun wise. You have to learn when not to."

"It's the money I'm worried about. I need that two thousand."

"That gal's life counts for more."

"If you say so."

Frowning, Aces looked out. McCarthy now had an arm around the woman's waist and was propelling her toward Tilly's shack. Aces didn't have a clear shot, so he didn't try.

Keeping the woman between him and the saloon, Mc-Carthy pounded on Tilly's door.

"Is that you, mister?" Tilly called out. "Did you come back for that poke?" She opened her door, smiling, then swore and tried to slam it shut.

McCarthy thrust the revolver at her and said something Aces didn't hear. They argued in low tones until suddenly McCarthy pressed the muzzle to the pretty woman's head.

"All right, all right," Tilly said. "I'll do it."

"What's happenin'?" Tyree said.

Aces would like to know himself. He began to ease the door open but stopped.

Tilly had come out of the shack and was heading toward them.

Chapter 19

Aces moved back, pushing against Tyree. "Out of the way," he said. "Let her in."

"Let who?" Tyree said.

The door opened and Tilly filled the doorway. She blinked in surprise, then glanced back at her shack and came in and closed the door behind her. "You want to be careful he doesn't see you or he'll kill Matilda."

"Did you know he was with her?"

"I did," Tilly admitted. "He told us he'd blow her brains out if we told you where he was." She frowned. "Sorry I had to lie to you. Matilda is a sweet gal. I can't let any harm come to her if I can help it." She took a step. "Now out of the way. I have things to do."

"Such as?" Aces said.

"I'm to gather up some food and water and take them to him. The two horses he rode in on are out back a ways from the shacks. He aims to hightail it as soon as he has the grub."

"And we'll be right on his heels," Tyree said.

"Like hell you will, boy," Tilly said. "He's takin' Matilda with him. Says he'll kill her if there's any sign of someone after him."

"We're not lettin' him get away," Tyree said.

"Matilda is not to be harmed," Tilly repeated. "I'll do

whatever I have to in order to keep that from happening"

"Fetch what you have to," Aces said.

Tilly lumbered toward them and they parted to let her by. She smelled of perfume and sweat, and her arms jiggled as she moved. It was a tight squeeze, as huge as she was.

When she was out of earshot, Tyree said, "Let's go out and end this. I don't care about the dove."

"We owe it to her not to get her killed," Aces said.

"We don't even know her," Tyree objected. "You don't owe anybody when you don't know them."

"You worry me, boy."

"I thought you'd stopped callin' me that."

Aces racked his brain. If McCarthy reached those horses, he stood a good chance of getting away. They couldn't track at night, not without torches, and it was tedious and slow. By morning McCarthy would be in the mountains, and from there he could go anywhere. West to Utah or Oregon country or east to the States. McCarthy might even go north into Canada. The border was thousands of miles long and easy to cross undetected.

"Step aside and I'll handle this," Tyree said.

"You'll do no such thing."

"Damn it, Aces," Tyree said. "I don't savvy you. One minute you're teachin' me to shoot and treatin' me like I matter, and the next you're treatin' me like a kid who doesn't know any better."

Aces was honest with him. "You don't. I see now that teachin' you to shoot isn't enough. You have to learn that there's a right and a wrong way of doing things, and we should always do the right."

"Right is what we think it is," Tyree said.

Aces sighed. "When you've lived a little longer you'll see that's not so. Was it right for those three to murder your ma and pa? Was it right for them to treat you so poorly at that orphanage?"

"This is different."

"No, it's not." Aces put a hand on Tyree's shoulder. "I'm askin' you, friend to friend, to do as I say in this."

Tyree fidgeted and nodded. "All right. For you I will. But it better work out. I need the money. I found a man in Cheyenne who says he knows who killed my folks. He'll tell me for five hundred dollars."

This was the first Aces had heard of it. He whistled and said, "That's a lot of money."

"Worth every penny if he knows."

Aces was tempted to point out that the man might be taking advantage of Tyree. The boy was so eager to track down the killers, he'd fall for anything. "I'd like to meet this fella."

"You're welcome to come along when I go see him," Tyree said.

Aces hadn't intended to become involved in the boy's hunt. Once they reached Cheyenne, he'd figured to part company and go about finding a rancher who was in need of punchers.

"I don't mind admittin' I could use your help," Tyree said. "You know a lot more than I do about things. I've had to learn as I go, and folks don't always take me as serious as they'd take you."

"I'll think about it," Aces said.

They had to wait a good ten minutes before Tilly reappeared carrying a burlap sack that bulged with whatever she'd picked. She was hurrying, which for her was a brisk waddle, and puffing like a steam engine. "Out of my way. It took longer than I thought and I have to get this to him."

Aces planted himself in her path. "I'm going with you."

"Like hell you are. You're forgettin' Matilda."

Aces told her what he had in mind.

"That's mighty clever," Tyree said, and laughed. "It should work, as wide as this female is."

"Don't call me wide," Tilly snapped. To Aces she said uncertainly, "I don't know. It could go wrong."

"We have to try," Aces said. "He might kill her anyway."

"I've been worried about that, to tell the truth," Tilly confessed. "His word don't mean much." She nodded and hefted the burlap sack. "Let's try it, and pray it works."

Aces let her go by. She stopped at the door and waited while he took off his hat and gave it to Tyree. Drawing his Colt, Aces cocked it, then pressed against Tilly's broad back and bent at the knees. "Go slow and act natural."

"Oh Lordy," Tilly said. She opened the door and stepped out.

Aces went with her, pressed close. The perfume smell was so strong it about gagged him. She was one of those who didn't bathe regularly and used perfume to mask the fact.

From her shack came a bellow. "Took you long enough. Did they try to stop you?"

"I got you things you can use," Tilly answered. "Jerky and bread and the like. Or did you just want me to grab any old thing, like pickles?"

"Don't sass me, woman. I don't like being sassed. My wife used to sass me and I'd slap her silly."

"Imagine that," Tilly said under her breath. "You pig." She slowly advanced, the sack held out where McCarthy could see it. "Matilda, how are you doing, girl? Has he hurt you?"

Aces heard a timid voice say that no, he hadn't.

"Did I give you permission to talk? Get over here, you tub of lard. You're slowing me down. I should have been gone by now."

"I can only move so fast," Tilly said.

"A snail could move faster, damn you," McCarthy said.

"I'm scared is why," Tilly said. "For all I know, you'll gun Matilda and me out of pure spite."

"All I want is the damn food," McCarthy said. "I wouldn't waste ammunition on a couple of whores."

"You have a mean mouth on you, but here I come."

Tilly went a little faster and Aces crouched lower. Everything depended on McCarthy not catching sight of him.

"Where are that kid and his friends?" McCarthy asked. "The gun hand and that lawman?"

"In the saloon."

"I'm surprised they let you bring me the grub."

"The kid didn't want to," Tilly said. "He wanted to march on out and have it out with you. But he was overruled."

"That stinking nuisance," McCarthy growled. "I was doing fine until he showed up. Everyone had forgotten about me."

"Is it true you strangled your missus?"

"Damn right I did. She cheated on me. And you know what? I enjoyed it. I'd do it again if I had it to live over."

"And you wonder why I'm scared of you."

"Quit jabbering and give me the damn sack. I don't have all night. Then you are to go in your shack and stay there until I'm gone."

"Yes, sir," Tilly said. "Whatever you say."

They were almost there.

Aces tensed to make his play. He must move fast. With any luck, McCarthy would be taken completely by surprise and not get off a shot.

"Hold it right there."

Tilly abruptly stopped. "What's the matter?"

"Set the sack down and take a few steps back," McCarthy commanded.

"Whatever for?"

"How do I know it's food?" McCarthy said. "It could be a beaver trap set to take my fingers off when I reach in."

"That's ridiculous," Tilly said.

"I saw traps hanging on the wall in there," McCarthy said. "And it would be something that tricky kid would do. Set the damn sack down and step back."

"It's not no beaver trap," Tilly insisted, "but I'll do whatever you want."

Aces took a quick step back so she wouldn't trip over him. He wasn't expecting her to take more than one, or to move as fast as she did. Her leg bumped his and she let out a squawk and began waving her arms to keep her balance.

"What the hell?" McCarthy said.

Teetering on her heels, Tilly glanced over her shoulder, her eyes widening with alarm. "Oh no," she said.

Aces knew she was going over. He tried to throw himself aside but only partly succeeded. Tilly crashed on top of him. The impact jarred his arm so hard he lost his hold on the Colt and it flew out of reach. He levered his arms to scramble to it but couldn't move. Tilly had him pinned from the waist down.

The next moment McCarthy stood over him, still with an arm around Matilda, smirking and pointing a revolver. "Well, look who it is. Nice try, gun hand. Any last words?"

Aces glared.

"Don't!" Tilly cried, struggling madly to sit up. She was like an upended turtle and couldn't twist far enough to get her hands under her.

"First him and then you, cow," McCarthy gloated. "And then this mouse."

"No!" Matilda screamed.

Shots blasted from the saloon. McCarthy glanced up, startled. He let go of Matilda and backed toward the shack, shooting as he went. Matilda said, "Oh!" and clutched herself.

"Matilda!" Tilly wailed.

Aces was struggling to slide out from under her. He heard Tyree shout something, and the boy and McCarthy traded more shots. Matilda was on her knees, her hand to her chest, her fingers wet with blood.

"No, no, no," Tilly cried.

Pushing against the ground, Aces strained every sinew. "You have to get off me, woman."

"I'm tryin', damn it. I can't help it I'm not delicate."

McCarthy disappeared around the shack. Flame stabbed the dark with a last shot, and boots drummed.

Tyree charged up, firing as he came. "You're not getting' away!" he bawled, and recklessly pounded after him.

Aces was practically beside himself. With a powerful wrench, he managed to extricate his legs. Crabbing to his Colt, he grabbed it and stood. Or tried to. His left leg spiked with pain and buckled. He had to thrust his arm down to keep his balance. Again he rose and this time his leg supported him, but his knee throbbed. Limping, he hobbled in pursuit.

Off in the night a six-shooter cracked and another replied.

"Tyree!" Aces hollered. He shouldn't have, since McCarthy might send lead his way, but the kid would get himself killed if he didn't use his head. Grimacing, he hobbled faster.

The night went quiet save for loud sobs from Tilly.

Aces stopped reluctantly. He had no idea where Tyree and McCarthy had gotten to. He flexed his leg, making sure nothing was broken.

Off a ways hooves drummed and rapidly receded. A last shot banged and someone cursed.

Aces waited. When a darkling figure materialized, he said, "You don't listen worth a damn."

"He got away," Tyree said.

"Didn't you hear me? You shouldn't have run off after him. You're lucky you're not dead."

"I saved your bacon and you do this?" Tyree said, and stalked past.

Aces didn't press it. The boy had saved him, and that was something. He followed him around the shack to where Tilly cradled Matilda and rocked back and forth, tears streaming her cheeks.

"He shot her!" Tilly sobbed.

Aces thought she meant Tyree. Then he saw a blood-rimmed bullet hole between Matilda's bony shoulder blades and realized she had been shot in the back, not the front. Tom McCarthy had been behind her; he'd done it.

"You have to go after him," Tilly said, sniffling. "You have to see he pays."

"Don't you worry, lady," Tyree said. "Tomorrow this ends, one way or the other."

Chapter 20

They set out at daybreak.

Aces refused to push as hard as they had before, which angered Tyree. Aces pointed out that their horses hadn't had enough rest, that McCarthy had an entire night's lead, and that haste might cause them to lose the tracks they were following. Tyree gave in but he wasn't happy.

Marshal Hitch, on the other hand, was in uncommonly good spirits. Aces mentioned as much when they were riding together.

"Why wouldn't I be in fine fettle?" Fred said. "It's a gorgeous day and no one is tryin' to kill me."

"Yet," Aces said, and grinned.

"To be honest, this is the most excitement I've had in my whole life. I'm used to sittin' in my office all day and not doing much of anything," Fred said. "When we started out for Cheyenne I wasn't pleased the mayor made me go. But now I'm sort of gettin' used to it. I'm not nearly as sore from all the ridin', and I find I like bein' out and about."

"I'm glad somebody is havin' a good time."

"The boy has been givin' you grief, I know. Remember he's young yet. He's not as patient as you or me."

"There's more to it than that," Aces said. He didn't elaborate.

Fred inhaled and beamed. "Isn't this day gorgeous? I'm beginnin' to understand what some people see in the outdoors."

"Took you long enough."

"Are you pokin' fun at my gray hairs?" Fred rejoined. "I admit I'm not the sharpest knife in the toolshed. It takes me a while to figure things out. I'm like the tortoise in that story about the tortoise and the hare."

"You don't say."

"I do. A man should know his limitations, and mine are that I'm slow but steady. I'll stick on McCarthy's trail from now until Armageddon if that's what it takes to bring him to bay."

"Tyree will be happy to hear that."

"He worries you, doesn't he?"

"Some," Aces admitted.

"Remember. People don't usually change overnight. Or in a week or two either. You've only known him a short while and you've done him more good than anybody else. Give it more time and I bet he'll change considerably."

Aces admired the lawman's attitude, but he was more practical. There was only so much he could do to help the boy. The rest, Tyree had to do on his own.

Toward noon they came on a herd of cattle. Aces spied several cowboys in the distance and figured the punchers would ride over to find out who they were, but the cowpokes were riding to the east and didn't spot them.

McCarthy's tracks continued north.

Aces wondered where the killer was bound. Certainly not to Sweetwater, where everyone knew what he had done.

"He's pushin' awful hard," Fred remarked at one point.

"Probably switchin' animals like he did before," Aces said.

"Even two will tire out after a while," Fred said. "He'll be lucky to make it to the mountains."

To Aces's immense frustration, McCarthy did.

That night they camped in a clearing by a stream, ringed by pines and spruce. The beans had lost their appeal. Aces hankered after a thick steak dripping with fat juice, and a mess of potatoes besides.

Gazing about them, Tyree said, "Here we are again. In two days we'll be in Sweetwater, and won't that tickle your mayor?"

"He'll make me a laughingstock," Fred predicted. "Tell everyone I can't do my job."

"Well, we have lost McCarthy twice," Tyree said. "It's not anything to crow about."

Aces was about to say that he would crow when McCarthy was behind bars in Cheyenne and not before, when a scream carried to them on a gust of wind, a faint, high-pitched shriek that hinted at unspeakable horror.

Fred shot to his feet. "Lord Almighty, did you hear that?"

"How could I not?" Tyree said. "It gave me goose bumps."

Standing, Aces turned into the wind. "It wasn't an animal."

Fred came around the fire to stand next to him. "You don't reckon it was McCarthy, do you?"

"It better not have been," Tyree declared. "They pay more if he's alive. Guess they want to put on a show with a trial and whatnot."

After a while they sat back down. Aces refilled his tin cup and thought about something he should have thought about sooner. "The Arapahos."

"What about them?" Fred said.

"It could be they're still around."

"You reckon they're to blame for that scream?" Tyree said.

"We'll take turns keepin' watch," Aces proposed.

No one objected. Fred offered to sit up first, and Tyree said he didn't mind being second.

So it was that along about two in the morning, Aces

was roused by a nudge on his leg. The fire had burned low and the horses were dozing. "Anything happen?"

"I was bored silly," Tyree said. "Heard some coyotes and a bear once, that was all." Yawning, he shuffled to his bedroll. "I'm losin' more sleep over McCarthy than I have over all the others I've gone after."

A brisk breeze had brought a chill. Aces huddled with his hands close to the flames. His knee had stopped hurting, but his leg was stiff and gave him twinges when he moved. He wouldn't be doing any running for a few days.

Other than the occasional chirp of a cricket, the night had gone unusually still.

Aces was glad he could sit there and relax. It had been one thing after another for days now, and the reprieve was welcome. He could use a deck of cards to pass the time. The thought brought back memories of his gambling days. He had no regrets about giving up a life of luck to tend cattle, although now and then he missed the excitement.

No sooner did that cross his mind than another scream pierced the night. As far off as the first, it was a tremulous wail of utter despair. Aces was on his feet before it died. He moved to the edge of the clearing, trying to gauge the direction and distance. To the northwest, he decided, maybe a mile or more. He was tempted to investigate, but it would be foolhardy to bumble around in the dark.

Neither Tyree nor Marshal Hitch stirred.

Aces scoured the mountains. In all that dark sprawl of untamed wilderness, there wasn't a light anywhere. It galvanized him into going to their fire and putting it out. He should have done it sooner.

The rest of the night crawled on the tiny feet of a centipede. In the gray of predawn, birds broke into chorus and deer came out of the undergrowth to graze and drink.

All appeared normal.

Aces woke his companions. No one was hungry. They

were saddled and ready when a golden arc blazed on the horizon.

Assuming the lead, Aces headed northwest. He went over a mile without finding anything and was about convinced that he'd been mistaken about the direction when he rounded a bend in a game trail and beheld a flat bank bordering a stream—and on it, staked out naked, a white man.

Tyree was first off his horse. "No, no, no," he said, running over. "You damn jackass. Why'd you have to go and run off?"

"I was afraid of this," Marshal Hitch said. "A man alone doesn't stand a prayer. He brought it on himself."

Alighting, Aces stood over the victim. "I reckon you're sorry that you didn't give yourself up at Sutter's Stump."

Tom McCarthy had been mutilated. Certain body parts had been cut off, and he'd been scalped. That he still had his tongue was a miracle, almost as big a miracle as the fact that he was still alive. "Is that you, Hitch? And Tyree?"

"It's us," Tyree said, moving closer. "What did they do to your eyes?"

"Cut them," McCarthy said.

"Was it the Arapahos?" Aces needed to know.

McCarthy nodded, and winced. "Caught me when my guard was down. I hadn't seen any sign of them, so I figured they were long gone." He licked lips that weren't there. "Never thought I would end like this."

"I could have told you," Fred said.

"You've cost me two thousand dollars, you stupid yack," Tyree said. "Good riddance." Turning his back, he walked off.

Aces hunkered. "Is there anything I can get you? Water? Food? You name it."

"Brains," McCarthy said, and laughed bitterly.

Aces fought down a wave of revulsion. "Tyree, you should join us."

"The hell I will," the boy replied. He was sulking and leaning against an oak. "He has spoiled everything."

"Come join us anyway."

Tyree cussed and smacked the oak. "I shouldn't, but for you I will." He came back and planted himself and folded his arms. "What do you want me to do?"

"Feel a little sorry for him."

"Now I've heard everything," Tyree said. "He's a murderer, for cryin' out loud. His wife, his friend, that dove. You want to feel sorry for someone; feel sorry for them."

"That's all right, kid," McCarthy said. "I was your age once." He closed his eyes and shuddered. "I'd like to be your age now, knowing what I know that I didn't back then. I'd like to live my whole life over and not make the mistakes I did the first time." He shuddered some more, his neck muscles bulging. "The pain," he said softly. "The pain."

"I can end it," Aces offered.

"No, thanks," McCarthy said. "I'll milk what's left to me, pain or no pain. I've never taken life for granted, and I won't start now."

"It was nice knowin' you back in Sweetwater," Fred said. "You always treated everyone decent."

"For a murderer?" McCarthy said.

"For a human being."

"That was kind of you, Fred. I won't forget it."

"For the love of heaven," Tyree said. "Did any of you bring a violin? You're dyin', mister. You've been cut to ribbons and it's what you deserve for what you did. Hell, you'd have been better off hanged."

"That'll be enough," Aces said.

"You wanted me to join you," Tyree said. "Here I am. Just don't expect me to weep and blubber."

"That's the spirit, kid," McCarthy said.

"I hate you," Tyree responded.

Aces changed the subject by asking, "Which way did the war party go? Those Arapahos?"

"I couldn't tell with my eyes put out."

"Ask him what the sky looks like, why don't you?" Tyree said.

Aces could have hit him.

"Would you like some words said over you?" Fred asked. "I've never read the Bible all the way through, but I know a few passages."

McCarthy showed some interest. Tilting his head toward the sound of Fred's voice, he said, "What would you say over me?"

"You want to hear it now?"

"I can't when I'm dead."

Flustered, Fred said, "I'll have to think about it some. I know Psalm Twenty-three, but that's hardly fittin'."

"Why not?" McCarthy said.

"Well, in that case," Fred said, and cleared his throat. "Let's see. How does it go again?" He paused. "'The Lord is my shepherd; I shall not want. He maketh me to lie down in green pastures: he leadeth me beside the still waters.'" Fred stopped and scratched his chin.

"Is that all you remember?" McCarthy said.

"No. Give me a minute." Fred did more scratching. "Now I recollect." He took a breath. "'He restoreth my soul: he leadeth me in the paths of righteousness for his name's sake—'"

"Oh, for Pete's sake," Tyree interrupted. "He strangled his wife and you're quotin' Scripture over him?"

"Even a strangler deserves that much," Fred said.

"Go on," Aces said.

"I'm not sure I remember it all, but I do this next part," Fred said. "'Yea, though I walk through the valley of the shadow of death, I will fear no evil: for thou art with me; thy rod and thy staff they comfort me.'" He started to go on, stopped, and sadly shook his head. "Dang. That's all I can recollect at the moment."

"That was fine," McCarthy said, and turned his sightless eyes to the sky. "God, please forgive me."

"Just die already," Tyree said.

"Death comes to all of us, boy," McCarthy said. He was weakening and they could barely hear him. "It'll come for you one day, like a thief in the night, and that'll be the end of you like this is the end of me." He gasped, stiffened, and gave up the ghost.

"Finally," Tyree said.

Chapter 21

Tyree was as mad as could be for three whole days.

He'd needed the two thousand he'd have been paid. He only had about forty to his name. To be so close to finally learning the name of his parents' murderers and then to be thwarted infuriated him.

Sometimes it seemed as if Tyree had been hunting their murderers forever. The hunt was everything to him. He lived it, breathed it. Some might say he was wasting himself, that he should come to terms with his loss and get on with his life. Especially since he had only been an infant when they were slain. He never knew his folks. He'd never heard their voices, never been hugged or hugged them in return. He had no idea whatsoever what they had been like. He didn't even know the color of their eyes.

So it made sense to get on with his life.

Problem was, Tyree couldn't forget them. Something inside him, something deep down that he couldn't account for, drove him to find their murderers. He'd tried to explain it to others and couldn't. It wasn't love. You couldn't love someone if you didn't know him. It wasn't out of fond memories. He didn't have any. It was something else. A compulsion he could no more resist than he could eating or sleeping.

It was why he became a bounty hunter. The men he

was after were criminals. Outlaws. To find them, he had to deal with others of their kind. He could ask around. Had they ever heard of an incident in Missouri? His hope was that one day he'd get lucky.

He was too young to wear a tin star or he might have become a lawman. A badge could sometimes get people to talk.

Since he couldn't tote tin, the bounty work seemed a smart way to conduct his hunt. He had dealings with the criminal element, and he wasn't tied to any one place. He could go wherever the trail led him.

It had been a tidbit of information from an outlaw he'd brought to bay in Kansas City that had brought Tyree to Cheyenne. The man bought his freedom with it. Tyree had asked his usual questions, and to his surprise, the outlaw claimed to know someone who knew the three men who were to blame. The outlaw had offered to tell him where to find the one who knew if Tyree let him go.

Tyree had agreed. He'd packed his saddlebags and left for Cheyenne the very next day. He looked for bounty work and a man offered him the chance to bring in Tom McCarthy.

He hadn't counted on McCarthy dying.

He hadn't counted on a lot of things this time.

First there was Marshal Fred Hitch. Tyree couldn't decide whether the lawman had taken a fatherly interest in him, or whether it was Hitch's natural niceness that accounted for him acting like a mother hen. Tyree liked the man, sort of, but he was next to worthless in a fight and had about as much vim and vinegar as a lump of clay.

Aces Connor was an entirely different matter. Tyree respected him, looked up to him. And why not? Aces was a bona fide gun hand. A man-killer. And for some reason he too had taken an interest in Tyree.

Tyree had leaped at the opportunity to learn gun handling from Aces. Learn from the best, people were always saying. He wasn't nearly as happy about his newfound mentor's constant carping to him about right and wrong.

He didn't share Aces's desire to always do right. To Tyree, right and wrong were fuzzy notions that seldom applied to the needs of the moment. He did what he had to when it needed to be done and didn't worry about whether he should or not.

Now, the morning after they'd buried Tom McCarthy, Tyree sat at the fire, nursing a cup of coffee and fuming. "I'll have to go after another bounty as soon as I get back to Cheyenne. That gent who knows one of the buzzards who killed my folks won't say who it is unless he gets that five hundred."

"If he even knows," Aces said.

"He said he does."

Marshal Hitch shook his head. "You're too trustin', son. Only pay him half and tell him he gets the rest when he proves he's not tryin' to trick you."

"I'm not your son, law dog," Tyree said. "And he won't tell me unless it's the full five hundred."

"He'll tell me," Aces said.

Tyree was mightily pleased but hid the fact. "You aim to tag along with me once we get there?"

"Why not?" Aces said. "I've got nothin' else to do. And you and me are pards now, aren't we?"

"I've never had a pard before," Tyree said, dazzled by the offer.

Marshal Hitch cleared his throat. "I reckon I'll tag along too."

Tyree was puzzled. "What on earth for? Your part in this is over. The mayor wanted you to help me take McCarthy to Cheyenne. Well, McCarthy's dead, so you have no reason to come along. Go back to Sweetwater and roost in that office of yours and sip your flask and be happy."

"To tell the truth, I'd like nothin' better," Fred said. "But I find I'd like to see this through."

"See what through? Me findin' the murderers? What are they to you?"

"Nothin'. It's not them. It's us. I've never, ever done

anything like this, Tyree. Common sense tells me I should do as you say. But part of me wants to go on. Helpin' you is only part of it. The rest has to do with me. With doing something I've never done before. With livin' for a change, and not hidin' from life. When it's over I'll go back to my hidey-hole."

"I don't know," Tyree said. He was skeptical the lawman could be of help. And he didn't like being mothered.

"You won't have any jurisdiction in Cheyenne," Aces mentioned.

"I'm still a marshal," Fred said. "People will be less likely to give you trouble if I'm along. Most won't buck a tin star."

"I don't know," Tyree said again.

"Give him a chance," Aces said. "What can it hurt?"

Tyree agreed, reluctantly, and was tilting his cup to his lips when he happened to gaze into the forest and saw a pair of eyes gazing back at him. Startled, he dropped the cup and leaped to his feet, drawing both Colts as he rose.

"What on earth?" Fred blurted.

"A redskin," Tyree said. "I saw him as plain as anything." Well, the eyes, at least, and some of the face.

Aces was up, his own Colt leveled. "One of the Arapahos?"

"It could be all of them," Fred said worriedly, scrambling up. "They came back to see if McCarthy had given up the ghost."

"Or they were out there the whole time," Aces said. "Watchin' and waitin' for a chance to jump us."

Tyree wasn't hankering to die. Not with his quest unfinished. "I have no quarrel with them. Let's light a shuck."

"And hope they don't come after us," Fred said.

Aces covered them while they saddled the horses, his included. Revolvers unlimbered, they made off to the south.

The skin on Tyree's back crawled. He kept expecting

to take an arrow. Head twisted, he didn't relax until they'd gone over half a mile. "No sign of them," he said in relief.

"Let's hope it stays that way," Aces said.

They rode until noon and stopped to rest their animals. Tyree walked in circles to stretch his legs, then went over to where Aces sat on a log watching their back trail.

"You sure are a worrier," Tyree teased.

"I'm fond of breathin'."

Reaching behind him to move his saber, Tyree joined him on the log.

"I've been meanin' to ask," Aces said. "Isn't it uncomfortable walkin' around with that armory of yours? You have to keep movin' the saber, and the bowie is always flappin' around."

"I'm used to it, I suppose."

"You look ridiculous."

"I told you before. The saber was my grandpa's. The bowie was my pa's. They're all I have of my past. I'm keepin' them with me until the day I die."

"You could put them somewhere for safekeepin'," Aces suggested. "Those derringers too."

"All that would leave me are my Colts."

"They should be all you need."

Tyree wasn't fond of being lectured to, and Aces had taken to doing that a lot lately. "You live your life your way. I'll live mine my own."

"You have a thick head, boy, and that's no lie," Aces said, but he grinned as he said it.

"I'm not used to someone givin' me advice," Tyree confessed. "I've been on my own my whole life."

"I only offer it when I think it will help."

Tyree fingered the bowie's sheath and looked over his shoulder at the saber's hilt.

He supposed he did look a mite silly toting them around. But he didn't have a normal keepsake like a watch or a ring. And the same compulsion that drove him to hunt down the murderers also made him want to cling to the only links he had to those who had brought him into the world.

Resting his chin in his hand, Tyree closed his eyes. Sometimes he wished he wasn't so driven. He should take a job as a clerk somewhere and live an ordinary life and forget about his pa and his ma. He should, but he couldn't. What sort of son would he be if he did? No son at all.

Opening his eyes, Tyree sighed.

"Something eatin' at you?" Aces asked.

"Just the usual."

Marshal Hitch walked over, looking worried. "They're after us. The war party. I feel it in my bones."

"There hasn't been any sign of them," Aces said.

"There won't be until they're ready to jump us," Fred said. "But they're out there, bidin' their time."

That was all Tyree needed. To be attacked and slain before he accomplished his life's purpose.

"It's your nerves talkin'," Aces said.

"I know what I know," Fred replied, "and nothin' you say can change my mind."

"You and Tyree have that in common," Aces said, chuckling.

Tyree wasn't amused. He was as unlike the law dog as a body could be. He wasn't timid. He didn't hide from the world. When things got rough, he got rough right back. Give as good as he got, that was his motto.

Presently they moved on.

Tyree rode alongside Aces. The cowboy seldom said much when they were on the go. The lawman, on the other hand, was a chatterbox. Always going on about this or that. It annoyed Tyree no end.

The middle of the afternoon found them winding down out of the mountains. Below stretched the plain that would take them to Sutter's Stump, and beyond. Tyree wondered out loud if they should stop when they got there.

"Are you loco?" Fred said. "Twice we barely got out with our lives. Give it a wide berth, I say."

They were descending the last slopes. Aces was in the lead, and as he went around a blue spruce he drew sharp rein. Bending low from the saddle, he said, "Look here."

Hoofprints pockmarked the earth.

Tyree knew fresh ones when he saw them. And he noticed something else. "They're not shod."

"No," Aces said.

"The Arapahos," Fred exclaimed, unlimbering his six-shooter. "They circled around in front of us, I'll bet. That's why we haven't seen any sign of them behind us."

"Be my guess," Aces said. Straightening in his saddle, he drew his ivory-handled Colt and held it on his thigh.

"When we reach the prairie," Fred said, "there won't be any cover."

"Which means they aim to jump us between here and there," Aces predicted.

"Oh, hell," Fred said.

Tyree didn't blame him for being anxious. His own mouth went dry at the prospect of fighting Indians. Drawing his right Colt, he said, "What if we do some circlin' of our own? Swing wide and go around them."

"Depends on how spread out they are," Aces said, "and how badly they want to count coup on us."

"They're young warriors," Fred said.

"So?" Tyree said.

It was Aces who answered. "So they have something to prove to themselves and to their tribe. If they take our scalps back, there will be a feast and a dance in their honor. They'll be praised as great warriors."

"I don't want my hair to end up hangin' in some lodge," Fred said. "Let's avoid them if we can."

"Stay close," Aces said, and reined to the east. For a quarter of a mile he rode parallel to the plain. "This should be far enough," he declared, and reined down.

"I hope you're right," Fred said.

Tyree was sure they'd outwitted the redskins. And once they reached the plain, the warriors could eat their dust.

A final slope was all that remained. Thick with timber, it was plunged in shadow. Their horses made little noise on the carpet of pine needles.

They came to the last rank of trees, and Fred laughed. "We did it," he said happily. "Will wonders never cease?"

That was when an arrow streaked out of nowhere and struck him in the shoulder.

Chapter 22

Tyree saw it as clear as anything. The barbed tip sheared into Hitch's right shoulder with a fleshy *thwip* and burst out his back. The impact twisted the lawman half around in his saddle. Hitch opened his mouth as if to scream, but didn't.

War whoops pierced the woods and buckskin-clad forms spilled from the shadows.

Tyree was a shade slow to react.

Not Aces Connor. The cowboy fanned his Colt in a blur of motion. An onrushing warrior, a lance raised to throw, seemed to slam into an invisible wall and crashed down. Swiveling, Aces fired at another warrior while hollering, "Ride! Ride like hell!"

Jabbing his spurs, Tyree broke for the prairie. He banged a shot at a long-haired figure, heard the whiz of a shaft past his ear, banged a second shot, and flew around a spruce. Too late, he saw a crouched warrior. He tried to take aim, but with a wolfish howl, the warrior sprang. One hand seized Tyree by the arm. The other swung a tomahawk. Tyree blocked the blow but was wrenched from his horse. Before he could recover his wits, he hit hard on his head and shoulder. Dazed, he made it to his knees.

Face aglow with bloodlust, the warrior leaped to his feet and raised the tomahawk for another try.

Tyree shot him. He wasn't conscious of doing it. He

wasn't even aware he still held the Colt. At the *crack*, the young Arapaho jerked and clutched himself, then howled anew and launched himself at Tyree. Tyree got his hand up to seize the other's wrist and stop the tomahawk from splitting his skull. Suddenly they were on the ground, grappling mightily.

Tyree punched the warrior on the jaw, but it had no effect. A knee to his own groin did, though. His vision spun and he nearly doubled over. Desperate to clear his head, he shoved the warrior away and scrambled back.

The Arapaho came after him.

Tyree got a leg up just as the warrior leaped. His boot caught the Arapaho on the chest and the warrior tumbled, enabling Tyree to heave onto his knees. Out of the corner of his eye he caught movement and turned to see another warrior coming at him with a knife. He fired and the warrior went down.

The first Arapaho was back up. With a cry of fury, he pounced.

Tyree was borne to earth. He felt a sharp pain in his left side. Jamming his Colt against the warrior's belly, he thumbed the hammer and squeezed. The Arapaho was jarred back but came at him again. Tyree fired, worked the hammer, fired.

The warrior dropped.

War whoops still sounded, and somewhere close by a gun thundered.

Tyree lurched erect, his left arm pressed to his ribs, and ran. The sorrel had kept going and was standing about ten yards from the forest, looking back. His life might depend on reaching it.

Racing out of the trees, Tyree sprinted like mad. The saber flopped against his back, and the bowie swung wildly. In the rush of conflict, he'd forgotten he had them. He reached the sorrel and flung a hand up to catch hold of the saddle horn, but the sorrel shied and moved forward. "Stop, damn you!" he fumed, and went after it.

A commotion in the forest drew his attention just as

Aces Connor exploded into the open. Aces had his Colt and reins in one hand, the reins to the marshal's bay in the other. Arrows were flying, and Aces was bent low. Marshal Hitch was clinging to his saddle horn with his good arm. His right appeared to be useless.

Tyree raised his Colts and fired at the vegetation to discourage the Arapahos. He didn't see any of them. He just shot. The sounds spooked the sorrel into moving again.

Backpedaling, Tyree was ready to let lead fly to protect his companions, but the Arapahos didn't come after them.

Aces reached him and bellowed, "Get on your horse!"

The sorrel had stopped, and Tyree wasted no time clambering on. He used his spurs, as did Aces. They galloped to the south, Tyree expecting to be pursued by the war party, but no one gave chase.

Aces didn't draw rein until they had gone better than a mile. Vaulting down, he moved to the bay. "How are you holdin' up?"

His teeth gritted, Marshal Hitch groaned and said, "Not so good. It hurts somethin' awful. You have to get it out."

About six inches of arrow, and the barbed tip, protruded from the lawman's back. The feathered end stuck out his front below the shoulder. He was bleeding but not profusely, and was in agony.

"We can't stop yet," Aces said. "They might come after us."

"How much farther?"

"Another mile should be enough."

"Too far," Fred said. "I'll pass out by then."

"We should tend to him here," Tyree spoke up. "He can keep up if we bandage him."

Rare uncertainty made Aces hesitate. "Have it your way. But you keep watch."

"Like a hawk," Tyree vowed. Dismounting, he examined his side. The tomahawk had scraped his ribs. The wound wasn't deep and it had already stopped bleeding, but it would hurt like Hades for a while.

"Are you keepin' watch or not?" Aces said. He had carefully lowered Marshal Hitch and now he was gathering dry grass and twigs for a fire.

"I got nicked," Tyree explained.

"I'll look at you next."

"No need," Tyree said. He refused to make a fuss over it. As wounds went, it was minor.

The lawman sat with his legs splayed, his hand on the arrow and his head hung low. "I'm so dizzy I can hardly sit."

"Hang on," Aces said.

The plain to the north stayed empty. Tyree was surprised that the war party hadn't come after them, and remarked as much.

"They lost four or more, wounded or dead," Aces said as he worked. "Odds are the others are tendin' to them like we're tendin' to the marshal."

"My first Injun scrape," Tyree said, marveling that he'd survived.

"May it be your last. I'd rather tangle with a snake-mean drunk than a warrior out to do me in."

"I should think drunks can be plenty dangerous," Tyree said.

"They can," Aces agreed, "but all that liquor makes them careless. They grandstand before they draw. Brag on how they're going to make worm food of you. That sort of thing."

"Can we concentrate on me?" Fred asked.

"I got the fire started, didn't I?" Aces replied.

The tiny flames grew rapidly.

Aces kneeled next to the lawman. "Tyree, do you reckon you can keep the fire going and watch for the Arapahos, both?"

"Easy as pie." Tyree stepped around the fire so he faced the distant mountains, and hunkered. The movement didn't help his side any.

"Now, then," Aces said as he examined the lawman. "The good news is it went clean through."

"I can see that," Fred said. "I want it out."

Aces bent over the barbed tip and sniffed loudly several times.

"What on earth are you doing?" Fred said.

"Sometimes Injuns dip their arrows in dead polecats or some other dead varmint to taint them. I heard of a Comanche once who liked to dip his in rattler venom."

"The Lord preserve me," Fred said.

"All I smell on this one is your blood," Aces said. "You might have lucked out twice over."

"I don't call bein' shot with an arrow any kind of luck at all."

Aces went to his palomino, groped in a saddlebag, and returned with a folding knife. Opening it, he tested the edge on his thumb. "This will do."

His face slick with sweat, Fred swayed. "Are you sure you know what you're doing?"

"I took an arrow out of a tree once. This shouldn't be much different."

Tyree laughed.

"Was that your idea of a joke?" Marshal Hitch said. "You pick a poor time for humor, sir."

"And you picked a poor time to get shot." Aces set down the folding knife and gripped the arrow below the barbed point. "I need to break it off. Brace yourself. This will hurt."

"I could use a sip from my flask first. It's in my saddlebag."

"Tyree, would you?" Aces said.

"What help will that be?" Tyree asked as he stood. "You should pour it on the wound."

"What a waste that would be," Fred said. "Are you a drinkin' man, boy?"

"I've never seen the point."

"Then keep quiet until you are. You should never criticize someone else's vices unless you have the same vice yourself."

"I never heard that before," Tyree said.

"Probably because you don't have any vices."

Aces snorted. "You have no shame, Hitch."

"Not a lick," Fred replied. Grimacing, he shuddered and said, "I can really use my flask."

Tyree brought it over. No sooner did he hold it out than the marshal snatched it and opened it and glued it to his lips. Hitch's throat bobbed and his expression became almost serene. "A person would reckon you'd died and gone to heaven," Tyree joked.

"Close," Fred said. He clutched the flask as if he were drowning and it was his only hope of staying afloat. "Now get to it, Mr. Connor, if you please."

Just like that, Aces broke the arrow. He did it so quickly, so unexpectedly that it took the lawman off guard. Hitch's eyes widened and he opened his mouth to cry out, but once again didn't. More shuddering ended with him doubled up and pale as a bedsheet.

"You were right," Fred husked. "It hurt like hell."

Aces tossed the broken end to the ground. "That's not the worst part. If you start to feel sick, I'd appreciate it if you vomited on something other than me."

"Sick?" Fred said.

Aces took a firm hold on the feathered end and commenced to slowly pull the arrow out. "Easy does it or it might set you to bleedin' worse."

"Sweet heaven," Fred exclaimed. Averting his face, he moaned. "That's the damnedest feelin'."

"So I've been told," Aces said.

Tyree felt his own gut churn and bitter bile rise in his throat. He had seen worse wounds, but something about extracting the arrow nauseated him. "Remind me to never take an arrow."

"It's not like I planned it," Fred said.

With a sickening squishy sound, the arrow came out.

So did more blood. Fred closed his eyes and sank onto his back. "If you'll excuse me, I reckon I'll pass out now."

"Not until we bandage you," Aces said.

"You are a cruel taskmaster," Fred said.

They used Tyree's bowie to cut a towel from the lawman's saddlebags into strips. Aces cleaned the entry and exit wounds and Tyree passed the strips to him and they were soon done.

Tying the last knot, Aces sat back and smiled. "There you go, law dog. How does it feel?"

Fred didn't reply. He was out to the world.

"Fetch a blanket," Aces said.

Tyree was going to ask why Aces couldn't get the blanket himself, but shrugged and did. He figured he owed the gun hand for helping him, but he sure didn't like being bossed around.

"We'll let him rest an hour or so," Aces said as he spread the blanket over Marshal Hitch.

"I reckon there's no hurry now, with McCarthy dead," Tyree said. "I just hope there's someone else with a sizable bounty on his head so I can raise the five hundred I need."

"That's a lot of money to pay for information," Aces mentioned.

"The son of a bitch won't take a cent less," Tyree said. "I tried to talk him down. But no. He said if I want to find the men I'm after, I pay him or I get lost. I considered tryin' to beat it out of him, but he's no mouse."

"What's this virtuous citizen's handle?"

"Moses," Tyree said. "Moses Tombs. He's an old-timer. Been on the wrong side of the law more often than not, and he claims to know nearly every owl-hoot who matters."

"And you believe him?"

Tyree squatted, plucked a blade of grass, and stuck it between his teeth. "I've been on the hunt for years now. Askin' questions of everyone I come across who might know somethin'. A few claimed they did, but none panned out. Now here comes old Moses, with all his big talk. Do I believe him? Not entirely, no. But I've been at this so long I reckon I'll grasp at any straw."

"With us to help you, things will change."

"How so?"

"You'll see."

"The murderers I'm after won't go down easy. They kill women and tried to kill me and I was just a baby. You get on me about how feeble my conscience is. They must have no conscience at all."

"Then we'll have no regrets when we blow them to hell."

"You'd help me do that?"

"What are pards for?" Aces said.

Chapter 23

Despite the clash with the war party and his hurt ribs and the death of Tom McCarthy, Tyree was in fine spirits.

He had been on his own for so long that he had gotten used to it being him against everyone else. He saw the world as a hostile place. No one cared for him—and he didn't care for them. People were always trying to take advantage of one another. It was dog-eat-dog, or as Tyree often thought of it, wolf-eat-sheep.

The few helping hands he got, people were using him. The man who sold him his first horse at half what it usually cost didn't tell him the horse couldn't trot a mile without becoming severely winded. The gent who offered him his first bounty job needed a certain bail jumper found or he would lose a lot of money. And so it went.

Then Tyree rode into Sweetwater and met an old lawman who seemed genuinely nice, and took to mothering him besides. Tyree figured Marshal Hitch was so nice because he was dumb. No one ever got ahead in the world by being nice. He was growing to like the old lawman, begrudgingly, but he could never be that nice himself.

Then the world surprised him again with something even more remarkable. A cowpoke with a reputation as a gun hand had taken him under his wing and had now gone so far as to call him his pard.

Tyree had never had a pard. For that matter, he'd never had a genuine friend. He'd never had anyone at all he could depend on, not in the way pards were supposed to depend on one another.

Tyree tried not to get excited over it. He told himself that it wouldn't last. That Aces would change his mind and go his own way.

Yet the cowboy seemed sincere, just like the lawman, and now Tyree found himself with the last thing in the world he ever expected to have: not one but two friends. It put him in a good spirits. So much so he'd catch himself grinning for no reason at all.

They spent two days waiting for the marshal to recover enough to be able to ride. Aces took Tyree aside and suggested they take Hitch back to Sweetwater. There was no reason for the marshal to go on to Cheyenne, and it would be weeks before he was fully recovered from his wounds.

They put it to Fred Hitch, and Hitch said no. He'd rather stick with them. Tyree knew that Aces was as surprised as he was.

"What are you tryin' to prove?" Aces asked.

"Nothin' at all," the lawman replied. "I just don't want to go back to Sweetwater just yet."

"That makes no kind of sense," Aces said bluntly.

"It does if you're me."

Aces and Tyree talked it over that night and were baffled. Tyree mentioned how Hitch had said he liked getting out in the world for a change, instead of hiding from it in his office. "Could be that's why."

"He's safer in his office," Aces said. "The world can kill you if you're not careful."

"Don't I know it?"

Aces shocked him by asking what he wanted to do. "We'll take him back if you say so, his wishes be damned. It's for his own good."

"You're leavin' it up to me?"

"We're after the buzzards who killed your folks. Seems to me you wouldn't want anything to interfere with that."

Aces was putting Tyree's wants above his own. No one in Tyree's entire existence had ever done that before. "I need to ponder on it some," he said.

That night, when he was sure Aces was asleep, Tyree went to Marshal Hitch, who lay staring into the fire. "We need to talk," he whispered.

"About what?"

"You. Aces says we should take you back. I think we should too. But you have your heart set on taggin' along."

"That's a good way of puttin' it," the marshal said. "I'm lettin' how I feel guide me and not my head."

"You nearly got killed. Didn't that teach you anything?"

"That it did," Fred replied. "To duck the next time."

Tyree chuckled. "I'm serious. You're a nuisance sometimes, but I don't want you dead on my account. I don't mind ridin' all the way back to Sweetwater for you. I owe you that much."

"That's damn decent of you, son," Fred said.

"Stop callin' me that."

"But I believe I'll go on with the two of you, if you'll have me. I know I'll slow you some for a while, but I promise not to let you down when it counts the most."

"Why are you doing this? We just don't savvy."

Fred Hitch eased onto his back, careful not to disturb his bandages. "Part of it is for me. I like being with the two of you. I like our adventures."

"Is that what you call havin' that Caleb out to split our skulls with an ax? Or that war party out to take our hair? An adventure?"

"For me they are. The only adventures I've ever had."

Tyree shook his head.

"The other part of it is you. I like you, son. You've had it rougher than most, yet you don't let that stop you. I want to help you find those you're after."

Tyree didn't know what to say to that. It choked him up a little, and hardly anything ever choked him up.

"So yes, I'd like to go on. If you think I'll be too much

of a burden, then by all means, take me back to Sweet-water. But I hope you'll prevail on Mr. Connor to let me come along."

Over breakfast Tyree informed Aces that he had thought about it and would like for the marshal to go on to Cheyenne with them. "It's what he wants, and he's a good old goat."

"He's a lunkhead and so are you. But you're my pard, and if that's what you want, that's what we'll do."

That was the moment it truly sank in. Tyree's entire world had changed. He had a pard and a mother hen. Two people he could count on. In a world where most folks were only out for themselves, it was like finding a vein of gold in ordinary rock. Tyree was suddenly rich in friends. It was enough to make a person giddy.

On their way to Cheyenne they avoided Sutter's Stump. Two visits had been enough.

The next day they ran into half a dozen cowhands Aces knew. The cowboys camped with them that night and stayed up late joshing and laughing. It was clear to Tyree that they accepted Aces as one of them, his repu-tation notwithstanding. It was equally clear that Aces liked the cowboy life, and was putting it aside to help him.

Five days later found them winding down out of the foothills to the Laramie Mountains.

Marshal Hitch was feeling a lot better. He still wore bandages, but he could ride for hours without it bother-ing him, and at night he could sleep straight through with-out the pain waking him. When they drew rein on a last crest and saw the sprawl of buildings and streets in the distance, he gave a slight whistle. "It sure has grown since I was here last."

"Cheyenne has pretty near ten thousand people," Tyree recalled hearing. That was small potatoes compared to St. Louis, which had over four hundred thousand. But Chey-enne was still one of the largest cities west of the Mississippi

River. People heading west, the cattle trade, the gold rush to the Black Hills, accounted for its growth.

They accounted for something else too. A quality Tyree liked about Cheyenne. St. Louis had been a quiet sort of city. An orderly city. A law-abiding city. There was nothing exciting about it.

Cheyenne was excitement, plus.

Its streets were always jammed, the people always bustling about. Frontiersmen and city folk, cowboys and the ranchers they worked for, tame Indians and Chinese railroad workers, and more, mixed and mingled and scurried all over like bustling ants in an anthill. Pistols and knives were as common as noses and ears, although often hidden under jackets or in pockets and sheaths. The threat of violence always hung in the air like a thunderhead about to unleash a storm.

When Tyree had first arrived, he drank in Cheyenne as a parched wanderer in a desert would drink cold water. It had a vigor St. Louis and other places lacked. If cities had hearts, then Cheyenne's heartbeat and his were a lot alike.

A large part of Cheyenne's wildness, Tyree had been told, had to do with it being a "drinkin' town," as one man put it. There were over two dozen saloons, four or five breweries, and other businesses, like social clubs, that catered to those who liked their liquor. At night Cheyenne was one big rowdy party, with piano playing to all hours, songs and dance onstage, and theaters for those with fancier tastes.

Yes, sir. Tyree liked Cheyenne a lot.

All of this went through his mind as they neared the city limits. A sign announced that the local laws would be strictly enforced. Every city had a sign like that. In Cheyenne, though, they didn't take it quite as seriously as other places. You could get away with more in Cheyenne, the saying went, if you were careful about it.

One thing Tyree didn't like about Cheyenne was how

the streets were laid out. In St. Louis there had been some sense to it, with many of the streets aligned with the four points of the compass and arranged in blocks. In Cheyenne, there wasn't any sense whatsoever. For one thing, instead of running north and south and east and west, Cheyenne's streets ran aslant of one another. If you wanted to tell direction, you had to keep an eye on the sun. It made Tyree wonder if whoever designed the town hadn't been hitting the liquor a little hard.

No sooner did they enter the outskirts than it was apparent something was going on. More folks were bustling about than Tyree had ever seen. The streets were practically packed with horse and wagon traffic. And nearly everyone was smiling and plainly in a good mood.

"What's all this?" Marshal Hitch wondered. "I've been to Cheyenne a few times and it wasn't ever this lively."

"Let's find out," Aces said. He reined over to where a pair of locals stood talking. "Howdy, gents."

The townsmen looked up.

"Mind tellin' us what all the fuss is about?" Aces asked. "We just got in."

"Then you haven't heard, cowpoke?" a man with a goatee replied. "Tomorrow is the big celebration. There will be fireworks and a parade and more goings-on than you can shake a stick at."

"What's bein' celebrated?" Aces said.

"Where have you been, cowboy?" the other man said, grinning. "Tomorrow is July tenth."

"So?"

"So Wyoming becomes a state," the man declared.

"Not only that," the man with the goatee said, "Cheyenne is to be the capital. They're building the new capitol buildings as we speak."

"Yes, sir," said the other proudly. "Tomorrow will be a day to beat all others. I can hardly wait."

"I'm obliged," Aces said, and reined back over to Tyree and Marshal Hitch. "You heard?"

"I plumb forgot about that state business," Tyree said. "It was all folks were talkin' about when I left."

Fred gazed up and down the busy street. "Findin' a place to stay might be difficult. Everywhere must be full up."

"I have a room," Tyree offered. "It's not much, but there's space on the floor where you can spread out your blankets."

The boardinghouse where Tyree was staying was on Seventeenth Street. He'd paid for a couple of months in advance, thinking it might take him that long to find the man he was looking for. It had barely taken a week. But the man wouldn't tell him what he wanted to know unless he came up with the five hundred dollars.

The lady who ran the boardinghouse was sweet Mrs. Watkins. Most any hour of the day she could be found in her rocking chair on her porch, knitting. She was there now, and greeted Tyree with her usual warm smile. She had white hair and wore a print dress and laced-up shoes polished to a sheen.

"Mr. Johnson, welcome back. You've been gone a week or two, I do believe. I haven't seen you at the dinner table or had to change your sheets."

"Yes, ma'am, I have," Tyree said.

Mrs. Watkins set her knitting needles in her lap. "Who are your friends?"

"This here is Mr. Connor," Tyree introduced his new pard, "and this other hombre is a lawman from . . ." He got no further.

Fred stepped past him, took Mrs. Watkins's hand, and gave a slight bow. "Marshal Frederick Hitch, from Sweetwater, at your service, madam."

"My word," Mrs. Watkins said, and blushed.

Tyree was astounded. "You're sure not timid around the ladies, are you?"

"Yes, well," Fred said, and coughed. "Mr. Johnson here has invited us to stay with him for a day or two. Would that be all right with you? We wouldn't want to impose. And we're willin' to pay you for your kindness."

Aces was looking at the lawman in amusement. "Don't you beat all?"

Mrs. Watkins smiled at Fred. "Ordinarily I wouldn't allow three men to that room. It's not very big and there's only the one bed. But with you being an officer of the law, and the statehood and all, it would be remiss of me to refuse you."

"My, you are eloquent, kind lady," Fred said. "And I think you for your kindness."

Fanning herself with her hand as if she were suddenly hot, Mrs. Watkins did some coughing of her own. "It is a pleasure to meet you. I hope we can sit down together and become better acquainted."

"I would like nothin' more."

Tyree led them inside before the marshal made a spectacle of himself. "I'll show you which room it is and then we can go find the gent who claims to know about my folks. Not that he'll tell us anything unless I pay him."

Aces Connor patted his ivory-handled Colt. "Have a little faith, pard," he said.

Chapter 24

"One thing I'd like to know," Marshal Hitch said as they threaded their way along the new capital's busy streets, "is why you call yourself Johnson when your last name is Larn."

"I thought I told you before," Tyree said. "Whoever shot my ma and pa might know their last name was Larn. And if they heard I'm a Larn and I'm askin' about them . . ." He shrugged.

They were near the railroad tracks, in a part of the city where the rougher element congregated. Tyree had learned shortly after he arrived that the saloon most hard cases favored, the one where those who lived on the shady side of the law showed up most nights to drink and swap tall tales, was called the Raging Bull. It was owned by a mousy little man by the name of Kierney. Gossip had it that in his younger days Kierney had been a thief who liked to slip into the homes of rich folks when they weren't there and help himself to their valuables. Apparently he'd been caught and sent to prison, and when he got out, used some money he'd stashed to open the Raging Bull and become respectable.

Tyree had never met anyone he disliked more. Kierney reminded him of a rat. The little man even had a ratlike face that was always twitching, and beady eyes that never held a hint of friendliness.

On this particular evening, the Raging Bull was outrageously crowded. The bar was lined shoulder to shoulder, all the tables were taken, and most of the floor space besides.

And talk about loud. The babble of voices, clinking chips and glasses, and gruff mirth assaulted Tyree's ears. "Didn't count on this," he had to say into one of Ace's since he wouldn't be heard otherwise.

Fred touched his shirt where his badge had been. "Good thing I took this off. I'd stand out like a sort thumb."

That he would. The flinty faces and cold stares, the abundance of revolvers and knives, warned anyone who came in that this saloon was the haunt of Cheyenne's wild and woolly crowd.

Tyree began rising onto his toes to see better. "Moses has to be here somewhere. He nearly always is."

"Moses?" Aces said. "Is that his real handle?"

"He's never said."

"You don't know if that's his real name yet you were set to give him five hundred dollars."

"What does his name have to do with it?"

"You are too young by half," Aces said.

Tyree didn't see why he kept carping about the five hundred. He'd hand over a thousand if it got him the information he needed. He'd been hunting the killers for years now. He'd like for it to finally be over so he could do something with his life. Exactly what, he wasn't sure. But it was a good thing, in a sense, that his parents were dead and not holding their breath waiting for him to avenge them. He was taking forever.

Tyree couldn't help it. As young as he was, a lot of people didn't take him seriously. He'd explain about his parents and ask for information and be treated as if he was a wet-nosed kid who didn't know any better than to go around imposing on folks.

A woman in a shiny green dress appeared as if out of nowhere and attached herself to Aces. Her face was made up with powder and rouge, and she had short blond curls that bounced when she moved her head. "Lookee what I found," she declared merrily. "Where have you been all my life, handsome?'

"Never heard that one before," Aces said.

"Now, now. Be nice. My name is Clementine. Why don't you buy me a drink and we'll become better acquainted?"

"Some other time," Aces said. "I'm here on business."

"Aren't they all?" Clementine said. "I just overheard a couple of gents talking about a stage somebody else robbed. And before that, I heard how Puck Tovey had his wick snuffed up to Sutter's Stump."

"They call that business?" Fred said.

"Honey, anything that has to do with the wrong side of the law is business to this bunch," Clementine said, and laughed.

"What's this about Puck Tovey?" Aces said.

"He was well-known in these parts. Came up from Texas, I think. Shot a man not long ago." Clementine pursed her ruby lips. "Him and another fella by the name of Bascomb were sent to their reward by some shootist from who knows where."

Tyree was taken aback when Aces hooked his thumbs in his gun belt and said, "At the moment he's standin' in front of you."

"What's that, handsome?" Clementine said. She was regarding one of her painted fingernails.

"Puck Tovey braced me and came down with a terrible case of slow."

"Wait a minute," Clementine said, looking up and stiffening. "Are you saying that *you're* the one who shot him?"

"And Ira Bascomb too," Aces said.

"Good heavens. And damn me if I don't believe you. Who are you anyhow? Anybody I'd have heard of?"

"Aces Connor," Aces said.

"Why, I believe I have heard your name. Didn't you shoot a drummer or a rustler some time ago?"

"Both," Aces said.

Clementine looked around at all the celebrants, then stepped up close to Aces. "Listen, you might want to keep it to yourself about Bascomb. He was well thought of by a lot of these curly wolves."

"Don't you worry, gal," Aces said, and playfully swatted her fanny. "Tell everybody I shot the both of them."

"You *want* everyone to know it was you?"

"It would help things, yes."

"It will get you buried in Boot Hill, you damn idiot. I'm trying to warn you to tread easy. You don't realize what you're in for."

"Ah, but I do," Aces said. Turning her around, he nodded toward the bar. "Start there and work your way around the room. Point me out to everybody, and when you come back, I'll buy you that drink and give you a couple of dollars besides."

"You're loco," Clementine said, but she giggled and sashayed off.

"I agree," Fred said. "You're askin' for trouble. Why draw a target on your chest?"

"For my new pard," Aces said, and clapped Tyree on the back.

"What?" Tyree was trying to make sense of it all. Until this moment, Aces had impressed him as having more sense than most. But this was reckless.

"Fear can loosen lips," Aces said.

Tyree still didn't understand, but evidently Marshal Hitch did.

"So that's why," Fred said. "I admire your grit and your cleverness, but there has to be a better way."

"If you have one let me hear it," Aces said.

"I don't, I'm sorry to say. Your bluster will have to do." Fred turned to Tyree. "I hope you appreciate what he's doing for you. Not many men would put themselves in a bullet's path for someone else, pard or no pard."

"I don't want him hurt on my account," Tyree said.

"Too late to stop it now," Fred said, and nodded toward the bar where Clementine was huddled with several drinkers. She looked in Aces's direction and pointed, and the drinkers excitedly began spreading the news themselves.

"You're too calm by half," Fred said to Aces.

"If it happens, it happens," Aces said. "But they'll be more curious than anything. They'll want to study me awhile. Gives us time to do what we came for and be gone."

"You hope."

Tyree saw Clementine go over to a table. As she bent, he noticed the face of a man at another table past her. His pulse quickened and he placed his hands on his Colts. "I knew he'd be here."

Aces said, "Is it Moses? Point him out."

Few in the Raging Bull had gray hair and a lot of wrinkles. Those on the wrong side of the law seldom lived to a ripe old age. Being an outlaw or a gunman just about ensured an early grave.

The man called Moses was an exception. He looked to be older than Methuselah, his face so cragged and seamed there wasn't a smooth spot anywhere. A bristly mustache and scraggily beard added to the impression of great age. His store-bought clothes had been patched and sewn so many times they nearly had as many wrinkles and creases as he did. His face was smudged from being unwashed; his fingernails were black from never being cleaned. When he opened his mouth he revealed yellow teeth, with more than a few missing.

Tyree worked his way around the table. On reaching the older man's elbow, he leaned down and said, "Remember me?"

Moses glanced up. His eyes were bloodshot and a wad of tobacco bulged his left cheek. "Well, look who it is. Got my money?"

"Not yet but—"

"Then we have nothin' to gab about. Come see me when you do." Moses held a hand over his cards, peeked at them, and added five dollars to the pot. "Are you still here, boy?"

Tyree turned to go. He didn't want to make an issue of it with so many people around.

"No," Aces said, and put a hand on his chest. "Stay put. He's going to talk to you whether he wants to or not."

Moses fixed his attention on Aces. "Who the hell are you to tell me what I will and won't do?"

As luck would have it, just then a townsman in a bowler rushed up to another of the players. The man in the bowler was so excited he didn't pay any mind to anyone else. "You won't believe what I just heard," he exclaimed. "Remember last week when we were told that Bascomb up to Sutter's Stump and a gun shark by the name of Tovey were bucked out in gore?"

"I do," the man at the table said.

"Well, word is being spread that the gun hand who did the bucking is here in the saloon."

The game came to a stop.

"Where is he?" the man at the table asked.

"Someone pointed him out to me a minute ago," the man in the bowler said. He straightened and looked around the room. "He's got a brown hat and looks to be a cowboy."

"Does his hat look like mine?" Aces asked.

The townsman in the bowler gazed across the table. "As a matter of fact it—" He stopped and his eyes seemed to bulge. "Lord in heaven, mister. I didn't mean nothing."

"Rafer?" the townsman at the table said.

Rafer had gone pale. Nervously licking his lips, he nodded at Aces. "That would be him right there."

Tyree would never forget their reaction. To a man, they betrayed a spark of awe or outright fear. To a man, they stared at Aces's ivory-handled Colt in a sort of wonderment that it had been the instrument of two deaths.

To Tyree, the effect was magical. He'd like to have that effect on folks. He'd like to be regarded with the same awe.

Aces was focused on Moses. "Suppose you cash in your chips."

"Suppose I don't want to?" Moses replied testily.

"I wasn't askin'," Aces said.

Moses glowered, his wrinkles folding in on themselves. "I don't know what gives you the right."

Aces placed his hand on his Colt. "I've shot five men in the past year or more. Is that enough right for you or would you like more?"

Moses was no coward, Tyree had to say that for him. Where most would have been intimidated, he growled, "There's law in this town. You can't go around doing as you damn well please."

"Any of that law in here?"

A hush had come over the nearest tables and those around them. Everyone was hanging on the exchange between Aces and Moses.

"I have half a mind to call your bluff," the latter said. "You cause trouble and the marshal will have you behind bars before you can blink."

"It won't be quite that quick," Aces said. "The trouble will be long over." He took half a step to one side so no one was between him and Moses. "My pard wants words with you. He'll have them, here and now, or you answer to me."

"Go to hell," Moses said, but he smacked his cards down and scooped up his pile of chips. Muttering, he stood. "You heard him, fellers. Deal me out, but I'll be back as soon as him and me finish up."

Tyree suddenly understood why Aces encouraged the dove to let everyone know Aces had curled up Tovey and Bascomb permanent. It was to impress Moses into doing what they wanted.

Tyree made up his mind then and there that he would like to be just like Aces Connor when he was older. A man could do worse.

The hush was spreading. Fully half the saloon had gone silent; half the heads were fixed on Aces.

Tyree decided to take their talk outside. Too many ears were listening. As he turned toward the batwings, it amazed him how quickly everyone got out of his way. All because he was with Aces. He smothered a laugh of delight. Here he was, a boy by most standards, and he was being treated as if he were one of the terrors of the territory. It was heady stuff.

Moses came after him, with Aces right behind, while Marshal Hitch brought up the rear, smiling at everybody and saying, "How do you do? How do you do? Pleased to meet you."

Tyree wanted to kick him. The lawman would spoil things, he was being so nice. Hard cases didn't act that way.

"That's a lovely dress you're wearin', ma'am," Fred said to a dove.

Shouldering a batwing, Tyree held it open and motioned for Moses to go ahead of him. Moses did, but no sooner did he step outside than he turned and shoved Tyree at Aces. Tyree would have fallen if Aces hadn't grabbed him, and before either could hope to prevent it, Moses whirled and bolted.

Chapter 25

Tyree was out of the saloon like a shot, and collided with a man walking past, nearly knocking him down.

"Watch where you're going, boy," the man declared, and went around.

Aces and Fred burst through the batwings and stood on either side, looking right and left.

"Where?" Aces said.

Tyree had no idea. Moses had disappeared into the flow of people and horses in the street. On an ordinary day it would be easy to spot him. But today, with every artery jammed with residents and visitors, it was like looking for a needle in a constantly moving haystack.

"He can't have gotten far," Fred said.

Tyree had an inspiration. Hopping off the boardwalk, he crouched low to the ground. This let him see under the horses and wagons and buckboards. A river of legs moved in each direction, some at a brisk pace, others more slowly. But only one pair of legs was moving like a bat out of hell.

"This way," Tyree said, and took off in pursuit.

"Wait for us, son," Fred called out.

Tyree wasn't about to. If Moses got away, he might never find him again, and lose the best chance he had of finding his parents' murderers. He weaved and dodged and twisted like a madman, drawing irate glares from those he brushed against or caused to draw up short. He darted into the path of a horse and bounded aside before it hit him, earning a curse from its rider.

Tyree was fortunate in that he was thin and agile. He could slip through the throng like quicksilver. But most of the adults were taller than he was, and to see over them he had to keep jumping into the air. He'd spotted Moses's hat, which was almost as old and worn as Moses, and tried to keep it in sight.

The chase went on for several blocks. Tyree was almost to an intersection when he jumped up yet again, and the hat was gone. He came to the junction and turned both ways. There weren't quite as many people—and no sign of Moses.

In a sudden panic Tyree turned left. He'd gone about twenty steps when something—instinct, a hunch, a feeling—caused him to whirl and run the other way. Darting over to the boardwalk to a post supporting an overhang, he quickly clambered up.

Eureka, Tyree congratulated himself. Moses was entering a building across the way. The old man was in such a hurry he didn't look back.

Sliding down, Tyree made a beeline for the building. He figured it must be where Moses was staying, but no. It appeared to be a warehouse. Twin doors had been left partly open, and within were crates and boxes and bins, plunged in dark shadow.

His hands on his Colts, Tyree slipped inside and stood with his back to a door to let his eyes adjust. After the hubbub of the streets, the warehouse seemed unnaturally still. There were two windows, but they were small and high on the side walls. Dust motes hung in the air, and a spiderweb was suspended from a rafter.

Tyree edged forward. He saw no sign of a back door, which meant he had the old geezer trapped.

Whoever owned the warehouse, and any workers, must be out and about, like everyone else.

Tyree placed each foot quietly. He probed the gloom between the piles and stacks, seeking telltale movement. Moses was too wily to give himself away. Finding him would take some doing.

Tyree thought of his ma and pa, and grew angry. All he wanted was to find their killers. In a decent world, Moses would help him out of the goodness of his heart. But the world wasn't a decent place. It was a maze of shadows and danger, just like the warehouse. And filled with vultures like Moses who didn't give a damn about anyone except themselves.

Tyree stopped and scowled. He was letting himself be distracted. That could prove fatal. Moses was old, but he wasn't a sheep. Moses was a crusty wolf, perfectly capable of killing someone should he have to.

Tyree debated calling out to him and asking him to come out of hiding. But no. The old man wouldn't come willingly.

Tyree was so intent on the spaces between the stuff stored there that he didn't realize the mistake he was making until a slight scraping sound came from above. He hadn't paid any attention to the tops of the piles and stacks. At the sound, he jerked his head up.

A heavy form slammed into him like a falling tree and he was smashed to the ground. Bony fingers wrapped around his throat and a seamed face split with malice filled his vision.

Tyree tried to rise, but Moses was straddling his chest and had his arms pinned. "Damn you!" Tyree bucked, but Moses stayed on top of him. Worse, he lost all the air in his lungs and couldn't get more because his windpipe was being choked off.

Tyree thrashed and kicked. His chest hurt and his throat throbbed with pain. He gasped for breath, but there wasn't any to be had. His vision swam and the warehouse darkened. He was being strangled to death and there wasn't a thing he could do.

Fear filled Tyree, the most potent fear he'd ever felt, fear that numbed his limbs and his brain. He didn't want to die. Not so young. Not with so much left undone. He exerted all his strength in one last attempt to heave Moses off, and failed.

Suddenly there was a hard voice and a flash of something metallic. Moses was knocked back and lost his hold. With an oath, Moses clawed for his six-gun, and the metal flashed again, sprawling him flat.

Tyree could breathe again. Wheezing and sputtering, he sucked in precious air. His throat hurt so bad he clutched it in agony. When a hand touched his shoulder he swatted at it, only to have his forearm gripped.

"It's all right, son. It's just me," Fred said. "Lie still and take deep breaths."

Tyree did as he advised. Gradually most of the hurt went away and his breathing returned to normal. With Fred helping him, he slowly sat up. "I'm obliged," he rasped. His throat felt raw, as if sand had been poured down it.

"You were lucky you weren't killed."

Tyree realized he had lost his hat and looked around for it.

"You shouldn't have run off like that," Fred said.

"Had to," Tyree said. His hat had been crumpled. Making a fist, he fixed that. "Damn that son of a bitch anyhow."

"He got his," the lawman said.

Tyree turned.

Moses was flat on his back, unconscious. A cheek had been opened and was bleeding badly, and he had a hen's egg on his temple.

Aces was standing over him, the ivory-handled Colt in his hand. "He almost had you." Aces had relieved Moses of his own revolver and now he tossed it into the shadows.

"That he did," Tyree admitted.

"He will find that was a mistake," Aces said. "Fred,

fetch some water from that trough out front, if you don't mind."

"Be right back."

Rising unsteadily, Tyree took several more deep breaths. He wasn't quite himself yet. "You saved my life."

Aces looked at him and grinned. "That's what pards do." His grin faded. "You should have used your pistols."

"He can't tell me what I need to know if he's dead."

"Shoot to wound, then," Aces said.

"I couldn't risk hittin' his vitals. I'm not as good a shot as you are yet."

On the ground, Moses groaned.

"What will you do to him?" Tyree asked.

"Whatever it takes."

Fred Hitch returned, his hat in hand, half-filled with water. Without saying a word, he upended it over Moses's face and stepped back.

Coughing and blinking, Moses sat up and gazed wildly about. He saw Tyree and glared, then saw Aces and his glare changed to a look of fright. "You!" he exclaimed. "It was you who struck me."

"I'll do it again if you try to get up."

Moses glanced toward the double doors. It was plain he wanted to bolt.

"You shouldn't have tried to kill him," Aces said.

"Go to hell," Moses blustered.

"My pard wants some answers."

"Go to hell twice and take him with you."

"Don't say I didn't ask nicely," Aces said, and slammed his Colt against the older man's face.

Crying out, Moses fell back. His other cheek was split and more blood flowed. Pressing both hands to his face, he cursed and shook.

"I can do this all day," Aces said.

Moses heaped a string of invective on him, ending with "It'll be a cold day in hell before I tell that brat anything. We had an agreement, him and me. He pays me five hundred dollars and I tell him what he wants to know."

"And you'll lie and take his money and skip town and he'll never see you again," Aces said.

"I gave my word," Moses said.

"Which isn't worth cow shit."

Fred Hitch squatted. "You'd be wise to cooperate, Mr. Moses. My friend here can be downright mean when he wants to be."

"Go to hell with them."

The marshal sighed. "There's just no talkin' sense to some people. They think they are different from everybody."

"I'm the same as anyone else," Moses said angrily.

"Are you?" Fred said. "You must not feel pain or you wouldn't make my friend mad. You must not mind spittin' up blood and busted teeth or havin' your ribs staved in or your fingers broke one by one."

Moses blanched. "You wouldn't do that. You wouldn't go that far."

"Oh no, I wouldn't," Fred said, and motioned at Aces. "But he would. You're lucky we're not out on the prairie somewhere. He'd probably shoot you in each knee and each elbow until you talked."

Tyree doubted Aces would do any such thing. He realized the marshal was trying to scare Moses into cooperating.

"Look, I was tryin' to help the kid—" Moses began.

"For five hundred dollars," Aces said.

"Maybe I asked for a little much," Moses said. "But it's worth it to him, and more. He said so."

Fred said, "Did Tyree tell you why he wants the information?"

"His folks were killed," Moses said.

"When he was an infant," Fred said. "That scar on his chin? They tried to kill him too."

Moses squirmed. "That has nothin' to do with me."

"How is it you know who he's after?" Aces asked.

"I get around. I hear things."

"Not good enough," Aces said.

Moses touched his left cheek and looked at the blood on his fingertips. "I know somebody. He was part of it."

"Still not good enough."

"You're not gettin' any more. Not for free. Not after you pistol-whipped me." Moses wiped the blood on his shirt. "You don't think that five hundred is fair. How much would be? Two hundred?"

Aces shook his head.

"One hundred? That's not hardly enough, but I'll take it so we can get this over with."

"If it's fairness you want," Aces said, "tell him for free."

"No, you don't," Moses said. "I'm not lettin' you horn-swoggle me. You give me something for my trouble or I don't tell you a thing."

"I'll give you your life."

Moses swallowed.

"That's worth more than five hundred, don't you think?" Aces pointed his Colt at Moses's face.

"You just hold on, mister," Moses said.

"I'm tired of your gab, old man. My pard will ask you questions and you'll answer him or I'll gun you where you sit."

"He won't learn a thing if I'm dead."

"True. We'll keep askin' around and sooner or later we'll run across someone else who knows about the murders. Or are you dumb enough to think you're the only one who does?"

Moses didn't answer.

"So, what will it be? I am plumb out of patience."

A crafty gleam came into Moses's dark eyes and he turned to Tyree. "You'd let him do this? Let him spoil your chance at catchin' the killers?"

"He's my pard," Tyree said with pride. "He can do what he wants."

"So long, old man," Aces said, and thumbed back the hammer.

Tyree wondered if Aces would really go through with it, but he didn't get to find out.

Bleating in fear, Moses thrust both hands up as if to ward off the slug. "All right! You win. I'll tell the kid what he wants to know."

"That wasn't so hard, was it?" Aces smiled and stepped back. "Tyree, it's your turn. Have at him."

Chapter 26

Tyree had been seeking clues to the murderers of his parents for so long—it seemed like his entire life—that now, on the verge of finding out, a jolt of excitement coursed through him. "Tell me everything," he said, moving closer to Moses. "Every little thing you can recollect."

Moses rubbed the hen's egg on his temple. "Before I do, I should tell you a few things. I was born in Missouri. Seems like a hundred years ago." He grinned, but no one grinned with him. "I was raised on a farm but hated farmin'. It was too much work. Always havin' to get up at the crack of dawn to milk the cows and feed the chickens. All that plowin' and plantin'. All the threshin' and pickin'. Farmers work themselves to the bone."

"What does this have to do with my folks?" Tyree snapped.

"Bear with me, boy. Your pard has beat on me and I'm doing this for free, so bear the hell with me."

"Get on with it," Aces said.

"Where was I? Oh yes, the farm. When I was about the boy's age here, I decided enough was enough. I was tired of workin' myself to the bone, and for what? Sure, the meals were good. My ma was a fine cook. Most farmin' ladies are. But my pa barely made enough money to get by. Farmers don't usually get rich, now, do they?"

Moses grinned again, then said, "Don't any of you have a sense of humor?"

Fred chuckled.

"Anyhow," Moses continued gloomily, "I left the farm to make my own way in the world. But little did I know."

"Let me guess," Fred said. "You found it was just as hard to make a livin' at everything else."

"That's what I learned," Moses said. "I tried diggin' ditches. I mended fences. I shoveled manure. Hated all of it. I thought bein' a clerk looked easy, so I got a job at a general store. The owner about worked me to death and paid me barely enough to buy my meals. It was one thing after another, and finally I learned my lesson."

"I can't wait to hear it," Fred said.

"I learned that workin' for a livin' is a fool's proposition," Moses said. "The smart thing to do is not to work. The smart thing is to take what you want by any means you can."

"Why am I not surprised?" Fred said.

Tyree wished he would stop interrupting. He was anxious to get to the part about his ma and pa.

"I robbed my first man the day I turned sixteen," Moses said. "Some old geezer who was walkin' home late one night, and I took a rock to the back of his noggin. Heard later that he was never the same. He couldn't talk right or somethin' like that. But the important thing was that the old bastard had sixty-two dollars in his poke." Moses brightened at the memory. "More money than I'd ever seen. More than my pa made in half a year of grubbin' at the land. I had found my callin'."

"Outlaw," Fred said.

"Not how you mean. Not at first," Moses said. "I robbed, mostly. I'd visit a town or settlement and stay a couple of days gettin' to know who was who and what was what, and then I'd pick a likely prospect and help myself to his poke or their purse and move on."

"The law didn't catch on?"

"There wasn't a lot of it back in those days," Moses said. "Only the big towns had marshals. Most of the law work was done by the sheriffs, and they had whole counties to cover. I was crafty enough not to do two robberies in a row in the same county. Took a lot of ridin', but I was young then and didn't mind."

"Did you shoot or knife anybody?" Fred asked.

Tyree looked at him.

"What?" Fred said.

"Not durin' my robbin' days, no," Moses said. "Most folks, you point a pistol at them, they'll hand over their valuables without much of a fuss."

"I wonder why," Fred said.

"Let him tell it," Aces said. "I don't aim to be here all day."

"Thank you," Tyree said.

Moses grew more at ease as he talked. Tyree got the impression the old man had never done this before, never opened up to others about his life of skullduggery and crime.

"I kept at it for a couple of years. The most I ever robbed was from some fella who had close to three hundred dollars on him. Usually it was less." Moses placed his hands in his lap and became thoughtful. "That was when I started to fall in with hard characters. I spent most of my time in saloons. Gambled a lot. Drank a lot. Met some who lived as I did, or worse."

"How worse?" Tyree found himself interrupting as Fred had done.

"I was never a killer, boy. I didn't harm anyone if I didn't have to. Not even when me and a gang robbed a few banks, and once a damn train." Moses paused. "But there are killers out there. Men who will snuff you as quick as look at you. They're the ones who are worse. The ones you have to tread easy around. Like your pard here." He nodded at Aces.

"I'm not no killer," Aces said.

"You told me yourself that you've shot five men in the past year or so," Moses said. "That don't make you no parson."

"It was them or me," Aces said. "When a man points a gun at you intendin' to do you in, you defend yourself."

"Well, there are some that don't need that excuse. They point their guns first. They are killers no matter how you cut it."

"Puck Tovey was a killer," Marshal Hitch said.

"Missouri had its share," Moses said. "I met more than a few. And about fifteen years ago, I think it was, I was playin' cards in Jefferson City with a friend by the name of Tucker. He was a lot like me. Grew up in a cabin in the woods and took to robbin'. He never killed anybody either. Then he fell in with a pair who had, and not once but a lot of times." Moses looked at Tyree. "Which almost brings us to your folks."

"Finally," Tyree said.

Moses glanced at the ivory-handled Colt Aces was still pointing at him, and sighed. "My friend was unhappy. Said he didn't know they were such a gun pair when he helped them rob a stage. They took him on other jobs. He didn't want to go, but he did. And just when he's tellin' me this, two fellas walk in and come over to our table. 'That's them,' Tucker whispered." Moses lowered his own voice. "That was when I first set eyes on Dunn and Lute."

"Were they brothers?" Fred asked.

"Hell no. What gave you that idea? Dunn is white and Lute is black. But they are peas in a pod. One look at them and you know—you *know*—that they are mad dogs who don't have a lick of love anywhere in their bodies."

"Love is a strange word comin' from you," Aces said.

"Why? I've had me a gal a time or three. I loved my folks. I just didn't want to be like them. No, you're mixin' apples and oranges. Dunn and Lute are ice inside. They have no feelin's for anybody. They will kill man or woman with no more regard than you would swat a fly."

"Or kill a baby, maybe?" Fred said.

Moses looked at Tyree. "That too."

For about a minute the old highwayman didn't speak and no one urged him to. Then Aces said, "Get on with it."

Moses nodded. "Dunn and Lute had come to get Tucker for a stage job. I learned about it later, the next time I ran into Tucker. That was pretty near a year later. I was passin' through a place called Monegaw Springs and had a powerful thirst, so I stopped at the saloon. And who should I see but my friend Tucker, sittin' by himself and chuggin' on a bottle? I went over and damn near couldn't believe my eyes when I saw he was cryin'."

"Cryin'?" Fred repeated.

"You heard me. Tucker sat there guzzlin' that whiskey with tears wettin' his cheeks. It spooked me, a grown man like him. I'd taken a chair and asked if he was all right and he looked at me and said he'd never be all right again."

Tyree and Aces and Fred waited.

"I asked him what the matter was, and he said it was Dunn and Lute. The law had posters out on them, and things were too hot in Missouri, so they were fixin' to leave and head west where there'd be easier pickin's."

"But why the cryin'?" Fred said.

"I'm gettin' to that."

"Fred, please," Tyree said.

Moses pressed a hand to his forehead. "I asked Tucker what there was to cry about if he was going to be shed of them, and he said he wasn't, that they'd told him he was going with them. I said he didn't have to if he didn't want to, and he said no one told Dunn and Lute no. He said they were camped outside the Springs and he had come in for a drink to get away from them for a while."

"So he was cryin' because he wanted to be shed of them," Fred said.

"No, you dang nuisance," Moses said angrily. Calming himself, he fixed on Tyree. "Tucker was cryin' on account of a baby."

Tyree thought his heart had stopped.

"It seems that Dunn and Lute were going around gettin' travelin' money, as they called it, by robbin' farms and whatnot. They'd come on a homestead with a farmer and his missus and the baby. Dunn shot the man and Lute shot the woman, and Dunn wanted Tucker to kill the kid. 'And did you?' I asked him. And Tucker looked at me, all wildlike, and stood up and walked out without sayin' so much as good-bye. And that was the last I saw of him for a good long while. I'd forgotten about the homesteader and the baby until the kid here showed up and started askin' around if anyone knew anything about a Missouri farmer and his family who'd been murdered years ago."

"All my askin' finally paid off," Tyree said. He'd done it in St. Louis. In Kansas City. In Denver. Now here in Cheyenne.

"I'll be honest, boy. I wasn't going to tell you a damn thing," Moses said. "But then I got a sign from heaven, as my ma used to say."

"An angel appeared to you in a dream?" Fred said.

"Ain't you funny?" Moses said. "No, it weren't that kind of sign. I was at the other end of town, or the city, I should say, and I went into a general store for some chaw. I saw someone with an apron sweepin' the floor, and it shocked me so much I turned around and walked back out."

"It must have been Dunn or Lute," Fred guessed.

"Sweepin' a floor? What do you use for brains? They'd no more work at clerkin' than they would herdin' sheep. They kill for a livin'. That's what they do."

"You saw Tucker," Tyree realized.

Moses nodded. "He looked a heap different. A lot of his hair is gone and what's left is mostly gray. And he's lost a lot of weight. But it was him. I'm as sure as anything."

"Dunn and Lute?" Tyree said. "Do you know where they are?"

"How would I, boy?"

"Tucker might," Aces said.

"If anyone does, it'd be him," Moses said. "And for five hundred dollars I was going to take you over there personally and introduce you. But now you've spoiled that. Now you can go yourself. And you know what? I hope he doesn't know. I hope he's no help at all."

"That's damn mean," Tyree said.

"What do you expect after your pard went and walloped me? I was going to play fair by you, as your pard likes to say, but now you both can go to hell. I want nothin' more to do with you."

"I like that idea," Aces said.

"About us bein' shed of him?" Tyree said.

"About him introducin' you to Tucker."

Moses sat up. "Didn't you hear me? I'm not doing any such thing. You know all you need to. You're on your own."

"How about you take us there right now?" Aces said.

A flush spread from Moses's chin to his hair. "You prod and you prod. I suppose if I don't, you'll pistol-whip me again."

"No," Tyree said. "He won't."

Both Aces and Moses said, "What?" at the same time.

Tyree regarded the old outlaw a few moments. "I'm much obliged for what you've told me. To be honest, I'd about given up hope of ever learnin' who was to blame. Like you say, comin' across you was a godsend. I don't blame you for being mad at us, what with us runnin' you down and all."

"You don't?" Moses said.

"You say you had a ma and pa, and you left them to be on your own," Tyree said in mild amazement. "I can't imagine doing that. I've gone my whole life without any parents. To me, you turned your back on the two people who should have mattered the most. The two who brought you into the world. The two who fed you and put clothes on your back. So what if it was hard work? You were a family. Don't you know how precious that was?"

"Hell, boy," Moses said.

"So go your own way," Tyree said. "I'd like for you to take me to this Tucker, but I won't have my pard force it on you. And as soon as I make some bail money, I'll pay you. Not the full five hundred. That's too much and you know it. But I'll pay you a hundred when I can, and that should make us even."

"You'd do that after I damn near choked you to death?"

"I would," Tyree said, not at all sure what was making him say it. By rights he should shoot the old goat.

"Well, now," Moses said, "if you can be that generous, so can I. I'll take you to Tucker. Just don't hold it against me later."

"Why would I?" Tyree said.

"Because if Tucker does know where you can find Dunn and Lute, you'll likely go after them and they will kill you dead."

Chapter 27

Tyree was glad that Moses had come around to doing as he wanted. The old man wasn't as coldhearted as he'd appeared.

They made their way along the busy streets of Cheyenne, Tyree only a few steps behind Moses, Aces and Fred Hitch trailing after.

Statehood had put most everyone in a festive mood. There was a lot of laughing and people whooping and hollering.

When someone nudged his elbow, Tyree assumed it must be one of the people who hemmed him. Then Aces materialized, looking grim.

"It's a trick," Aces said so only Tyree would hear.

Distracted by all the commotion, Tyree said absently, "What is?"

"Are you turnin' into a simpleton? Moses is up to somethin'. Don't let your guard down."

Tyree was all interest. "What makes you think so?" He'd pegged Moses as being sincere.

"He did all he could to get away from us and wouldn't cooperate until I threatened to shoot him."

Tyree shrugged. "He had a change of heart, is all."

"Not him. He's a chip of flint inside. A lot of the old-timers are like that. They don't back down, ever. And they sure don't betray their friends."

"I don't know as I agree."

"You want to believe him, fine. Just be careful. Fred and I have your back, but there's no tellin' what Moses will do." Aces dropped back to be with the marshal.

Tyree grew uneasy. His newfound pard was a good judge of character. If Aces said not to trust Moses, then he shouldn't.

But Moses sure was acting friendly. He looked at Tyree every now and again and gave a slight smile.

They rounded a corner and started up another street. A particularly loud crowd filled it, and Tyree found himself completely surrounded. He lost sight of Moses. He tried to shoulder through those ahead of him, but they were slow to give way. "Let me by," he said. Hardly anyone paid attention.

Panic set in. Tyree rose onto the tips of his toes but couldn't see Moses. He jumped up and down and still didn't. He commenced to push and shove, and more than a few glares were thrown his way.

"Watch what you're doing, boy," a burly man warned.

"No pushing," another snapped.

Tyree ignored them. If he lost Moses, all the trouble he had gone to would be for nothing. All the years of going from city to city, all his time spent tracking down wanted men, all the hours of mingling with those on the wrong side of the law to ask if any had ever heard of his folks.

A dandy in a suit and derby suddenly barred Tyree's way. He sought to go around, but the wall of people prevented him. "Let me pass," he hollered, but the dandy didn't so much as look at him.

Tyree was losing his temper. The celebration was no excuse for people to be rude. He attempted to squeeze between the dandy and another man and the dandy pushed him.

"Watch what you're doing, youngster."

"Out of my damn way," Tyree bristled.

The dandy was talking to a friend and smiling, but now he looked sharply at Tyree and lost the smile. "Don't cuss at me, boy. And don't tell me what to do."

"I'm tryin' to get past."

"You'll have to be patient," the dandy said. "Everyone is moving as slow as turtles."

"Just move a little."

"Quit pestering me," the dandy said, and turned back to his friend.

Tyree placed his hands on his Colts, but just then Moses appeared in front of the dandy and wagged a finger in his face.

"Let the kid past, consarn you."

"What are you, his grandpa?" the dandy said, but he moved enough that Tyree could move on.

"I'm obliged," Tyree said to Moses.

The old man wheeled. "Keep up, boy. I'm doing this against my better judgment and I want to get it over with."

It continued to be slow going. Tyree chafed at the delay every step of the way. He distinctly recalled Moses saying that Tucker worked at a general store, so he was surprised when the old man veered toward the right side of the street and made as if to enter a saloon. He snatched Moses by the arm.

"What are you doing? That's not a general store."

"The store is farther on," Moses said. "I don't know if Tucker is workin' today. When he's not, this is where he comes."

Tyree was instantly suspicious. Moses had told them he didn't talk to Tucker. He would have grabbed him and demanded to know what was really going on, but Moses pulled ahead and gained the batwings. "Hold on," Tyree hollered.

Moses pushed on in.

"What is this?" Aces asked, suddenly at Tyree's side. "He didn't say anything about a saloon."

"I don't know," Tyree said.

Fred was at his other elbow. "He gave in too easy. It has to be a trick."

"Or worse," Aces said.

Barreling in, they stopped and looked about. The place was almost as jammed as the street.

"I don't see him," Marshal Hitch said.

Neither did Tyree. Panic set in again and he bulled his way deeper in, not caring who he had to shove. He went clear across to the bar and there was no sign of Moses. "We've lost him!"

Aces said, "What have I told you about losin' your head? Moments like these are when you need to think clearly."

"Easy for you to say."

One of the bartenders came over and said to Aces and Fred, "What will it be, gents?"

"Did you see an old man come in here?" the lawman asked.

"You have to be joshing."

"It's important."

"Do you want drinks or not?"

Tyree was about to reach over and grab the barkeep by his apron, but a hand fell on his shoulder.

Aces pointed toward the back.

Tyree glimpsed someone going through a door. From the back it looked a lot like Moses. "Damn him anyhow."

Aces started to follow, but Tyree beat him to it, darting past and weaving like mad. The door was to a narrow hall. He ran down it, looking into the rooms he passed. One was a storeroom for the liquor. Another had a desk in it.

The rear door hung partly open. Tyree burst outside and blinked in the glare of the sun. An alley ran in both directions. And there, running toward the far end, was Moses.

"Stop!" Tyree cried.

Moses glanced over his shoulder and grinned.

Tyree took off after him. He heard Aces yell for him to wait, but he would be damned if he would. The old man had played them for fools. Moses must never have intended to help all along but had strung them like a fisherman playing out a fish line, waiting for an opportunity like this to slip away.

Tyree felt a powerful impulse to shoot him. But no, that wouldn't help them find Tucker. And it would bring the law down on their heads.

So Tyree ran. He reached the end of the alley and was confronted by another river of people. A crate sat against a wall. Climbing onto it, he scanned the street.

Moses was gone.

Tyree's frustration knew no bounds. To be so close, and to be thwarted. He sagged against the wall, momentarily crushed.

"No sign of him?" Aces asked.

Tyree bleakly shook his head.

"He hoodwinked us," Fred said, "and we fell for it."

"Speak for yourself," Aces said.

Tears of frustration filled Tyree's eyes and he wiped them away with his sleeve. "I see him again, I'll kill him."

"You should always let the other fella start it," Aces said, "or you'll be the one behind bars."

"I don't care," Tyree said. "Not with him."

"Don't give up," Aces said. "I suspect he wasn't a complete liar."

Tyree would clutch at any straw. "How do you mean?"

"He might have really seen Tucker workin' at a general store," Aces speculated. "We look for the nearest one, and if Tucker's not there, go on to the next."

"That's better than givin' up," Fred said.

They retraced their steps down the alley into the saloon and out the front to the street. Aces assumed the lead. Tyree found that following his wake was a lot easier than following Moses. Aces only had to ask once for someone to move aside and he usually did.

The entire city was in fine fettle. Statehood was the

goal of every territory. It took years, and a lot of work. Wyoming would become the forty-fourth state, Tyree had heard tell. There had been a lot of talk about what to call it. A nickname of sorts. All the states had them. The newspaper said they should call Wyoming the Equality State on account of Wyoming being the first place in the country where women were granted the right to vote. Others wanted to call it the Cowboy State on account of all the ranches and the cattle trade. Tyree reckoned the Saloon State would be a great name since Wyoming had more saloons than anywhere he'd ever been. He was thinking of that when Aces abruptly angled to the left and motioned for them to catch up.

AVERALL'S GENERAL MERCHANDISE, a large sign on a false front proclaimed. Under that was GOODS OF ALL KINDS. And under that was CASH ONLY.

The place was doing brisk business, with people buying things for the celebration. A rake-thin man who must have been the owner and his young helper were kept busy answering questions and taking payment.

Aces went down a side aisle and along a wall to a spot where they could watch the front counter.

"What are we doing?" Tyree wanted to know. "Let's go ask if Tucker works here."

"And risk him being warned that someone is lookin' for him?" Aces shook his head. "Let's wait and see if he's around."

"He might be off for the day," Fred said.

"As busy as it is? Not likely," Aces replied.

Tyree hated waiting. He kept shifting his weight from one foot to the other and running his hands over the handles of his Colts.

"You're a bundle of nerves," Aces remarked at one point.

"Can't help it," Tyree said.

"Don't be discouraged," Fred said. "If it's not this store, it might be the next or the one after that. A city this size, there has to be quite a few."

"And we'll check them all," Aces said.

They were trying to help, but that didn't put Tyree at ease. It could be that Moses had lied about everything. There was no Tucker. There might not even be a Dunn and a Lute. It could be that Moses had killed his ma and pa. At that idea, Tyree burned under his collar.

Just then another man in an apron came out of the back. He was carrying a lot of fireworks and took them to a display near the front window.

"I'll be damned," Fred Hitch said.

The man fit Moses's description. He was old. A lot of his hair was gone. He set the fireworks down and began arranging them in the display.

Tyree took a step, but Aces grabbed him by the shoulder.

"Not yet."

"He's right there," Tyree said. To be so close and have to wait was more than he could bear. "Give me a good reason."

"He might take one look and bolt."

"Why should he?" Tyree argued. "He doesn't know me from Adam. And he has no idea anyone is lookin' for him."

"I have an idea," Fred said. "You two stay put." Plastering a smile on his face, he went over to the man working on the display.

"He better not give us away," Tyree said.

"Give him more credit," Aces said. "He's not you."

Fred and the man talked a bit, but they couldn't hear what was being said. Finally Fred said something that made the other man laugh, and then came back around to where they waited.

"Well?" Tyree said impatiently.

"He says he likes brandy more than whiskey and he does his nightly drinkin' at the very saloon we were at a while ago," Fred related.

"*That's* what you talked about? Drinkin'?" Tyree could have hit him.

"I mentioned how I was a drinkin' man and new in town and asked him if there was a saloon he'd recommend."

"Smart," Aces said.

"Dumb," Tyree said. "We don't know if he's Tucker or not."

"He says his name is Finch," Fred revealed. "And when I asked where he's from, guess what he told me?"

"Missouri," Aces said.

Marshal Hitch smiled. "The very same." He clapped Tyree on the arm. "I believe you have found your man."

Chapter 28

It took Aces and Fred both to keep Tyree from barging on over. They each grabbed an arm and Aces moved in front of him.

"Not here, pard."

"Why in hell not?" Tyree demanded. He was so close to at long last finding his parents' killers.

"Keep your voice down, you lunkhead," Fred said.

Tyree saw the man working on the display raise his head and idly look around, but he didn't look in their direction.

"Didn't you learn anything from Moses?" Aces said. "If that's Tucker, you can't confront him here, with all these people around. We lay a finger on him, and someone is bound to holler for the law."

"True," Fred said.

"And even if he's friendly and will talk to you," Aces went on, "his boss ain't about to let him stand around jawin' when he should be workin'."

"True again," Fred said.

"We follow him when he gets off for the day," Aces proposed. "When the time and place are right, he'll be all yours."

"Take his advice, son."

Tyree had stopped struggling. As much as it galled him, they were right. A public fracas might bring a badge.

And it was better where no one could overhear. "If it's not chickens, it's feathers," he complained.

"That's life," Fred said. "It's always throwin' obstacles at us. Why do you reckon I like Sweetwater so much? The obstacles are few and far between."

"Anything gets in your way, you bust on through it," Tyree said.

"Some folks think that way," Fred said. "Some folks thrive on it. They like the challenge. Me, I like peace and quiet. The only challenge I want in my day is makin' up my mind what to eat."

"Yet here you are, you faker," Aces said, grinning.

"If I didn't feel sorry for Tyree, I wouldn't be," Fred said.

"I don't need anybody's pity," Tyree said.

"You have it anyway. You've earned my respect, son. I'll see this to the end with you and then I'm going back to my office and my flask and life without obstacles."

Reluctantly Tyree let them lead him out. He deliberately turned his head away from the man called Finch so Finch wouldn't see his face. Once they were outdoors Aces led them along the boardwalk to a bench. No one was using it, so they claimed it for themselves.

"Here is as good as anywhere," Aces announced.

"What if he goes out the back way?" Marshal Hitch said. "It's unlikely but you never know."

"We'd lose him," Tyree said, immediately furious at the prospect.

"Rein in that temper of yours," Aces said. "We lose him today, we come back tomorrow, or the next day after, if we have to. But since Fred will watch the back way out, we won't lose him."

"I will?" Fred said, and sighed. "I will indeed." He stood and took a couple of steps. "But what do we do if he comes out the front and I'm still back there?"

"If the store closes and you find us gone, park yourself on this bench. We'll come fetch you as soon as we can," Aces suggested.

Fred pulled his hat brim lower. "I hope this gent really is Tucker. I hope he can point us at Dunn and Lute. I want this over more than anything."

"Not more than me," Tyree said.

"Don't take me wrong," Fred said. "I'll stick with you come what may." He smiled and took a couple more steps. "Oh. I almost forgot. I saw a sign that said the store closes at seven. We've got until then, at least." He gave a little wave and ambled toward the general store.

"Nice man," Aces said.

"Too nice," Tyree said.

Aces sat back and rested his arms on the back of the bench. "Folks like Hitch make life bearable. If everybody was like you and me, we'd all be at each other's throats."

Tyree knew the cowboy was only making a joke, but he disagreed. "Not you and me. If everybody was like Dunn and Lute."

"Or Puck Tovey and Bascomb."

"I never thought about it much," Tyree said. Not about how people in it made the world good or bad.

"At your age I didn't either," Aces said.

"You're not that old. You're not Fred."

"It's not the years, it's the experience. Some folks haven't lived half as long as him and yet lived twice as much."

Tyree pondered that awhile. It seemed to him to be part right. It wasn't just living and doing a lot; it was learning from what you did. Take Dunn and Lute. They must have done a lot of vile things in their time, but what did they learn from them? That question sparked another. Were they still the killers they'd been when they murdered his ma and pa? From what Moses had said, he gathered they were. He hoped so. It would make what he aimed to do easier.

By a clock across the street it was four o'clock when Finch came out of the general store. Tyree started to rise, thinking that Finch was calling it quits for the day. But no, Finch stepped to a barrel full of hoes and shovels. He picked a hoe and went back in. For a customer, Tyree guessed, and sure enough, not long after a man in bib overalls walked out with the hoe and other items.

Tyree let the passersby entertain him. They were quite a collection. City folks, farm folks, frontiersmen, cowboys—an awful lot of cowboys—now and then tame Indians and once a dozen troopers in uniform with a sergeant at their head.

Aces was doing the same. "I've always like to study on folks," he remarked. "You never know what you'll see. Take that rainbow yonder."

Tyree laughed.

A big woman was coming down the street. She lumbered like a bear and had a face that could by no means be called pretty, but for all that, she dressed as feminine as anything. Her dress was pink and gold, her hat, with an ostrich feather waving in the air, was green and purple, her parasol was striped with six or seven colors. She held her head high in dignity and was one of the few not in a hurry.

"I think I'm in love," Aces said.

"Her?" Tyree said.

"It's not the size or the looks," Aces said. "It's the heart."

"Did you think about that a lot too?" Tyree teased. He'd never met anyone who thought so much. And Aces a cowboy, to boot.

"Ridin' herd gives a man a lot of time for ponderin'."

"I'd imagine you'd be a thinker no matter what work you did."

"And I thank you for the compliment."

Tyree wasn't so sure it was. There was such a thing as too much thinking. He'd as soon live life as think about it.

A buckboard clattered past with a passel of squealing, laughing kids in homespun in the back. Shortly after, along came an elegant carriage, the best money could purchase, with leather everywhere and brass trim and even lanterns hanging from brass posts. The driver wore a uniform.

"Rich folks," Aces said.

Seven o'clock didn't come quickly enough to suit Tyree. By then a lot of the traffic had thinned. It was suppertime for those with families, and workers were heading home to be with their loved ones.

Finch and the younger clerk came out of the store and took the barrel and other displays inside.

Tyree stood. It wouldn't be long now, he told himself. He was surprised when Marshal Hitch came around the side of the general store and over to their bench.

"Miss me?" Fred said.

"You were to watch the back," Aces said.

"No need. The owner came out and discarded some trash. When he went back in, I heard him throw the bolt. No one is comin' out that way."

"You better be right," Tyree said.

The last of the customers straggled out. The owner escorted an elderly woman and pecked her on the cheek. She patted his and left.

Next was the young clerk. He was as happy as could be to get off work and scampered away like a shot.

Last to emerge were the owner again, and Finch. The owner locked the door and shook it as if to be certain it was really locked. Then he said a few words to Finch and they parted company.

"He's comin' our way," Fred said.

Tyree turned his back to the street, placed his boot on the bench, and pretended to be doing something to it. Out of the corner of his eye he glimpsed his quarry go past.

Finch was wearing a bowler and had a folded newspaper under his arm. His suit was plain and cheap, his shoes the same. He looked downright dowdy, as unremarkable as dishwater. That the man had had a hand in the slaying of his parents seemed preposterous.

They let Finch get half a block ahead. There was no danger of losing him, the traffic had thinned so much.

Still, Tyree was uneasy. He worried that Finch somehow knew they were stalking him and had a trick up his
sleeve to shake them, as Moses had done.

Presently Finch turned and entered a small saloon
called the Silver Spur. They saw him through the window; he went to the bar and the bartender greeted him
warmly. Apparently they knew each other. A whiskey
glass was set in front of him and half-filled.

"Wonderful," Fred said. "He'll spend all night drinkin'.
Not that I have cause to complain, mind you."

The marshal was proven wrong. Finch only downed
the one glass, taking his sweet time.

They made it a point to be under an overhang across
the street when Finch came out. Without so much as a
glance their way, he was off again, strolling contentedly
along.

"First time I've seen him happy all day," Fred said.

Finch left the center of the city for the outskirts. He
picked up his pace when he came to a quiet side street
lined with quaint homes, some with picket fences. Opening a gate, he was almost to the porch when the front
door opened and out came a woman about the same age
in a print dress. She greeted him with a hug and a kiss
and together they went inside.

"Well, now," Fred said. "He has a missus."

"Didn't expect this," Aces said.

Tyree frowned. That made two of them. It never occurred to him that the old outlaw had turned a new leaf
and somewhere along the line become respectable.

"Maybe Moses was lyin'." Fred voiced Tyree's own
fear. "Maybe this isn't Tucker at all."

"Only one way to find out," Aces said, looking at
Tyree. "It's up to you how we go about it."

"What if he has young'uns?" Fred said. "We can't
brace a family."

"All I want is to talk to him," Tyree said. And he
would be damned if he would wait another minute. Tug-
ging at his gun belt, he marched to the gate, opened it,

and strode up the steps to the porch. At the door he hesitated.

The curtains that covered the windows glowed with lamplight, and from within came soft voices.

"We can do it tomorrow on his way to work," Aces said.

"No." Tyree knocked louder than was called for, waited barely five seconds, and pounded again.

"Get ready," Fred said.

The door opened and Finch stood there, smiling. "Yes?" he said uncertainly, looking from one of them to the other. "May I help you?"

The man was so polite, so earnest, that Tyree couldn't find the right words to say. He mustered the will to demand if his name was really Tucker, but the woman appeared and placed her hand on her husband's arm.

"What is it, Charles? Who are these people?"

"I don't know, dear," Finch said. "They haven't told me yet."

"I'm . . . ," Tyree got out, and stopped, struck speechless.

Charles Finch was staring at Tyree's face, at his jaw. Finch's eyes widened and every drop of blood in his head must have drained away because he became as white as paper. Taking half a step back, Finch clutched at his throat and bleated in a whisper, "No. It can't be."

"Charles?" the woman said.

"Who . . . ?" Finch said, and had to swallow twice before he could finish. "Who are you, young man?"

"Tyree Larn."

"Merciful God," Finch said, and put a hand to the wall for support.

"Charles?" the woman said anxiously. "What on earth is going on? You look as if you've seen a ghost."

"Oh, Ethel," Finch said. Recovering, he smiled and patted her. "Everything is fine, dear. Don't you worry." He faced his visitors. "Are you hungry? We're about to sit down to supper, and you and your friends are welcome to join us."

"They are?" Ethel said.

Tyree wasn't the least bit hungry. He wanted answers, not food, but Aces answered for him.

"We'd be right happy to share your meal. We've come a long way and have a lot to talk about later."

"That we do," Charles Finch said. Then again, more to himself than to them, "That we surely do."

Chapter 29

Ethel Finch didn't hide how puzzled she was by the turn of events. To her credit, she didn't pester her husband with questions or demand to know more about their guests. She simply remarked that she needed to spend a little time in the kitchen. She had cooked for two and now there were five and she wanted to add to the vegetables and whatnot.

With a polite smile, she excused herself.

Charles Finch bade them take seats in the parlor. He seemed fascinated by Tyree and hardly took his eyes off him.

Marshal Hitch and Aces sat in chairs. Tyree was about to claim the last one when Finch roosted on a settee and patted it. "Why don't you sit over here, young man? That way we won't have to holler."

Tyree suspected there was more to it. They wouldn't need to raise their voices if he was in the settee, and the wife wouldn't overhear them. He sat and shifted so he faced the man, his right hand on his Colt.

Finch noticed. "There's no need for that. I'm not heeled."

"There is if you're who I think you are," Tyree said.

"I'm George Tucker."

The declaration took Tyree by surprise. Even though he'd suspected the truth, even though he came here to demand it, the forthright admission left him momentarily startled.

"But you already know that," Tucker said, "or you wouldn't be here. I don't know how you found me, but I've always dreaded this day would happen. I've dreaded it since I saved your life."

"Saved it?" Tyree blurted louder than he intended.

Tucker glanced at the hall to the kitchen. "Please keep your voice down. Ethel doesn't know any of it. She would be upset if she did. Frankly I don't know if she would accept what I did. She might walk out on me, and I can't lose her. I love her. I love that woman more than anything."

"That's all right," Fred Hitch said. "We won't tell her."

"Speak for yourself, law dog," Tyree growled. He wasn't making any promises. Touching his scar, he said, "Was it you who did this or one of the others? Was it Dunn or Lute?"

"You know about them too?" Tucker bent to see the scar better, and a great sorrow came over him. "Dear Lord. Is that what I did to you?"

"It was you?" Before Tyree could stop himself, he had his Colt out and cocked and shoved it against Tucker's chest. He came close to shooting. If the man had jerked back or resisted, he might have. As it was, it took tremendous will on his part to lower the Colt again when it was obvious Tucker wasn't going to do anything. "I should fill you with holes."

"By rights you should, yes," Tucker said.

"Put the smoke wagon away, pard," Aces said.

"I thought you were on my side," Tyree replied sullenly, but he shoved the Colt into its holster.

Tucker glanced at the hall again. "I'd imagine you want answers. And I want to give them to you. But I don't know how much time we have. Can you wait until after the meal? Until after Ethel turns in? I'll stay up as late as need be and tell you all you want to know. You have my word."

"The word of a man who cuts babies," Tyree said.

Tucker seemed to shrivel in on himself, and bowed his head. "It was the most awful thing I've ever done. At the same time, it put me on the road to a better life." He looked up and there were tears in his eyes. "Will you be patient with me, Mr. Larn? Please?"

"Yes, he will," Marshal Hitch said. "Won't you, son?"

"I don't see why I should." Tyree was growing mad. Here was the man who could end his years-long search. He wanted answers *now*.

"I'm askin' you to be patient too, pard," Aces said.

Tyree wasn't a simpleton. He knew that Aces kept bringing up that they were partners to persuade him to go along. "Damn it all."

"Please don't swear," Tucker said. "Ethel doesn't like profanity. She was brought up in a religious house."

"As if I care," Tyree said.

"Please," Tucker pleaded.

Tyree might have told him to go to hell, but the old outlaw had unexpected allies.

"You're bein' childish, and unreasonable to boot," Fred said. "Can't you see what you've done to this man?"

"What *I've* done to *him*? Don't you have that backward?"

"He's given his word, pard," Aces said. "That should be enough for now."

"For you, maybe," Tyree said. But he gave in. Every nerve in him screamed not to, but he said, "I'll wait until after we eat, Tucker, but know this. Try to run off on us like Moses did, and I'll gun you. It won't matter if your wife is there. You had a hand in the killin' of my folks and I hate you for that."

Tucker looked sickly. He coughed and wiped at his eyes. "I suppose I'd feel the same if I were in your boots. But I won't run. I'm too old for that. And I have Ethel. I'd never leave her. Not for any reason. Not in a million years."

Just then his wife appeared wearing an apron. "It

won't be but two minutes yet. George, if you would be so kind as to help me set the table?"

"Certainly, dear."

Tyree almost got up to go with them. He didn't want the man out of his sight. Restraining himself, he sat there with his fingers twitching.

"That was decent of you, son," Fred said.

"Decent, hell," Tyree said.

"You have to rein your feelin's in," Aces advised. "Hide your hate for the time being."

"You heard him," Tyree said. "He was the one who cut me." He ran a finger along the scar he'd had his whole life long, the scar that constantly reminded him of the horror that turned his life into a living hell.

"To save you, he said," Fred reminded him. "I wonder."

"He'd say anything to save his own skin."

"It's been fifteen years," Aces said. "You can be patient a little longer."

"If you want to find Dunn and Lute, it's what I'd do," Fred said.

"Enough." Tyree was tired of talking about it. "I said I would and I will. But I don't have to like it."

"Ethel sounds like a good woman," Fred remarked.

"That she does," Aces said.

Tyree got it then. They wanted him to act nice for the wife's benefit, to be considerate to spare her any suffering. But what about his own suffering? he asked himself.

"Your ma was a good woman, wasn't she?" Fred said.

Tyree gave him a cold stare. "That was low."

"She was, don't you reckon?"

"Don't you dare compare them," Tyree said. "It won't soften me. Did Tucker stop Dunn and Lute from killin' them? He did not."

"Ethel wasn't there," Fred said.

"So you're sayin' I shouldn't cause her misery over somethin' her husband did or didn't do."

"That's only fair," Fred said.

"And right," Aces echoed.

"As friends you are pitiful," Tyree declared.

"You don't mean that," Fred said, "so we won't hold it against you."

No, Tyree didn't, but it still irritated him that they preferred he tread easy when he yearned to storm into the kitchen, seize Tucker by the throat, and shake him until his teeth rattled.

"If Tucker knows where to find Dunn and Lute, you're going after them, aren't you?" Aces said.

"Need you even ask?"

"I reckon I'll hold off lookin' for work for a while, then," the cowboy said, and grinned.

Tyree slumped in the settee. Aces was only trying to cheer him up, but he was beyond that. His emotions were all in a whirl. It was if he were being torn in all different directions at once.

"I've heard a good woman can do that to a man," Fred said to Aces. "First time I came across it."

"He loves her—that's for sure," Aces said.

"I never could find a woman for me," Fred said. "Too particular, I reckon. Or too set in my ways. Females like a man they can change to suit them. One look at me and women see I'm hopeless."

"I have hopes, one day," Aces said.

"You do?" Fred chuckled. "Why, you romantic cowpoke, you."

"There comes a time when a feller gets tired of keepin' his own company under the blankets at night," Aces said wistfully. "A lot of late, I've thought about findin' a filly and hangin' out the feed bag."

"That's all she'd be to you?" Fred teased. "A cook?"

"A good woman can be everything to a man," Aces said. "His reason for gettin' up in the mornin'. Hell, his reason for breathin'."

"Listen to yourself," Tyree said.

"What do you know, youngster?" Fred said. "When you're old like us, then you can talk. We know what we know. And I tell you now that if you ever find a woman as good as this Ethel, you hold on to her like she was the rarest jewel on earth. Because, as God is my witness, she is."

"Amen," Aces said.

That was when Ethel appeared, her apron gone, smiling timidly. "Supper is served, gentlemen. If you would follow me?"

Tyree jumped up. "Where's your husband?" he demanded, afraid that Tucker had done the same as Moses and taken flight.

"Carving the beef. I would do it myself, but he's much better with a butcher knife." Ethel held up a hand and moved her fingers. "I have a touch of arthritis. It impairs me sometimes."

"With me it's gout," Fred Hitch said. "Some days my feet pain me so I want to chop them off."

"That would be gruesome," Ethel said.

"Show us your husband," Tyree said, earning pointed glances from both Fred and Aces.

A troubled look came over Ethel, but she smiled and motioned. "Right this way. Mind the cat if he's around. He likes to rub against your leg. I nearly trip over him on occasion. His name is Whiskers."

Tyree was in no mood for a cat on top of everything else. Fortunately for the feline it didn't appear. Tyree made it a point to hook a thumb in his gun belt close to his holster as he entered the kitchen. A butcher knife could carve more than beef.

George Tucker was just setting a large plate with slices of meat on the table. "All set, dearest," he announced. "I filled the water glasses too."

"Isn't he wonderful?" Ethel said to them.

"A good man is like a good woman," Fred said. "They make each other's lives a lot happier."

"Why, Mr. Hitch," Ethel said. "That was sweet."

"Did you call him good?" Tyree said to Fred.

Everyone froze except for Ethel. "My George has

been good to me, yes." She came to Fred's defense. "All these years, I've never had a complaint. So I'll thank you not to take that tone. It seems to me you have a burr under your skin, Mr. Larn, and it would please me greatly if you would pluck it out."

Tyree hovered on the cusp of fury. He couldn't help himself. Now after so long, after enduring so much.

Unwittingly Ethel said the very thing it would take to cool the heat of his resentment. "I'd warrant your own mother would say that going around mad at the world is a poor way to be."

"My mother would," Fred said quickly. "All good mothers feel that way, and your ma was a good woman, wasn't she, Tyree? Just like Mrs. Finch here."

Tyree felt a constriction in his throat. "I'd imagine so," he said, coming out of himself. "I apologize, ma'am. I reckon I have a burr, at that."

Relief showed on Fred's and Aces's faces.

On George Tucker's too, who patted the top of a chair. "Have a seat, gentlemen, and we can begin."

It was a fine meal. Tyree couldn't remember the last time he had home cooking, unless it was when he had made the acquaintance of that man in St. Louis who told him there was money to be made in bounty work.

The beef had been bought that very day, Ethel mentioned. There were potatoes smeared in butter and carrots and peas. She'd baked the bread that morning. For dessert there was pudding Tyree had never tasted—butterscotch. He forgot himself so much he ate fit to burst.

George Tucker seemed pleased by that. "You have quite the appetite, son," he remarked.

Just like that, Tyree's anger came crashing back. He realized Tucker was doing as Fred always did, that calling him "son" didn't mean anything. But he couldn't stop himself from saying harshly, "Don't ever call me that, you hear?"

"I didn't mean anything," Tucker said.

"There you go with your burr again, young man," Ethel said.

Tyree felt the need to explain. "I lost my folks when I was little. I don't like for anyone to call me son. Not even Marshal Hitch there, and we've been ridin' together for a while now."

"Mr. Hitch is a lawman?"

"That I am," Fred said cheerfully. Reaching into his pocket, he produced his badge and pinned it on. "I keep forgettin' to wear this."

"Does whatever you have to talk to my husband about have to do with the law?" Ethel asked in obvious concern.

Fred laughed. "I'm not here to arrest him, if that's what you're thinkin'."

"It has to do with me," Tyree said.

"Oh. Well. That's a relief," Ethel said.

Tyree did something he hadn't done all night. He laughed too.

Chapter 30

The moment, at long last, came.

After supper they sat in the parlor making small talk. Marshal Hitch did most of the talking. He brought up the celebration for statehood, the railroad, even how ladies didn't wear bonnets as often as they used to. That last, Tyree figured, was for Ethel's benefit.

Tyree hardly said a word. Aces wasn't very gabby either.

By the grandfather clock in the corner, it was pushing ten o'clock when Ethel announced that she must excuse herself. She was so tired she could hardly keep her eyes open. She added, pointedly, that she hoped their guests didn't keep her husband up much longer, as he needed his rest too.

"We'll be going soon, ma'am," Fred assured her.

Tucker rose, tenderly clasped her hand, and guided her to the hall. "Off you go, my dear. I'll be up shortly."

"I'm so sorry," Ethel said.

"Nonsense. You gave us a fine meal and fine company." Tucker kissed her on the cheek. "Now please. I shouldn't be more than half an hour. I promise."

"Very well," Ethel said, not sounding happy about it. She glanced nervously at Tyree. "Good night to you, Mr. Larn. I do hope that burr is gone."

"Pleasant dreams," Tyree forced himself to say.

Tucker kissed her other cheek and Ethel made for the stairs. He waited as she climbed.

"Half an hour, no more," Ethel called down.

Tucker smiled and nodded and slowly returned to the settee, moving as might a man walking to the gallows. Taking a seat, he folded his hands in his lap. "I reckon we should get on with it."

"About damn time," Tyree said. Sitting out supper had been bad enough. Listening to their gab had tested his patience to its limits, and he was simmering. "No more delays, you hear? I want to know about my ma and my pa, and I want to know *now*."

"First I have to ask," Tucker said, "how did Moses know where I am?"

"He's here in Cheyenne," Fred said. "He saw you at the store."

"How did you find him?"

Tyree held up a hand to stop the lawman from answering. "Didn't you hear me, mister? Forget that old bastard. He's an outlaw, like you, and doesn't count for anything."

"Like I was, you mean," Tucker said. "I gave up the wild life a long time ago. The day I met Ethel, in fact. She—"

"I swear," Tyree said.

Aces had been quiet a long while, but now he stirred. "Mr. Tucker, you'd be right smart to get to it. You can see how much it means to him."

"We know that a couple of gents named Dunn and Lute were involved," Fred said, "but that's all we know."

"Dunn and Lute," Tucker said, and shuddered. "As evil a pair as ever drew breath. I'm not exaggeratin' either. They are evil through and through. Some folks like to say there's no such thing as evil, but I've rode with it and talked to it and seen it with my very own eyes." He looked at Tyree. "It was evil that killed your folks, and that evil is still alive."

"Start with them," Tyree said. "Start with why."

"Why else?" Tuckered said. "For the valuables. The law was after Dunn and Lute and they needed travelin' money. So they went around robbin' most everyone they came across. That night it was your pa's farm. He invited us to supper, and . . ." Tucker stopped.

"I want it all," Tyree said.

"I rode some with Dunn and Lute in those days," Tucker said. "I didn't like either, but I was scared not to. I was afraid they'd kill me if I crossed them. That's how evil they are."

"Enough about the evil," Tyree said.

"If I'd had more gumption, I wouldn't have been with them that night. As it was, what happened at your pa's place gave me the gumption I needed to mend my ways. You see—"

"You've strayed again," Tyree said. "My pa and my ma and me."

"Oh. As I just told you, we rode up and your pa asked us to supper. He had no idea who we were. He was just being friendly. But Dunn didn't like it when your folks wouldn't let Lute in, and that might be what set him off."

"Back up," Tyree said. "Why not?"

"They didn't want a black man at their table. Somethin' to do with the War Between the States, and how it would upset your ma."

Tyree vaguely recollected his uncle telling him that their family fought for the South and lost some of their menfolk to Yankee bullets.

"Anyway, Dunn shot your pa, Lute shot your ma, and that left you, a swaddlin' infant. Dunn said since they'd killed the others, it was my turn. He wanted me to kill you right there in front of him."

"The hell you say," Fred said. "And Tyree a baby."

"I felt the same," Tucker said. He closed his eyes and put his fingers to them. "It haunts me. I see it when I'm awake. I dream it when I'm asleep. I see the blood, and feel it on my hands. I feel the same fear. But I had to do it, or they'd have shot me."

"You mentioned tryin' to save him," Fred said.

Tyree wished the lawman would shut up.

Tucker lowered his hand and nodded bleakly. He looked Tyree in the eye, his own eyes misting again. "Dunn wanted me to shoot you. One shot to the head and it would have been over. But I said no, I'd rather just slit your throat."

"Awful kind of you," Tyree said.

"Hear me out," Tucker said. "I was thinkin' fast, faster than I've ever thought in my life. Rackin' my brain for some way to spare you. You were a baby, for Pete's sake. I didn't want that on my conscience."

"I think I see where this is going," Fred said.

Tyree didn't. "How was slittin' my throat any different from shootin' me in the head?"

"I couldn't fake the shootin'," Tucker said. "I'd have to point the gun at you and squeeze the trigger and they'd see the slug splatter your brains. But with a knife there was a chance I could fool them." He paused, and a tear trickled down a cheek. "What I did was I drew my clasp knife and opened it. When I hesitated, Dunn said he knew I didn't have it in me, that I was a weak sister, and he had half a mind to do me and the baby both. So I held you close to me"—and Tucker imitated how he had held Tyree close to his chest—"but turned some, so Dunn didn't have a good look at your face and neck. And I cut you, quick-like."

"You miserable buzzard."

"I saved your life," Tucker declared, and uttered a low sob. "I cut you along your jawbone instead of across your throat. Cut you deep so there was a lot of blood. So much of it Dunn couldn't tell if I had or I hadn't. The shock made you pass out, so when I showed you to him, it looked as if I'd done the deed."

"That was damn clever," Fred said.

"And dangerous," Aces said.

Tyree let the revelation sink in. All these years, he'd

thought the killers had botched killing him. Now he learned that it had been botched on purpose to save him.

"I set you on the floor and suggested we get the hell out of there," Tucker related. "That if we were caught with a dead baby, we'd be strung up faster than Dunn could blink." He swallowed, hard. "I was afraid he'd take a look at you and see that I had tried to trick them."

"You rode off and left a baby lyin' in its own blood," Tyree said in undisguised disgust.

"If I hadn't, I'd have been lyin' there with you." Tucker pressed his hands together as if he were about to pray. "Don't you see, boy? If I hadn't done anything, Dunn or Lute or both would have killed you and me. That's how evil they are."

"We're back to that again."

"We never left it. Evil is real. And there are evil people in this world. People like Dunn and Lute. They have no regard for anyone. They murder and they steal and to them it's nothin'. It's just what they do."

"I feel sorry for what those two put you through," Fred said.

"I brought it on myself," Tucker said. "I should have refused to ride with them. Or left Missouri. But Dunn was right. I was a weak sister. I didn't have the gumption. Not until he made me cut the baby." He wrung his hands. "I couldn't take it anymore. I had to be shed of them. So when we reached St. Louis, I slipped away one night and headed west on my own. I gave up the owl-hoot trail once and for good."

"From outlaw to clerk," Tyree said.

"It doesn't pay much, but it's good, honest work and we get by, Ethel and me. She helps by sewin' and knittin'. Truth is, she's everything to me. I wouldn't want to live without her."

"You said that already," Tyree said.

"Cut that out," Fred scolded him. "He came clean with you, didn't he? Show some respect."

"For the man who gave me this?" Tyree touched his scar.

"You say you don't like to be called a boy," Marshal Hitch said. "Fine. Act like a man, then. And a man would forgive Tucker for what he did."

"A man would, pard," Aces said.

Tyree didn't know what to say, so he said nothing. He'd held on to his hate for so long, he couldn't just shed it the way he shed his socks.

Tucker wasn't paying attention to them. He said quietly, "I got a scare about three years ago. I found out Dunn and Lute were in Wyoming Territory. For a while I thought they might be after me, but I haven't seen hide nor hair of them. They've left me be, thank goodness."

"Where are they?" Fred asked.

"Up in the Teton country," Tucker said. "They have their own gang. They raid a lot up in Montana and over in Utah and always come back to Robbers Roost, as it's called. A town of nothin' but robbers and killers."

"Where is the law in all this?" Aces asked.

"I've heard where federal marshals go into the Roost from time to time, but those who are wanted always scatter before the marshals get there and come back after the marshals are gone."

"Now that Wyoming is a state, maybe the government will form a company of rangers like they have down to Texas," Fred said.

"That wouldn't stop or scare Dunn and Lute," Tucker said.

Tyree was making up his mind about something. All these years, he'd longed to put a slug into the man who'd cut him. He'd imagined it countless times, daydreamed about how fine it would feel. Here the man sat. All he had to do was pull a Colt and shoot. But now that he'd learned the truth, he couldn't bring himself to do it. "I am mightily confused," he said out loud.

"About what?" Fred asked.

Not wanting to admit his weakness, Tyree said to Tucker, "Tell me more about this Robbers Roost."

"It's way back in the Tetons," Tucker replied. "I've never been there, but from what I gather, it's high up near the snow line, with secret ways in and out. Cabins and shacks, mostly, and a saloon."

"I've heard of it," Aces mentioned. "No self-respectin' cowhand ever goes there. It's said that if you ride in with a full poke, you might make it out but the poke won't."

"That's where I have to go," Tyree said.

Tucker went to put a hand on Tyree's arm but caught himself. "I was afraid you might say that. Listen, youngster. You go in there after Dunn and Lute, it'll be the last anybody sees of you."

"You're positive that's where they are?"

"As sure as I'm sittin' here."

"Then I have no choice," Tyree said, and his own words hit him like a sack of rocks. *He had no choice.* Just as Tucker had no choice fifteen years ago. Either murder a baby . . . or pretend to.

"You don't understand," Tucker was saying. "It won't be only Dunn and Lute. They have a gang. Men as evil as they are. Men who will do you in if Dunn or Lute so much as snaps his fingers."

"What else would you have me do? Twiddle my thumbs until they die of old age?"

"Why does it have to be you? A lawman might plant them toes up someday. Or they could be shot on one of their raids. Or they could go up against a gun hand as good as they are. You never know what could happen."

"Could, could, and could," Tyree said, and shook his head. "That won't do. They have to pay for my ma and my pa. By my own hand. So I see them die with my own eyes, and I can spit in their faces."

"Oh, Tyree," Fred said.

"I'm going to Robbers Roost," Tyree announced. "I'm going to find Dunn and Lute and bed them down permanent."

"Ask a federal marshal to go with you," Tucker suggested. "If you explain things, he'll be happy to."

"Who are you tryin' to kid?" Tyree replied. "A marshal would try to stop me. No, I'll go it alone if I have to."

"You don't," Aces said. "You have a pard now, remember?"

"I wish the both of you wouldn't," Tucker said.

"The three of us," Fred said. "I've come this far, I might as well see it all the way through."

"Your badge won't do you any good there," Aces said. "They find out you're a law dog, they're liable to string you up."

"Then we won't tell them," Fred said, grinning. He turned to Tyree and his expression became somber. "Since I took up with you, I've been shot at and hit and taken an arrow. Anyone with any sense would be shed of you. But I never claimed to have all that much in the way of brains, and besides, you and me are friends now, and while a friend ain't the same as a pard, it's enough that I'll go along and try to keep you out of trouble. What do you say?"

Tyree was feeling warm inside, in a good way. First Aces, now Fred. Smiling, he said, "I say you jabber worse than a biddy, but you're welcome to come get killed like Aces and me."

"Thank you," Fred said.

Chapter 31

The Teton Range, it was sometimes said, was one of God's gifts to creation.

A spectacular display of nature at its grandest, many of the towering peaks rose more than two miles into the sky. The Shoshones called them "the mountains of high pinnacles." The early French, more amorously inclined, called them "the three breasts," after the highest in the range.

Everyone else called them magnificent.

Part of that was due to a geological feature rarely found anywhere in the world. The Teton Mountains lacked foothills. Seeing them for the first time was often a shock; they rose so stark and clear they took the breath away.

Located south of the geyser country, a wonderment in itself, the Tetons were as remote as any range on the continent. Few whites had ever beheld them. Trappers, in the early days. Then the mountain men. Now ranchers had moved in, but the ranches were few and far between. Several small towns had sprung up along the edge of the range but not in the range itself. Robbers Roost was a notorious exception. To reach it was a challenge.

Marshal Fred Hitch was of the opinion they should follow the Gros Ventre River into the southern extremity of the range, then head north by northwest until they reached the Roost. His reasoning was that it would be easier on their horses and they wouldn't want for water or game.

Aces consulted a map with the lawman, and agreed.

Tyree didn't care how they got there so long as they did. He burned with his desire to hunt down Dunn and Lute and repay them for what they had done to his folks. It was all he thought about.

Them, and George Tucker.

Tyree had surprised himself considerably by letting Tucker live. After he'd heard the former outlaw's account, which he didn't doubt was genuine, Tyree's resolve to shoot him faded. The man had actually saved him. Scarred him for life, but saved him. For years he'd hankered to shoot the man who had done that to him—but he'd be shooting someone who risked his hide to spare his.

"Now, there's irony for you," Marshal Hitch had commented.

It sure as hell was.

Tyree consoled himself with the thought that with Dunn and Lute it would be different. According to Tucker, they were pure evil, as vile and vicious as human beings could be. Shooting them would be no problem at all. Tyree relished the prospect, and cleaned his Colts every other night even though they didn't need it.

The Gros Ventre proved to be a scenic waterway. Bordered by lush flatland with low banks, the rapids were few, the river not all that deep, and the fishing, so everyone claimed, excellent.

Not that Tyree had any interest in fish. He barely noticed the buffalo they came on either, or the eagles that winged high in the air, or the elk and deer that made the region a hunter's paradise.

Each night after supper they sat around their fire relaxing after their long hours in the saddle. Aces and Fred did most of the talking. Tyree had one thing and one thing only on his mind, and had to be drawn into their conversations.

It got so that one night Fred peered across the crackling flames at Tyree and cleared his throat. He'd grown to like the boy a lot over the past few weeks, and had to say what was on his mind. "You worry me, son. You truly do."

"What is it now?" Tyree asked.

"You're obsessed," Fred said. "You're sittin' here with Aces and me, but you're not really here. You're off in the Tetons, killin' Dunn and Lute."

"Nicely put," Aces said. He was concerned too but had held off saying anything. His new pard might see it as pestering.

"Call it whatever you want," Tyree said. "If you were me, you'd feel the same."

"Likely I would," Fred conceded. "But I'd like to think I'd take some time to smell the roses."

"Roses?" Tyree repeated. "What do flowers have to do with it?"

"You're so caught up in your vengeance you don't notice the world around you." Fred gestured. "There's so much beauty here."

"Says the gent who likes to hide in his office all day."

Fred laughed. "You've got me there. Maybe that's why I admire all this so much. I haven't gotten out into the world in a coon's age, so I appreciate it that much more."

"I'll appreciate it once Dunn and Lute are dead."

"I wonder," Fred said.

"What *will* you do, pard, once it's over?" Aces asked.

Tyree hadn't thought that far ahead. "How would I know? I take things one day at a time."

"Here's a notion," Aces said. "You can become a cowhand like me. I'll teach you all you need to know. It's not the most exciting work in the world, but it beats sittin' behind a desk."

"Thanks heaps," Fred said.

"We'll find a ranch where the cook is a marvel and a boss who pays well and cowboy for as long as our bodies hold out."

"That would do, I suppose." Tyree couldn't think of anything else he wanted to do with his life anyway.

The next day, at the river's edge, they came on the tracks of unshod ponies.

"Injuns," Aces announced. "They could be Shoshones, who are friendly. Or the Blackfeet, who aren't."

They stayed on their guard after that.

Not two days later they struck more sign. Only this time it was wagon tracks, miles from any trail.

"Who could be so foolish as to come in this far with wagons?" Fred marveled. It never ceased to amaze him, the things people did.

"There are three altogether," Aces deduced. "They came in from the south and are headin' for the Tetons. Pilgrims from the Oregon Trail, would be my guess."

"Are they lost?" Fred wondered.

"We'll find out soon enough," Aces said. "They're not that far ahead."

"I wouldn't mind the company for a night," Fred remarked. He missed town life. The one part of his job he liked the most was helping other people.

Were it up to Tyree, they'd avoid contact. For that matter, were it up to him, they wouldn't stop until they reached Robbers Roost. "One night won't hurt," he said. But no more, he vowed.

Evening was approaching when glimmers of firelight appeared in the distance.

"There they are," Aces said. He found himself hoping there were women, preferably unattached, whom he could strike up an acquaintance with. He enjoyed females, unlike some cowpokes he knew. Women were strange, but they could be a delight.

Fred took off his hat and slapped at his shirt and his sleeves.

"What are you doing?" Tyree asked.

"Sprucin' up."

"It would serve you right if you spooked your horse and fell and broke your neck."

"A joke?" Fred said. "There's hope for you yet."

The wagons were in a circle on a flat by the river. Conestogas, with canvas tops, the kind emigrants used. The teams had been picketed outside the circle and tripods had been set up in it. Large black pots hung from hooks over the cook fires.

Aces counted thirteen people. Drawing rein in the dark beyond the firelight, he hallooed them with "Hello the camp! There are three of us and we're friendly and we'd be obliged if we could come on in."

The chaos it caused was almost comical. The men scrambled for their rifles; the women grabbed their young ones and scooted to a wagon on the opposite side.

Five men then advanced, three of them young and wearing homespun and workers' boots. Everything about them said *farmers*.

The other two were different. One wore buckskins and a beaver hat, the other a wool shirt more fitting for winter than summer, and a short-brimmed hat that looked to be fairly new.

"Be careful with those long guns," Aces said, his hand on his Colt.

A farmer with hair the color of corn motioned with his shotgun. "Come out where we can see you, mister. For all we know you could be owl-hoots."

Fred gigged his bay past Aces, saying, "Let me." He thrust out his chest so his badge caught the firelight and plastered a friendly smile on his face. "Marshal Fred Hitch, gentlemen," he declared. "We mean you no harm."

The sight of his tin star had an immediate effect. The three farmers lowered their weapons.

But not the other two.

The man in buckskins trained a Sharps on Fred. "What are you doing here, law dog? Are you federal?"

"I'm from Sweetwater," Fred revealed. "On the trail of outlaws."

Aces came up beside him. "Lower that buffalo gun," he commanded.

"The hell I will," the man in buckskins replied.

"Mr. Creech, please," the farmer with the shotgun said.

"We can't take no chances," Creech said.

"They are officers of the law."

Aces didn't correct the farmer's mistake. He was watching the one in the wool shirt, who had a thick beard and a hooked nose, and a Spencer he was raising to his shoulder. Aces drew, flicking his Colt up and out. "You raise that any higher and I'll splatter your brains."

"Hold on, there," the farmer who appeared to be in charge said. "There's no need for that."

Tyree came out of the dark, his hands on his Colts. "What's the matter with you people? We said we were friendly."

"Why, it's a boy," a beefy farmer said.

"I'm not neither," Tyree said. He was so sick of being called that he could scream. "Put down those damn rifles," he snapped at the pair who hadn't done so.

"Tyree," Fred said. He was afraid the youngster would provoke them into shooting. Smiling at the man in buckskins, he said, "But I'd do as he says. You shoot a lawman and there will be hell to pay."

"That boy's no lawman," the man said, but he jerked his Sharps down and nodded at the man in the wool shirt, who did the same with his Spencer.

Dismounting, Fred offered his hand to the farmer with the shotgun. "Pleased to make your acquaintance."

"Same here," the farmer said, shaking. "I'm Luther Hays. We're out of Pittsburg, Pennsylvania. This here is my brother, Thad, and my cousin, Orpheus."

Fred shook hands all around. The farmers returned his smile and were friendly, but the other two gave him hard stares, as if they resented his being there. That struck him as peculiar. Men didn't resent the law unless they had cause.

Aces slid his Colt into his holster and alighted. He didn't shake. He wanted his gun hand free.

The women timidly came forward with their young ones clustered at their legs like young chicks to mother hens. They stopped at the tripods.

Tyree had no interest in any of it. Not the farmers or their families or their food. He had one thing and one thing only on his mind: Robbers Roost.

"We never expected to run into a lawman way out here," Luther Hays was saying. "Our guides told us there aren't any settlements for a hundred miles."

"Guides?" Fred said.

Hays pointed. "Mr. Creech and Mr. Sterns here. They know this country like the backs of their hands. We were fortunate they came across us. We were on our way to Oregon, but they've convinced us there is better land to be had a lot nearer."

"You don't say," Fred said.

Creech cradled his Sharps and scowled. "You don't need to tell them everything, Mr. Hays."

"He's a lawman," Hays said.

"Out here that doesn't mean much," Sterns said with a sneer.

"It does to us," Hays said. "We are law-abiding folk, and I'll thank you to show a little more respect." He motioned at Fred. "Would you like to meet our families, Marshal Hitch? We have soup on, and there's plenty for everyone."

"By heaven, you're a kind soul," Fred said. "We'd be delighted." As hungry as he was, he took the liberty of speaking for Aces and Tyree.

Aces strolled after them, leading his palomino. He noticed that Creech and Sterns moved off and huddled together. The pair raised his hackles, and he'd learned to trust his instincts.

Tyree dismounted near the cook fires. Putting a hand on the small of his back, he arched it to relieve a kink.

Hays was making introductions. The wives were reserved, their young ones curious but timid.

Fred accepted a china cup brimming with coffee. "You

folks are the salt of the earth," he complimented them. "To your health," he said, and swallowed.

"So, who is it you and your posse are after, Marshal, if you don't mind my asking?" Frank Hays said.

"We're not exactly a posse," Fred said. "But we're bound for a place where outlaws are as thick as fleas on a hound dog. It's called Robbers Roost."

Aces had turned sideways so he could keep one eye on Creech and Stern. He was the only one who saw them whip around and regard Fred Hitch as if he were a gnat they'd like to swat.

"Where exactly is this better land you're bound for, if you don't mind *my* askin'?" Fred had gone on.

"North a ways." Hays gestured in the direction of the Tetons. "Up in those mountains. There's a valley, Mr. Creech says, ten miles long and five miles wide, and the earth so fertile our crops won't hardly need tending."

Aces had never been to the Tetons, but he had heard a lot about them, and one of the things he'd learned was that if these pilgrims were after farmland, they'd be better off farming on the moon.

Something was wrong. Very wrong.

And there was only one thing for Aces to do.

Chapter 32

Tyree didn't care about the farmers. He didn't care about their guides. He didn't pay much attention to what anyone was doing or saying, so he was considerably surprised when Aces Connor came over beside him, squatted, and said so only he would hear, "Back my play, pard."

A farmer's wife had just given Tyree a bowl of soup and a spoon to eat it with. Pausing in the act of dipping the spoon into the broth, he said, "How's that again?"

Aces made sure Creech and Sterns weren't listening. The pair was several yards away, talking to Frank Hays. "I have my suspicions about the guides," he said quietly.

"Suspicions how?"

"Keep your voice down." Aces leaned in and whispered, "I'm countin' on you not to let them back-shoot me." Rising, he moved off.

Tyree was startled. He'd had no inkling that a shooting affray was brewing. The pair had struck him as surly, but grumpiness was no reason to shoot them. He set the bowl and the spoon down and stood, his thumbs in his gun belt close to his Colts.

Aces went around the fire to Marshal Hitch, who was complimenting one of the wives on her tasty soup, saying how he hadn't had soup this good in ages. Hunkering, Aces nudged him. "Since you like these folks so much, you might want to help them some more."

"They're decent people," Fred said. Nice people. The kind he liked. The kind who never caused trouble for anyone. The kind who made his job as a marshal easier. He'd often thought it was a shame that more people weren't as nice as he was. "How can I help them?"

Careful not to be overheard, Aces shared his suspicion.

"How will you go about provin' it?" Fred asked.

"By seizin' the bull by the horns," Aces said. "Be ready."

"I'll do my best."

Standing, Aces went over to Luther Hays and the so-called guides and interrupted them with "I have a question for Mr. Creech and Mr. Sterns."

Hays turned. "I have one for you too. Mr. Creech here says I shouldn't be so willing to trust you. He thinks it's strange a marshal from Sweetwater is wandering around these parts."

"It's no stranger than their valley that isn't," Aces said.

"I beg your pardon?"

"Their valley that's supposed to be ten miles long and five miles wide and perfect for growin' crops," Aces said. "There ain't one."

Creech and Sterns both scowled, Creech with his Sharps cradled, Sterns with his Spencer pointing at the ground.

"What's that you're sayin'?" Creech said.

"Are you callin' us liars?" Sterns demanded.

"Poor ones, at that," Aces said. "How much are Mr. Hays and his people payin' you to lead them to your make-believe valley?"

A smug smile spread Creech's stubble. "Nary a cent," he said. "We're doing it for free."

Sterns nodded. "We're only tryin' to help these folks."

Aces had been certain the unsavory pair was out to fleece the farmers. Now another, more sinister, notion occurred to him, sparked by a discussion in the Circle H bunkhouse nearly a year ago. "Into an early grave, most likely," he said.

"What are you on about?" Hays wanted to know.

"We've only just met you and you accuse these men we've been traveling with for better than a week of being out to kill us?"

"You're new to these parts, Mr. Hays." Aces was patient with him. "It could be you haven't heard about the outlaws hereabouts. There are some, I've been told, that like to waylay emigrants like yourselves. Rumor has it these outlaws trick pilgrims into going off into the mountains and no one ever hears from them again."

"I never heard any such rumor," Creech declared.

"Me either," Sterns echoed angrily.

"What are you up to, Mr. Connor?" Luther Hays said. "If this is your idea of humor, it's in poor taste."

Aces realized he should have let the farmers get to know him a little better before he made his accusation. But now that he had jumped in with both feet, it was sink or swim. Raising his voice so everyone in the circle would hear, he said, "I'm tryin' to spare you from harm, or worse. I've been in Wyoming for years and I've never heard tell of this valley these two vultures claim you should go to."

"What did you call us?" Sterns said.

"Don't let him rile you," Creech said.

"What is this, Luther?" the woman who had passed out the soup asked. "What is it this man is saying?"

"I think," Hays answered, "that Mr. Connor believes our guides are up to no good."

Sterns was glaring at Aces. He was the one Aces watched, the one who would lose his temper. Creech was more crafty, and more wary.

"To what end, Mr. Hays?" the latter now asked the farmer. "Why would we lead you and your families off into the middle of nowhere?"

"That's easy," Aces said. "To rob them and put windows in their skulls."

"The women and children too?" Hays said in disbelief.

"You're not in Pennsylvania anymore." Aces sought to

enlighten him. "Out here there are vermin who will murder anybody. Take young Tyree over there. His ma and pa were killed when he was a baby by two polecats who happen to be up in the Tetons right this minute. Their handles are Dunn and Lute, and they are scum. Just like anyone who'd ride with them." Aces said that last to get a reaction; he got more than he bargained for.

Sterns turned red in the face and blurted to Creech, "Did you hear what he just called them?"

"Hush, damn you," Creech said.

"No, Mr. Hays," Aces said. "If I were you, I'd turn around and head for the Oregon Trail and be shed of these guides of yours. They are curly wolves, and you and yours are the sheep they aim to shear."

"I won't be talked to like that, you son of a bitch," Sterns growled.

"Mr. Sterns, please, your language," Hays said.

"I won't, I tell you." Sterns took a step back, his body coiled. "I have half a mind to blow him in two."

"Calm down, you jackass," Creech said. "He can't prove that we haven't been honest with these folks."

"Sure I can," Aces said.

"How?" Creech demanded.

"All Mr. Hays has to do is look at your pard's ugly face. It's as plain as his big nose that he's lyin' through his teeth."

Sterns let out a howl of fury. Jerking his Spencer up, he worked the lever to feed a cartridge into the chamber.

Aces shot him. He drew and fanned a single shot that slammed into Sterns's sternum and knocked him back a step. Sterns stayed on his feet, though, and gamely brought his Spencer to bear. He'd have been wiser to fire from the hip. That was what Aces did, fanning the Colt's hammer, two swift shots that crumpled Sterns where he stood and caused one of the women to scream and a little girl to wail at the top of her lungs.

In the aftermath, none of the emigrants moved. They were in shock.

Aces pointed his Colt at Creech. "How about you, buckskin?"

"No, you don't," Creech said, not making any move to use his Sharps. "You gun me, you're the murderer. These folks are witnesses."

Luther Hays found his voice. "Enough, I say. There will be no more shooting." He stepped over to Sterns and felt for a pulse. "He's dead," he said to the woman who had addressed him and must be his wife. "He's really dead."

The other farmers picked up the rifles they had set down, and one cocked his, the click unnaturally loud.

Tyree moved over beside Aces, ready to resort to his pistols should it prove necessary.

Fred Hitch stayed where he was. "This is good soup," he exclaimed loudly. "Everyone should help themselves while it's hot."

The emigrants regarded him as if he were insane.

"How can you sit there eating?" Luther Hays said. "A man has just been killed right in front of your eyes."

"That happens a lot out here," Fred said, and tapped his badge. "I'm used to it." Which was a bald-faced lie. "Mr. Connor was only tryin' to protect you. I'd trust him with my life, and I agree with him that your guides were plumb suspicious."

"Here, now," Creech said. "Don't be makin' wild accusations."

"If I could prove you are in cahoots with Dunn and Lute, I'd let Mr. Connor do the same to you," Fred said.

"You call that law?" Hays said.

"I call it justice," Fred said.

Creech was remarkably composed, given his situation. "Don't worry, Mr. Hays. He can't prove a thing. But I'll be damned if I'm stickin' around. I'm going to take my friend and go."

"Where to?" another farmer asked.

"Away from here," was all Creech would say. Handing his Sharps to Hays, he proceeded to saddle two horses and brought them over. The farmers offered to help lift Sterns, but Creech refused their aid and did it himself, placing Sterns belly down and tying Sterns's wrists to his ankles so the body wouldn't slide off. Reclaiming his Sharps, Creech climbed onto his mount, glared at Aces and Tyree, and jabbed his heels. In no time the night swallowed him and presently the hoofbeats faded.

"We should have done something," a woman said.

"He wouldn't let us," Hays said.

While all that was going on, Fred finished his first bowl and started in on a second. He was content to stay with the emigrants until morning and maybe prevail on them for breakfast as well. Aces dashed his hopes.

"At first light we'll head out and follow him."

"We will?" Tyree said.

"Whatever for?" Fred asked. "You saved these good folks. Let him go his way and good riddance."

"Use your noggin," Aces said, and touched a finger to his. "Didn't you see Creech's face when I mentioned Dunn and Lute? Where do you reckon he'll head from here?"

"By golly," Fred said. "He'll light a shuck for Robbers Roost."

"And we'll be right behind him," Aces said, "trackin' him the whole way."

"You planned that?" Fred said in amazement. Killing one man to track the other? He would never have thought of such a ruse.

"Let's just say it worked out well," Aces said.

Tyree was enormously pleased. They could have spent a month of Sundays scouring the Tetons for the outlaw sanctuary. Few knew exactly where it was, and the Tetons covered a lot of territory, five or six hundred square miles, Fred had told him.

"How can you sit there eating soup when a man has just been killed?" Hays said to Fred.

"I'm hungry."

"But a man has *died*," a woman said.

"People do it all the time," Fred replied. "It's not worth losin' your appetite over."

Hays's wife stepped to his side and took his hand. "I wouldn't stay here now even if there is a valley. Wyoming isn't for us, Luther. It's too violent. Take us on to Oregon as we intended. We never should have let those two change our minds."

"No," Hays said, "we shouldn't."

It was a subdued bunch of farmers who sat down to supper. The small children clung to their mothers; the women were anxious and troubled, the men uncommonly quiet.

Fred felt guilty imposing on their good graces. Finishing his second bowl, he set it aside and stood. "I think we have worn out our welcome," he said to Aces.

Aces nodded. "I reckon so."

Turning to the farmers, Fred smiled and said, "We'll be partin' company with you folks. We thank you for your kindness, but we must be going."

That was fine by Tyree. He'd never wanted to spend time with them anyway. "We're grateful for the food," he said to be polite.

Aces hadn't bothered to help himself and none of the ladies had offered him a bowl—or venture anywhere near him. Without a word, he touched his hat brim, climbed onto the palomino, and rode off.

"That was a shame," Fred said when he caught up. "I heard one of the kids say their mother had made dumplings."

"Liquor and food, that's all you think of," Tyree said.

"You're a fine one to criticize," Fred said. "All you think of is revenge."

"Speakin' of which," Aces said, "we need to be clear on how we deal with Creech. With any luck, he'll lead us right where we want to go."

"What's to deal with?" Tyree asked.

"We can't let him talk to Dunn and Lute," Aces said. "When they ask how Sterns died, Creech will tell them about us, and how I mentioned their names."

"Oh, hell no," Fred said.

"We'll let him lead us there and stop him before he can ride in," Aces said. He wasn't as confident as he sounded, but he always had been one to take potential disasters lightly.

"I don't care if they know we're comin'," Tyree said. "I aim to walk right up to Dunn and Lute and start shootin'."

"Wow," Fred said. "That's dumb."

"Is it ever?" Aces said. "How many times do I have to say that we must do this smart?"

"I want them dead," Tyree said petulantly.

"It won't be just them," Fred said. "There's the not-so-little matter of the ten to twenty outlaws who might be there with them."

"The lead will fly fast and furious," Aces predicted.

"I hope so," Tyree said.

Chapter 33

Tyree had every confidence their plan would work. Luck was on their side. It was luck that he'd met Moses, luck that Moses led them to Tucker, luck that brought them to the Tetons at the same time as the emigrants were being led to the slaughter by Creech and Sterns.

Although, after he thought about it awhile, he realized that the years of effort and sweat on his part had a lot to do with it too. There had been days when it seemed as if he had been hunting for his parents' killers forever. So maybe it wasn't just luck. Maybe all his hunting had simply finally paid off.

Creech headed north into the Tetons, and they followed. Aces did most of the tracking. Tyree could track if the prints were fresh enough. Fred wasn't much good at it at all. Too much "desk-ridin'," Tyree joked.

Aces figured Creech would bury Sterns since it would take days to penetrate into the dark heart of the Tetons where Robbers Roost was supposed to be, and by then the body would be awfully ripe. But Creech surprised him.

Creech dumped the body over a cliff.

They were staying well back to keep Creech from discovering he was being trailed. They spotted several buzzards circling over a ridge they were climbing but didn't think much of it.

At the crest, a cliff yawned, a sheer drop of hundreds

of feet. Creech had skirted the top and ridden on up into heavy timber.

Midway, Tyree happened to look down and gave a start. "Is that what I think it is?"

Shifting in his saddle, Aces peered over the edge. "I'll be damned."

Fred risked a peek. He didn't like heights. Never had. Just climbing a tall ladder made him queasy. But he peeked and beheld a smashed body lying on jagged boulders far below. The head had burst like a melon, decorating a boulder with brains and hair, and one of the arms wasn't attached.

Vultures were pecking and tearing at the remains. One was perched on Sterns's chest and was prying at an eye with its beak. Suddenly the eye popped free and the vulture raised its ugly head and gulped the eyeball down its gullet.

Fred thought he'd be sick.

"Did you see that?" Tyree said, and laughed. Buzzards had always struck him as comical.

"I thought those two were pards, but Creech just dumped him there," Fred said, looking away.

"Anything ever happens to me," Aces said to Tyree, "I'd appreciate better treatment. Bury me if you can take the time."

"I don't care what happens to me," Tyree said. "You can feed me to hogs for all I care."

"How hideous," Fred said, imagining a hog tearing at human flesh and gulping it as the vulture had done.

"Dead is dead," Tyree said. "It's not like you feel anything."

The tracks told them that Creech was in a hurry to get where he was going. He trotted when he could. And since he had two horses, he switched mounts whenever one became tired.

By the end of the day they were farther behind than Aces liked. Fortunately the sky showed no sign of thunderheads. A heavy rain would erase the sign.

That night they camped in a clearing under a host of sparkling stars. Wolves howled and a mountain lion screamed. The Tetons were largely untouched by man, and predators and prey thrived in great numbers.

The next day they came on sign of a different kind, tracks of an enormous beast that crossed Creech's trail and went off to the west.

Tyree whistled in astonishment.

"Will you look at the size of those?" Fred marveled. "The thing must be a monster."

The "thing" had been a roving grizzly. The clearest prints were almost a foot long and half again as wide.

"It's a big one—that's for sure," Aces said. He'd encountered a few grizzlies while working the range. The bears, thank goodness, always took one whiff and went the other way. They weren't as numerous as they'd been, and it was generally believed that it wouldn't be long before the only grizzlies left were those that lived deep in the mountains, like this one.

"And you poke fun at me for likin' to sit at my desk?" Fred said to Tyree. "The most fearsome critters I have to deal with are flies and mice. They beat grizzlies all hollow."

Aces regretted that they didn't have a spyglass so they could keep better track of Creech. He hoped Creech didn't have one or Creech might know they were after him. But the outlaw never once tried to hide his trail. That told Aces that they were safe enough, provided they continued to be cautious.

Several days passed. The daytime temperature became cooler at the higher elevation, giving them a welcome respite from the summer heat. The hard travel wore at them, though. And at their horses. Their mounts weren't accustomed to mountain riding; the steep slopes and switchbacks took a toll.

One afternoon they crested a spiny ridge and drew rein in surprise. Below lay a narrow valley bisected by a stream.

"Lookee there," Fred said.

Smoke from a campfire coiled into the air.

"Quick," Aces said. "Back into the trees." He had seen figures moving about, and horses.

Climbing down, they shucked their rifles and crawled to where they had a clear view.

Fred counted seven men. Two appeared to be Indians, or partly so.

Creech stood out, as he was the only one dressed entirely in buckskins. He was seated at their fire, drinking coffee and talking.

"More outlaws, you reckon?" Fred said.

"It could be anybody," Tyree said. The delay annoyed him. He was so close to finding Dunn and Lute that the last thing he wanted was another delay.

"No, the marshal is right," Aces said. "Whoever they are, they're bad men. Creech wouldn't hobnob like that with ordinary folk."

"He did with the emigrants," Tyree mentioned.

"He was a wolf mixin' with sheep so he could shear them." Aces nodded at the group below. "Do they strike you as sheep?"

"Enough argument, boys," Fred said. "It appears they're breakin' camp."

That they were. The fire was doused, they saddled their horses, and Creech and the new bunch parted company. Creech went on to the northwest. His new acquaintances crossed the valley and started up the ridge.

"Tarnation, they're comin' our way," Fred declared in alarm. If Aces was right about them and they caught sight of his badge, he'd be a goner.

"We hide," Aces said, crabbing backward. "Hurry."

From the shadowy recess of a phalanx of firs, they watched the seven men come over the crest, riding in single file.

Fred swallowed. He'd seldom seen such vicious-looking individuals. Hard cases, each and every one. The very hardest. Some men bore their natures like a stamp, and these bore the stamp of killers.

Aces was worried that Creech had sicced the men on them, but none of the seven were looking for sign.

Tyree was tempted to shoot them. He'd come to have a powerful dislike for outlaws. It seemed to him that if all the lawbreakers in the world were rounded up and hanged, the world would be a better place. A place where a homesteader and his wife wouldn't be murdered by those they'd invited to supper. A place where a baby wouldn't be scarred for life. He put his hands on his Colts.

"Don't you dare, pard," Aces whispered.

They waited awhile after the seven were out of sight, just in case.

Fred didn't breathe easy again until they had descended to the valley floor. They went to where the camp had been, the charred embers of the fire still giving off a little smoke.

Fred was past it and almost to the stream when his horse nickered and shied. He had strayed a little to the left of the others, near to some brush. Glancing over, he felt his skin crawl. "Tarnation!" he exclaimed.

Aces and Tyree reined around.

A body lay sprawled on its back. Long black hair and a beaded buckskin dress showed it was female. Little else was recognizable. Someone had taken a hatchet or a tomahawk to her, chopping and mutilating.

"That poor woman," Fred said.

"Who do you reckon she was?" Tyree asked.

"I can't tell which tribe," Aces said. "Those men must have stole her and used her until they tired of her or else she made one of them mad, and there she is."

"Should we bury the body?" Fred said.

"Hell no," Tyree replied. They had lost enough time as it was. To his relief, Aces agreed.

"Whoever she was, we'll let the coyotes have her. We can't afford to lose Creech. Let's push on."

They thought it had been rough going so far, but it became worse. Creech appeared to be heading for a clus-

ter of peaks that thrust at the sky like granite spear tips.
They were so far in the range that the peaks didn't have
names. Not white names anyhow. In the winter they
would be capped with snow, but now they were barren
and gray.

"I should get out of my office more often," Fred said
in awe. Not that he would. If this trip had taught him
anything, it was that he had no business traipsing over
the countryside after a couple of killers. He was a town
body, through and through. Give him his comforts, and
his whiskey, and he would live out his days perfectly content. But he was also a man of his word. He'd said he
would help Tyree and Aces, and he would.

Aces was captivated by the peaks, but not so fascinated that he'd give up the life of a cowboy to become a
mountain man. To each his own, he'd always said, and for
him, the prairie and a herd of cattle were as good as life
got. Still, the mountains were beautiful, and he commented as much.

Tyree didn't see what the fuss was about. Rock was
rock and trees were trees. When Fred mentioned that
he'd heard of a famous artist from Europe or someplace
who once came to the Tetons to paint them, Tyree shook
his head. One man's beauty was another man's ordinary,
he reckoned.

Their climb brought them to a cleft wide enough for a
Conestoga. On either hand reared stone ramparts, walls
so high they had to crane their necks to see the tops.

"A pass, by heaven," Fred said.

Aces regarded the lengthening shadows. "It's almost
sundown. We'll make camp in those pines yonder and go
through the pass in the mornin'."

"Why not now?" Tyree said. His impatience was
worse than ever. They were *so* close. He could feel it.

"Because dark will fall soon and we don't know what's
waitin' for us on the other side," Aces answered.

Once the sun went down, the air turned chill. A wind
from out of the north made it colder still.

The night was strangely quiet. Huddled close to their fire, they were quiet themselves until Fred cleared his throat.

"Tomorrow could see the end of our journey."

"Could indeed," Aces allowed.

"Anything happens to me," Fred said, "I want you two to do me a favor. Send my badge to Sweetwater, to Mayor Crittendon, along with a note that he can go to hell and burn for all eternity."

Tyree laughed.

"We never know what a new day will bring," Aces said, and indicated the peaks and the vast wilderness below. "I never reckoned on ever being in the Tetons."

"Me either," Fred said.

"Old hens, the both of you," Tyree said. "Marshal Hitch, I expect it. But, Aces, you surprise me."

"All we're sayin' is that we never know what life will do to us," Aces said. "You should know that better than anybody."

"You're welcome to go back, the both of you," Tyree said. "If you don't want to be here, you should have said so."

"Damn it, Tyree," Aces said. "That's not what we're sayin' at all."

"Through thick and thin," Fred said, "we'll be at your side."

Tyree had draped his blanket over his shoulders to ward off the cold and now he pulled it tighter and bent toward the fire. "Don't think I'm not grateful," he said. "I am. I never had friends like you, and it would pain me if you wound up like that Injun gal."

"It would pain me too," Fred said.

Tyree looked up and for a moment thought he was seeing things. A figure in buckskins stood just within the circle of firelight, behind Aces, pointing a rifle at them. "Creech!" Tyree bawled, and went to unwrap his blanket.

"Don't, you!" the outlaw declared. "Give me any excuse, any of you, and I'll blow your head clean off."

Fred was too shocked to do anything.

Aces twisted around, and froze.

Creech's mouth split in a sinister smirk. "Have to ad-mit, I was mighty surprised when my horse picked up a stone and I was pryin' it out with my knife and looked back and spotted you. Careless of me not to have caught on sooner."

Tyree was tempted to try him. If he could slip his hands under his blanket unnoticed . . .

"Go ahead, boy," Creech said. "Die if you want to."

"Tyree," Fred said.

"He's fixin' to kill us anyway," Tyree said. And he'd be damned if he'd sit there and let himself be shot.

"That's where you're wrong, boy," Creech said. "You three don't know it, but you can spare me from havin' my throat slit." He laughed, then added, "And have your own slit instead."

Chapter 34

Aces surprised himself sometimes. There stood an outlaw who had no qualms about blowing him to Hades, and he felt no fear whatsoever. It was the same as all the other times he'd had guns pointed at him, or arrows were sent whizzing his way. He never felt afraid. Once a puncher he knew told him that wasn't natural. People should be scared when their life was in danger. If they weren't, something peculiar was going on inside their head.

Aces didn't see it that way. He'd always prided himself on staying calm in a crisis. Even back when he was a boy, he practiced at it, to where now it came naturally. Most folks would cringe in fright at having that Sharps pointed at them. Not him. His first thought was *stay calm*.

Ace had a sister to thank, in part, for his calmness. She had been prone to hysterics, they were called. Fits of fear that paralyzed her or set her to trembling uncontrollably and sobbing in panic. Her grandmother was that way, their mother said, and his sister had inherited her fragile disposition.

His father had shocked Aces by informing him that some men were prone to hysterics too. That they would weep like babies or curl into a ball, and there was nothing they could do.

Aces had worried that if hysterics were in the family's blood and his grandmother and sister had them, then he might come down with them too. So from an early age he'd made it his life's purpose to always stay calm no matter what. Some might say that was silly. Some might say it was childish. He liked to think of it as keeping his head when all those around him lost theirs.

Aces kept his head now. He stayed still as Creech came closer, his gaze locked on the Sharps. He was the only one who noticed something. For the moment, he kept it to himself.

"What was that about slit throats?" Tyree asked. He was stalling, hoping the outlaw would make a mistake and he could resort to his Colts.

"Dunn and Lute, those gents the law dog mentioned," Creech said. "They won't be happy about your cowpoke friend there shootin' Sterns. They might take it into their heads that I'm partly to blame. That I should have done something. That if I'd been quicker, I'd have shot your friend before he shot mine."

"They'd slit your throat over that?" Fred said, struggling to hide the tremor in his voice.

"Those two are the most snake-mean two-legged critters I ever met," Creech said. "Give them an excuse, any little excuse at all, and they will buck you out in gore. Thing is, you can't ever tell what will set them off."

"Yet you ride with them?" Fred said.

"They rule Robbers Roost, the only place in all the West where a man like me can go and not have to worry about a tin star takin' him into custody. The only law in the Roost are Dunn and Lute."

"I have never savvied the outlaw mind," Fred said.

"Savvy this," Creech said. "I aim to tie you three and take you with me. When Dunn and Lute hear about the cowpoke shootin' Sterns, they'll vent their spleens on him and not on me."

"Clever," Fred said.

"*I* think so." Creech wagged his Sharps. "On your feet one at a time and shuck your hardware."

"I'll go first," Aces said.

Marshal Hitch and Tyree glanced at him in surprise. "Do it," Creech barked.

Aces slowly stood, his hands out from his sides. Just as slowly, he moved his right hand to the buckle to his gun belt, and stopped.

"What are you waitin' for?" Creech said. "Unhitch the damn belt and let it drop and step back."

"I reckon I won't," Aces said.

Creech raised the Sharps halfway to his shoulder. "If you think this is a bluff, you're addlepated. I've killed before. Plenty of times. One more won't matter."

"I agree there," Aces said. "But I still won't."

Tyree started to rise but caught himself. "What are you doing, pard?"

"Shut up, boy," Creech commanded. He appeared puzzled more than mad, and was looking Aces up and down. "You'd rather be shot than have your throat slit? Is that why you're balkin'?"

"Most outlaws are amateurs," Aces said. "I heard that somewhere and it's true. If outlaws were smart they wouldn't be outlaws."

"Are you lecturin' me?" Creech said in amazement.

"Take your friend Sterns. If he'd been smart, he wouldn't have been on the prod. He would have ridden off with you and still be alive."

"Are you drunk?" Creech sniffed a few times. "I don't smell any alcohol."

"No, I'm smart," Aces said.

"Is that right?" Creech replied, and laughed.

"Remember the James-Younger Gang?" Aces said. "They rode all the way from Missouri to Minnesota to rob the Northfield bank and were practically wiped out. That wasn't smart."

"What the hell?" Creech said.

"Or how about the Renos? They went and hid in Canada but made such a nuisance of themselves they were brought back and hanged by vigilantes. That wasn't smart."

"You better stop," Creech said.

"I have one more," Aces said. "All of them were stupid, but not as stupid as you. You saw me shoot your pard, yet here you are."

"Remindin' me of that is just plain dumb. It only makes me mad."

"You're missin' the point," Aces said.

"What the hell is it?" Creech demanded angrily.

"You march in here and point your cannon at us yet you don't have the brains to cock it."

Creech glanced at the Sharp's hammer and then at Ace's right hand, inches from his holster. "Son of a bitch."

"See what I mean?" Aces said.

"I reckon I'm stupid at that." Creech grinned, and flicked his thumb.

Aces drew in a blur. He fired just as the Sharps went off with a thunderous blast, the slug kicking up dust at his feet. He fired again, and a third time, putting all three within a hair of one another over where the heart would be.

Creech tottered. A look of incredulity came over him. He tried to speak, tried to raise the Sharps even though it was a single-shot. He sputtered, spitting blood and red spittle. His knees buckled, his eyes rolled up into his head, and he pitched to the ground with a thud.

"Whew." Fred let out a long breath.

"Slick as anything," Tyree said, and laughed.

"We were lucky," Aces said. If Creech had cocked the Sharps before showing himself, he might be the one lying in the dust. He began to reload.

Luck, Tyree thought. There it was again. "I don't even carry around a four-leaf clover," he said out loud.

"How's that?" Fred asked. He was rattled. He couldn't get over how casual and quick the bloodshed had become. It didn't bode well for when they reached Robbers Roost.

"If this were a card game I'd win every pot," Tyree boasted.

"Don't get cocky," Fred advised. The boy wasn't taking things seriously enough to suit him.

"So far my plan is workin' out," Aces said as he slid a cartridge into the cylinder. "All that's left is bracin' Dunn and Lute in their lair."

"Is that all?" Fred said.

Tyree helped Aces drag the body away in case the scent of blood drew a grizzly or wolves. He went through Creech's pocket and found a poke with over forty dollars. He gave a third to Aces and offered a share to Fred Hitch, but the lawman refused.

"I couldn't take tainted money."

"You're loco," Tyree said bluntly. "How is it tainted? By Aces shootin' him? He was an outlaw and had it comin'."

"The money is probably stolen," Fred said.

"So?" Tyree said. It wasn't as if they could give it back to its rightful owners. "I hope I never become a stickler for always doing right like you are."

"My pa used to say that a man who always does right doesn't ever need to fret about being in the wrong."

Tyree snickered. "So that's where you get it from."

"You shouldn't insult him," Aces said.

"By sayin' he's silly?" Tyree chuckled, and said to Fred, "I like you, Marshal. I truly do. You've stood by me where I doubt few would. So don't take it wrong of me if I laugh a little at some of the things you do."

"I was young once," Fred said.

"What happened to you?"

"Isn't it obvious? I grew old."

They took turns keeping watch. Tyree offered to go first and sat drinking coffee to keep him awake. He was excited that they might finally reach Robbers Roost the next day. His quest for revenge could soon be over.

Marshal Hitch was slow to wake to take his turn. He listened to a pack of wolves serenade the night and moodily mused on how best to stay alive when the final fight came. He had no illusions about being a match for

Dunn and Lute. His wits would serve him better than his pistol, but his wits weren't cooperating.

When it came time for Fred to wake Aces, he didn't. Fred let him sleep another hour or so. Of all of them, Aces needed to be sharp as a honed bowie when they rode into the Roost. Aces could use the extra rest.

His own eyes were drooping when Fred shook his friend's shoulder. "Nothin' much doing," he reported.

Aces stood and walked in a circle a few times to get his blood to flow. The coffeepot held enough for a last cup, and he nursed it as the wind gradually died and the sky to the east went from black to gray.

Aces always liked sunrise. It was his favorite time of the day. The rising sun never failed to fill him with a mix of pleasure and vigor that the whole world was new again.

Most days were mysteries of opportunity, but not this one. Today there was Robbers Roost. Today there were Dunn and Lute. Today might be the day he drew his last breath.

"Up and at 'em," Aces hollered to wake the others. "We have an outlaw town to tree."

No one was hungry. No one cared for coffee.

They spent a fruitless half hour searching for Creech's animals and were about to give up and head for the pass when a whinny drew them to a dry wash, and there they were.

"We should strip the saddles, smack them on the rump, and let them run free," Fred suggested.

"No." Aces had been struck by a brainstorm. "I have plans for them."

"You have a plan for everything," Fred said.

Tyree hardly said a word. The biggest day of his life, a day he had yearned for since he could remember, was at long last about to take place. He thought only of Dunn and Lute, and his ma and pa.

Fred came last, leading the extra animals. He wasn't in any hurry. The blood they were about to spill, or have spilled, was blood he could do without. He wondered how he'd let himself be roped into this, and then remembered. He'd roped himself.

Aces concentrated on staying calm. That he had to showed he wasn't. The calmness should come without being forced. The truth was, though, he was a mite on edge. Tangling with Dunn and Lute was perilous enough. If ten to twenty other outlaws were with them, it'd be a miracle to make it out alive.

Despite all the revolver fights he'd been in, Aces had never given much thought to dying. He did now. There was such a thing as biting off more than you could chew. Ten to twenty outlaws was a big bite.

Just then a raven screeched, and they looked up to see one of the big black birds gliding overhead.

"That's a bad omen," Fred said. "My grandmother used to say that crows and ravens are what she called harbingers of death."

"Spare me your superstitions," Tyree said.

"You're the one who believes in luck," Fred said. "Me, I believe in stayin' alive. You can't enjoy life if you're dead."

"Wise words," Tyree said, and chuckled.

Aces expected to emerge from the far end of the pass high on the divide, with slopes below, stretching on forever. He was wrong.

Before them was a grassy tableland dotted by islands of aspens and belts of cottonwoods. In the distance were buildings. Most were made of logs.

"I'll be switched," Tyree exclaimed, drawing rein. "We're here."

"Another fifteen minutes yet," Aces said, his estimate of how long it would take to cover that distance.

Fred unpinned his badge and stuck it in a pocket. There was no sense in advertising he was a lawman. "What was that quote I gave from the Bible? Into the valley of the shadow we go."

"That's not no valley," Tyree said.

Aces turned in his saddle. "I may not have the chance to say this later, so here goes." He smiled at Tyree and Fred. "It's been an honor to ride with you. That day you found me in . . ." He stopped, his mouth open, looking past them.

Tyree and Fred twisted around.

A man had come from behind a giant boulder. His hat had a hole in it and was frayed around the brim, and he had a beard that fell to his waist. The beard was gray, but there was nothing old about how he moved or the menace in his eyes. He had trained a Winchester on them. "What do we have here?"

"Howdy," Fred said, smiling to give the impression they were friendly. "You must be posted as a sentry to keep an eye on the pass."

"That I am, mister," the outlaw said, sounding amused that Fred had said something so obvious. "And to shoot those who have no business being here."

Chapter 35

Tyree was mad at being thwarted so close to his goal. He was tempted to try for his Colts but didn't. The sentry had already cocked the Winchester and, that close, wouldn't miss.

Aces wanted to kick himself. He should have expected the outlaws to have a guard or two. His hands happened to be on his saddle horn, and fast as he was, he couldn't possibly draw and shoot before the man put a round in him. Simmering, he had to submit to being told that they were to raise their arms and slide from their mounts using only their legs.

Fred Hitch was awkward at it. He got his arms up and his right leg over the saddle horn, but when he went to slide, he lost his balance and fell to his hands and knees. "Sorry," he blurted as the muzzle of the man's Winchester was trained on him.

"I thought you were tryin' something," the sentry said.

"Not me," Fred said. "I'm just clumsy."

"I want all of you to face your animals and put your hands on your saddles. I'm going to disarm you. Any of you so much as twitch, you're dead."

Fred believed him. Standing, he faced his bay and placed his hands on his saddle.

He winced when the Winchester was jammed into his spine. He felt his six-shooter being snatched from its holster and heard the thud of it being tossed away. Then a hand patted him down searching for more weapons.

"Stay right where you are."

"Yes, sir," Fred said.

Tyree had contrived to face his horse so that one hand was on his saddle and the other on the end of his bedroll. He tensed as boots crunched behind him, and frowned when the Winchester's muzzle gouged his back. "Go easy there, mister."

"Shut the hell up, boy."

Tyree's Colts were jerked and thrown.

"You totin' any other sidearms?"

"No." Tyree's derringers were in his saddlebags. So was his bowie. His saber too was no longer on him. He'd taken his pard's advice about not going around like a walking arsenal.

The man laughed. "Now, why don't I believe you?"

Tyree was patted down from his neck to his ankles. He turned his head enough to see the sentry step back.

"I reckon you were tellin' the truth, boy." The man turned to go to Aces and finish disarming them.

Tyree slid his hand into the bedroll. The hilt of the saber was right where it should be. Gripping the hilt, he struck like lightning, yanking the saber out and thrusting it at the sentry's neck. The man sensed the attack and spun just as the saber sheared into his neck and out the other side. With an inarticulate cry, the outlaw attempted to point the Winchester, but Tyree swatted the barrel aside. Suddenly one of the man's hands was on his throat, the fingers digging deep. Tyree twisted the saber and the man gurgled but didn't go down.

Aces leaped to help. Drawing his Colt, he clubbed the sentry even as he grabbed the Winchester and wrenched. Fortunately the rifle didn't go off. He tore it from the man's grasp and went to club him again, but there was no need.

The sentry was folding. Blood streaming from his neck, he collapsed onto his side. Already his shirt was soaked.

He tried to say something, but all that came out was more blood.

Tyree had held on to his saber. Now, placing a foot on the sentry's chest, he sliced outward, severing half the man's throat in the process. Stepping back, he grinned. "Pretty slick if I say so myself."

"You're being cocky again," Fred said, but he was impressed. The boy had acted quickly and decisively.

"Get your guns," Aces said. He was gazing toward Robbers Roost. There was no sign of anyone coming their way. As far off as it was, he doubted they'd been seen. But he didn't like being out in the open.

They hoisted the body over one of the extra horses, which had the good sense not to shy, and took off toward some cottonwoods.

Only when they were under cover did Aces breathe a little easier. He tied the palomino and moved to where he could see the Roost. They were within rifle range, but there was no one to shoot. The place looked deserted.

"No one is there," Tyree said, shocked. After they'd come all this way, it simply couldn't be.

"What do you know?" Fred said. Secretly he was pleased. It could be that all the outlaws were off robbing a stage or a train. Maybe they could still get out of there alive.

"No, wait," Aces said.

A couple of men came out of a log building with batwings. They each had bottles and were grinning and talking. Almost at the same time, a slovenly-looking woman opened a cabin door, stepped out, shook a blanket, and went back in.

"They're there all right," Aces said. "At least some of them."

"Thank goodness," Tyree said.

Fred sighed and said, "I should have known."

"Where are their horses?" Tyree wondered.

"There," Aces said, pointing. "At the side of the saloon. You can just make out their tails."

"How do we do this?" Fred was concerned to find out. "We can't just ride on in. They don't cotton to strangers."

"My plan was to give the extra horses swats on their rumps and send them in," Aces revealed. "The outlaws would come out to investigate, givin' us some idea of how many are there. But I've changed my mind."

Fred was glad. Drawing the outlaws out was the last thing they should do. It would put them on their guard.

"What else, then?" Tyree asked.

Aces cocked his head at the sky. "The day is too young yet to wait for dark. So we crawl on over through the grass."

Fred thought of his poor knees. "That's a long crawl. It must be pretty near two hundred yards."

"More like a hundred."

"Well, that makes a difference," Fred said. But he got his rifle when the others did, and before he knew it, he was slithering through the grass and scraping his belly. He hated it, but he trusted that Aces knew what he was doing.

Tyree was near giddy. At long last, he'd have Dunn and Lute in his sights. He would show them no mercy but shoot them down like the dogs they were.

Aces hoped he wasn't making a mistake. Should anyone be looking out a window, they might be spotted and hell would break loose.

Fred kept his head as low to the ground as he could. The grass wasn't all that high and he was afraid the top of his hat showed. He almost took it off, but he refused to go around bareheaded.

Feminine laughter wafted from the saloon, followed by a man's gruff voice.

By Aces's reckoning they weren't more than thirty yards out when another cabin door opened and out strode a black man. His hat and his vest were black, and he walked with a swagger. He wore a brace of pistols and a big knife as well.

"Lute!" Tyree exclaimed, tingling all over. It had to be. There weren't that many black men in those parts.

"Hush, consarn you," Aces said.

Fred was impressed by how the outlaw carried himself. Lute had a deadly air about him, if such a thing were possible.

The black man was almost to the saloon when he abruptly stopped. He stared toward the pass for an unusually long time, then stepped to the batwings and shoved on in.

"What was that about?" Fred whispered.

"He was lookin' to see if anyone was comin'," Tyree guessed.

Aces prayed the boy was right. "Keep movin'." He quickly crawled to the side of the saloon. Thankfully there was no window. Rising into a crouch, he brushed grass from his Winchester.

Tyree was still tingling. On the other side of that wall were the two men he was after. It took all his self-control not to go barging in.

Fred reached the wall last. His elbows and knees were scuffed and his belly was sore. "I'm glad I wasn't born a snake," he muttered.

"We need to see in," Aces said. "We go in blind, we're askin' for trouble."

Just being there, Fred reflected, was asking for trouble, but he didn't say anything.

"Remember," Tyree said. "Dunn and Lute are mine."

"We can't make any promises, pard," Aces said. "Once the lead starts flyin', it will be hard to pick and choose."

Tyree didn't like the sound of that. He had to be the one to deal with Dunn and Lute. He just had to.

Aces led them around to the rear. Again, there was no window. There wasn't even a door. "Can it be?"

"What?" Fred said.

"There's only the one way in and out."

"So?"

"Don't you see? They've made it easy for us. We have them trapped." Aces crooked a finger. "Come on."

Seven horses were tied to the hitch rail.

"Only seven to three," Tyree said, encouraged. Things were looking better and better.

"Don't take that for granted," Fred warned. "There could be more."

Aces moved to the front but didn't show himself. No one was out and about. Smoke rose from a cabin chimney, the only sign of life.

"I'll go first," Tyree said. He was tired of waiting. The time had come to end his hunt.

"Not so fast," Aces said. "We do this smart, like we've done everything else." He contemplated, then said, "Marshal, I'd like for you to stay here and keep an eye on the cabins and shacks. Anyone pops out, you discourage them."

"Without being killed, of course," Fred said.

"Tyree, as much as you want this to all be on you, we do this as pards. We go in together and start shootin' together and we don't let a damn one of those coyotes make it out alive."

Tyree nodded. His mouth had gone dry and his pulse had quickened.

"Don't wait for them to start it," Aces said. "We drop as many as we can before they collect their wits."

"Enough talk," Tyree said. "Let's do it, damn it."

Aces nodded.

Shoulder to shoulder they walked to the batwings. Without slowing, without any hesitation, they pushed on in.

There were nine men, not just seven, and two women.

Aces fired first. He shot a bucktoothed man who had a glass to his mouth, worked his rifle's lever, and shot a hairy man in the act of pouring from a bottle. He shot a third who was fondling a dove.

Tyree was slower to act. As he came in he spotted a pair of men at a corner table. One was Lute. The other, big and broad with blond hair and the hardest face he'd ever seen, must be Dunn. The two weren't amateurs. They heaved out of their chairs and stabbed for their six-shooters, and Tyree started toward them. He should have stayed close to Aces, but something snapped inside him. His mind stopped working and his body grew hot, and he advanced as if in a dream. He aimed the Winchester and fired at Dunn, shifted, and fired at Lute. He got off his shots before they could get off any, but then they were shooting back. Pain seared his shoulder and his arm. He jacked the lever, fired, jacked the lever, fired. Dimly did he hear the boom of other guns. All he saw were Dunn and Lute. They seemed to fill his vision, to be his whole world. He shot at Dunn and he shot at Lute and his left leg exploded with pain, but he kept advancing and shooting. Everything was a haze except the two men he hated. The men who had murdered his ma and his pa. He wanted to scream at them, to shriek that he was paying them back for his folks, but he shot instead. He shot and he shot, and then his Winchester went empty or jammed because it wouldn't shoot and he dropped it and grabbed his Colts.

Aces saw the boy move toward the table, but there was nothing he could do to help. His own hands were full. An outlaw in a bear-hide coat produced a revolver from a pocket and Aces shot him in the forehead. Two men rolling dice pushed to their feet, scrambling to draw, and Aces shot one in the chest and the other in the temple. The bartender brought a scattergun from under the bar but had to thumb back the hammers to shoot. Aces drilled him in the face.

Outside, Fred saw the slovenly woman step from her cabin. He pointed his Winchester and she went back in again. "That was easy," he said.

Tyree had tears in his eyes. He didn't know where they came from, but they were there and his vision was blurring. Dunn and Lute were still on their feet, but Lute had a hand on the table to keep from falling. Tyree fired at him and then at Dunn. He was struck an invisible blow in the ribs that rocked him, but he continued to walk and shoot and now he was so close to the table that he could have reached out and touched it. Lute was sprawled over the top and Dunn had sagged against the wall and was sluggishly raising his six-shooter.

"For my ma and pa," Tyree said, blinking the tears away. He shot Dunn in the chest, methodically, one shot after the other, shot and shot until both his Colts clicked empty. A hand squeezed his arm.

"They're dead," Aces said. He had rushed over to help, but it wasn't needed. The killers had been shot to pieces. So had his pard.

Tyree looked down at himself. He had taken lead in the shoulder and the arm and been hit in the ribs and his legs. "I'm still breathin'," he marveled.

The batwings creaked and Fred barreled in. He swung his Winchester from side to side and declared, "God in heaven."

"We need to take a look at you," Aces told Tyree, "and see about patchin' you up."

"Sure," Tyree said, nodding absently. "Whatever you say, pard."

Fred ran up to them. "Is that it?" he said. "It's over already?"

Aces stared at him.

"What?" Fred said.

"I'm mighty tired," Tyree announced. He felt as if he were slipping into a deep, dark hole.

"Don't die on us, son," Fred said.

"I'll try not to," Tyree said, and the dark hole claimed him.

Chapter 36

Years after

Frederick Hitch returned to Sweetwater and spent the next ten years as their marshal. He didn't spend nearly as much time in his office as he used to, and he hardly ever was seen with his flask. He was over sixty when he turned in his badge. The town honored his long service with a watch and a plaque. He'd bought a small house and he spent his declining years enjoying a few beers at the saloon now and then or rocking on his porch and gazing to the west in the direction of the Tetons.

Aces Connor hired on with the Bar T. Within two years he was foreman. He married a pretty gal and they had two sons. No one remembered his gun hand days, and he liked it that way. He taught his sons to shoot but impressed on them that they must never, ever take another's life unless they had no choice. Neither son followed in his boot steps. The older became a lawyer. The other took to retailing and went to Chicago to work for Sears, Roebuck and Company in their mail order business.

Tyree Larn became a U.S. federal marshal and served with distinction. He was conscientious in his pursuit of outlaws and became known for always taking them alive. Not once in his long career did he shoot a lawbreaker.

Tyree met a woman from Tennessee and married when he was twenty-five. His wife was fiercely proud of him and stayed devoted to him all their days. They had three daughters.

His wife only asked him once about his scars. It was their wedding night. She had never seen him without his shirt on, and certainly not without his pants. The worst scar was on his side, six inches long or better.

Tyree told her he got it in a shoot-out, and that was all he was going to say. He never revealed how his parents died. He only said they'd died when he was a boy, and he didn't remember much about them.

In his fiftieth year Tyree took her to the Tetons, to a tableland on the west side of a high pass. She loved the mountains, thought they were beautiful, and thanked him for bringing her.

The saloon and cabins had long since fallen into disrepair from neglect, and the shacks were in ruins.

Tyree stood in the doorway of the saloon, his hands clasped behind his back. One of the batwings was missing; the other hung by a single hinge. Brushing at a cobweb, he went in.

"What was a saloon doing way out here?" his wife wondered.

The tables had been overturned, the chairs busted. The mirror, what was left of it, was lined with cracks.

His wife swatted at the dust and coughed. "I can't say I like it in here. It's too dim and dingy." She tugged on his sleeve. "Let's go, husband mine." That was her pet expression for him.

"In a minute." Tyree went to a corner table. Three of the legs had snapped off and it lay on its side.

"What's going on? What is this place to you?"

"I was here once."

"You and your secrets," she said. "How come you never told me?"

"It was another time," Tyree said. "Another life."

"Silly man," his wife said lightheartedly. "We each live one life, not two or three."

Tyree touched the table and looked at the dust on his fingertips. "That's where you're mistaken, my dear. Some of us live more than one life. We're one person when we're young and another person when we're older."

"Oh, really? And who were you when you were younger, if I might ask?"

"I was different. You wouldn't have liked me."

"Says you." His wife playfully caressed his chin. "I bet you were as adorable as anything."

Tyree stared at a bullet hole in the table and another in the wall. "I don't know as I'd go that far." He took her hand and they walked back out into the sunlight.

Swollen by an unseasonable snowmelt across the Great Plains that early December of 1872, the Big Muddy threw itself against an arrow-shaped sandbar three miles downstream of Lexington, Missouri. The river was turned aside, white water foaming in angry impotence around the northern bank of the promontory. Frustrated, the Missouri channeled a swift torrent of brown water and ice around the bar and hurled it venomously into the path of the 212-foot stern-wheeler *Rajah*.

Rajah was firing hard, preparing to skirt the sandbar. Capt. Amos Buell, commanding, was anxious to reach the city and unload his two hundred tons of freight and twenty-six passengers.

Rajah's boilers were glowing cherry red, her exhausts hammering, but Buell called for more power to the boat's two engines.

The river was coming at him fast and furious, challenging the stern-wheeler to reach its goal, no sure thing for a craft that drew just twenty inches and had 80 percent of her ramshackle bulk above the waterline.

The paddle wheel had been rotating at twenty times a minute. Now the cast-iron-and-wood monster, twenty-five feet wide and eighteen feet in diameter, churned faster, increasing its revolutions to twenty-three a minute. Startled fountains of foam were thrown up as high as the boiler deck as the wheel's paddles dipped into the river 168 times every sixty seconds.

Captain Buell recklessly hurled his boat against the flood. Huge chunks of ice slammed into *Rajah*'s bow and banged against her iron sides, to be slowly washed astern. Her exhausts, located on the foam-lashed boiler deck, were pounding now, rattling the stabilizing hog chain that ran from the stern to the wheelhouse.

Time and time again *Rajah* made a few feet of headway, only to be driven back by the river, the powerful torrent twisting the boat's bow violently toward shore.

Buell called for more power, but the *Rajah* had given all she had. There was nothing left to give.

The boilers would not take a pound more pressure than they were carrying, and the engineer warned that the boat was in danger of being blown apart.

Buell decided against another attempt to round the sandbar where the river narrowed and thus concentrated its mighty strength. He'd smash right through the bar, trusting *Rajah*'s weight and momentum to carry her through.

The captain reversed engines and *Rajah* backed up, going with the current, shuddering as huge slabs of ice thudded into her, threatening to buckle her thin plates.

Standing on the boat's hurricane deck, Buck Fletcher watched all this with interest but little joy. He was familiar with the stately floating palaces that plied the Mississippi, but this boat was smaller and slower. However, he knew enough of river navigation to piece together Amos Buell's strategy and the thoughts running through the man's head.

As *Rajah* continued to reverse, Fletcher guessed that the captain was going to let her pick up speed and meet the sandbar head-on.

He did not give much for their chances, especially if the boilers burst and blew them all to smithereens.

But then, a man shackled hand and foot, guarded by a nine-man infantry detail, had little to lose, including his life. He faced twenty years' hard labor in the hell of the Wyoming Territorial Prison, and that was just another kind of death, slower certainly, but just as certain.

"What's he going to do, Major?"

Fletcher turned as 2d Lt. Elisha Simpson stepped closer to him, his round, freckled face anxious, revealing the infantry soldier's instinctive distrust of anything that floated on water. The boy was a West Pointer and looked to be about eighteen years old.

Fletcher's bleak smile lit up his long, lean, and hard face, still brown from the sun and untouched as yet by the gray pallor of prison, his wide, mobile mouth revealing teeth that were very white under a sweeping dragoon mustache.

"I guess the captain is going to climb right over that sandbar ahead," Fletcher said. "He knows he can't buck this current and that's the only way he can make Lexington this side of spring."

Fletcher shook his head. "And, Lieutenant, don't call me Major. The War Between the States is long over."

"Yes, Major," Simpson said, only half listening as he studied the ice-studded river beyond the bow of the boat. The boy stood in silence for a few moments, his face screwed up in thought; then he turned his head and called out over his shoulder, "Corporal Burke!"

The corporal, a grizzled veteran in his early fifties, stepped smartly beside the young officer and saluted. "Yes, sorr."

"Strike those chains from the major," he said. "If we have to swim for it, I don't want him weighed down by thirty pounds of iron."

Burke's face was a study in confusion. "Sorr," he said, his Irish accent strong, "does the lieutenant think that's wise?"

Such was the reputation of Buck Fletcher as a skilled and ruthless gunfighter and convicted murderer that the corporal was completely taken aback, an understandable reaction not unmixed with a certain amount of fear.

"Yes, Corporal," Simpson said, "the lieutenant is sure."

The officer studied Fletcher closely, taking in the amused blue eyes in the hard hatchet blade of a face. "Major, will you give me your word as an officer and a gentlemen you won't try to escape if we have to swim?"

Fletcher smiled again. "Lieutenant, if this tub blows up, we'll all be dead and it won't matter a damn whether you have my word or not. If we have to swim, we'd last about two minutes in that freezing water, so it won't matter a damn that way either." As he saw doubt cloud the boy's eyes, Fletcher's smile widened and he nodded. "Sure, Lieutenant, you have my word."

That was all it took. The young officer didn't question Fletcher any further. This man had once been a major of horse artillery in the army of the United States and he had given his word. That he might be lying did not, for even a single moment, enter into Simpson's thinking.

"Corporal Burke," the lieutenant said, "strike those chains."

Grumbling under his breath, Burke unlocked the padlock that held the chains together, releasing Fletcher's leg irons and then the manacles around his wrists.

The soldier gathered up the chains and laid them, clanking, on the deck. Burke gave Fletcher a sidelong glance, his black eyes ugly. "Sorr, permission to fix bayonets."

The young officer hesitated for a few moments, then nodded, saying nothing, his cheeks reddening a little as he refused to look Fletcher in the eye. Burke gave the order and the detail fixed twenty-inch-long spiked bayonets to their newly issued Springfield rifles. The young soldiers stood alert and wary, mindful that they were guarding a dangerous prisoner, a gunfighter who was said to have killed a dozen men in shooting scrapes from Texas to Kansas and beyond. Such men were deadly, certain, and almighty sudden, and there was no taking even the slightest chance with them, especially now that Fletcher's chains had been removed.

Despite the cold, as he shivered in his prison-issue canvas pants and shirt, Fletcher was amused. He understood how the soldiers felt. Most of them were raw recruits, and he knew he'd feel the same way if he were in their shoes.

"She's slowing," Simpson said, looking back at the paddle wheel.

"Now the captain will order full speed ahead and challenge that sandbar," Fletcher said. He rubbed his wrists where the manacles had chafed them raw, a small motion nevertheless noticed by Simpson, who threw Fletcher an apologetic glance.

"Better brace yourself, Major," the young officer said. "When we hit, this boat could come to a mighty quick stop."

Fletcher grasped the rail in front of him and spread his feet wider.

Rajah's wheel was turning faster now, biting into the muddy water, propelling her forward. Thick black smoke and showers of sparks poured from her twin stacks, and her exhausts were thumping loud again.

Chunks of ice, some of them as big as river barges, slammed into *Rajah*'s bow and sides, and the little boat shuddered and recoiled under the impact. Up in the wheelhouse Buell blasted the whistle, defying the river to do its worst. The whistle's screams echoed along miles of the winding river valley, penetrating even the dank, crowded back alleys of Lexington. The ship's bell was pealing, adding its incessant clamor to that of the whistle.

It was said, Simpson yelled to Fletcher over the din, that Buell had melted five hundred silver dollars into the metal from which the bell was cast to improve its tone.

"Sounds like six hundred to me," Fletcher said, but the lieutenant didn't hear.

Rajah charged ahead, her paddles churning, shouldering aside ice as she rammed through coffee-colored water, the sandbar getting closer with every revolution of the wheel. . . .

*　　*　　*

"Life is just one big wheel," Fletcher recalled Warden Nathaniel K. Boswell saying to him just before he was taken under escort from the newly opened Wyoming Territorial Prison in Laramie two weeks before. "One day you're on top of the world; then the wheel turns and you're at the bottom again. That's where you are, Fletcher, at the bottom, and you can't get any lower."

The man had not gone into details about why Fletcher had served only a month of his twenty-year sentence before he was dragged from his cell and told he was being taken under army escort to Lexington, there to meet a man he didn't know.

"This man has a proposition for you, Fletcher," Boswell had said. "I'm told there could be a great deal of danger involved, but I think you'd be very wise to take it."

Boswell shrugged, scratched under his beard with the stem of his pipe, then waved an indifferent hand. Apparently bored, he added, "Take this man's proposition or stay here and rot with all the rest. The decision is yours, and I don't give a damn one way or the other."

It was a choice of a sort, but really no choice at all, and Fletcher had jumped at it.

"Who is this man?" he'd asked. "And why in Lexington?"

Again the warden shrugged. "I have no idea, but he has considerable power and influence. I know that." Boswell was a former United States deputy marshal and his eyes were cold and unforgiving. "If it was up to me, I'd pen you up forever, Fletcher, you and all your kind, paid killers and plunderers. But President Grant himself signed the order for your temporary release, and I can't ignore that kind of authority."

The warden nodded to the guards who flanked Fletcher. "Take him out of my sight until his army escort arrives." As Fletcher was shuffling from the man's office, his heavy leg irons clanking, Boswell had called out after him, "Do us all a favor, Fletcher. Get yourself killed."

*   *   *

"A man could get killed this way, Major," Lieutenant Simpson yelled to Fletcher above the roar of *Rajah*'s engines and her shrieking whistle, bringing him back to the present. "I've never had much love for boats."

Fletcher nodded and placed his mouth next to the young officer's ear. "Best you tell those boys of yours to find something to hold on to," he said. "When she hits the bar some of those men could end up going over the side."

Simpson half raised his arm in salute, then realized what he was doing and his face colored again. "Corporal Burke!" he yelled more loudly than necessary, covering up his mistake. "Get the men braced for a collision."

Thirty seconds later *Rajah* hit the sandbar hard. She rammed through half the bar's width and came to a jolting stop. Her wheel was still churning, throwing up high fountains of muddy water, black drops spattering Fletcher and the soldiers far forward on the hurricane deck.

Buell backed his boat off, readying *Rajah* for another try. It seemed that more ice was banging against her hull, driven by raging, ugly water, and now, adding to everyone's misery, sleet began to fall, driven by a rising wind from the north.

It had gotten progressively colder since the day began, and as the gray afternoon slowly shaded into night, the temperature plunged, surely ending any hope of residents along both banks of the Missouri that the recent snowmelt portended an extended Indian summer.

Rajah charged the sandbar again, backed off, charged a second time. Then a third, and a fourth.

Finally, her straining hull plates groaning, threatening any minute to tear away from their rivets, the boat rammed through the bar. *Rajah* brushed aside the white trunk of a dead dogwood tree that angled up from the sand, its branches spread wide like thin, surrendering arms, and, as she cleared the bar, fussily straightened her bow like an old dowager straightening her bonnet. Then, gathering around her what was left of her shabby, rickety dignity, she floated into calmer water.

Buell nosed his battered craft into a Lexington wharf, vented *Rajah*'s steam, and tied her up. As Buell ran out the gangplank for the passengers, mulatto dockworkers were already scrambling on board to unload her cargo, and the captain, somber, thin, and bearded, left the wheelhouse to oversee the operation.

Lieutenant Simpson turned to Fletcher, his eyes miserable. "Major, I must . . ." The young officer stumbled, trying to find the words, and Fletcher smiled.

"You have a duty to do, Lieutenant. Best you do it."

Relieved, Simpson nodded and turned to Corporal Burke. "The shackles, Corporal."

"There's no need for that."

Every head swiveled toward the tall man who had just stepped onto the hurricane deck. He wore a black overcoat with an astrakhan collar, his eyes shaded by the brim of his top hat. The man took a step toward Simpson. "We must be discreet, Lieutenant," he said. "I don't want this man brought to my home in chains."

"I have my orders, sir," the young officer said, his face stiff. "I was instructed to conduct Major . . . uh . . . this prisoner by train and stage to Missouri, join the steamship *Rajah* in Jefferson City, and when we disembarked in Lexington, remove him in chains to the home of Senator Falcon Stark."

"You've done well, Lieutenant," the man said. "I am Senator Stark, and I will take custody of the prisoner."

"Sir, I think I should provide an escort and remain with you until your business with the prisoner is concluded."

"I'll be quite safe, I assure you, Lieutenant," Stark said. His voice was as smooth as watered silk but it was edged by impatience and not a little anger.

This, Fletcher thought, *is a man grown well used to the*

arrogance of power, a man who cuts a wide path and expects lesser men to scramble out of his way.

A sleet flurry scattered wet drops between Stark and Fletcher and the others. Through this shifting gray curtain a man as tall as Stark but dressed in a wide-brimmed hat and sheepskin mackinaw, a red woolen scarf wrapped around his neck, stepped to the senator's side.

The man's cold eyes swept the green young soldiers, dismissed them as unimportant and irrelevant, then came to rest on Fletcher.

"Been a long time, Buck," he said, without friendliness.

Fletcher nodded. "Wes Slaughter. You're a long way from El Paso."

The gunman shrugged. "You know how it is; in our line of work we go where somebody's doing the hiring."

"I don't know how it is," Fletcher said, his eyes changing from blue to a hard gunmetal gray. "In my line of work I meet my enemies face-to-face. What's your line of work, Wes?"

The gunman was stung and he let it show. "Damn you, Fletcher. Someday I'm going to take great pleasure in killing you."

Fletcher nodded, his smile thin and humorless. "You told me that same thing in the Sideboard Saloon in Cheyenne not two months ago. But when we came right down to it and the talking was done, you wouldn't draw. I guess it will have to be in the back, a specialty of yours, I believe."

"Cheyenne wasn't the right time or the right place, is all, Fletcher," Slaughter said, refusing to be baited further. "If we ever meet again when the talking is done and it's the Colts' turn to speak, it will be face-to-face, all right. I've seen you draw, Fletcher, and on your best day you couldn't come close to shading me."

"The day I can't shade a back-shooting polecat like you, Wes, is the day I hang up my guns for good," Fletcher said, his eyes holding a challenge he knew the other man could not ignore.

Angry, Slaughter opened his mouth to speak again, but Stark waved an irritable hand. "Mr. Slaughter, if you wish to remain an associate of mine, don't bandy words with a convicted criminal."

He turned to Simpson, who seemed baffled by this exchange. "Lieutenant, surely you understand that I don't want to attract the unwanted attention you and your men would cause by leading this prisoner to my home in chains. I have a carriage waiting, and I assure you Fletcher will be quite secure with me and Mr. Slaughter."

"I have my orders, sir," Simpson said, but this time he sounded uncertain.

"I'm countermanding them, Lieutenant," Stark snapped. "Or do I have to go over your head to your commanding officer?"

Fletcher smiled. "His commanding officer is in Wyoming, Stark. I'd say that's a fair piece from here."

Stark turned on Fletcher, his face black with anger. "You will address me as senator or not at all." Then to Simpson: "Captain Buell sails at first light tomorrow morning for Jefferson City. Make sure you and your men are on board." His voice softened a little. "I will personally inform President Grant how well you performed your duty. Ah, what is your name, Lieutenant?"

Defeated by this man's air of command, backed up by the real power and influence he wielded, the officer let his shoulders slump. "Well," he said, "my orders were to deliver the prisoner to you, Senator. I guess I've done that. And my name is Simpson."

"You've carried out your duty, Lieutenant Simpson, and again let me say most excellently."

The young officer turned to Fletcher. "Major," he said, "I've been meaning to tell you this before, but somehow I never quite got around to it. It was a long war and I guess you've no call to remember, but at Antietam your guns covered the retreat of a surrounded infantry brigade from the West Woods, despite the fact that you were under heavy fire yourself. You saved not only the brigade but also the reputation of the colonel in command." He stuck out his hand. "That colonel was my father. It's many years after the event, but on his behalf I wish to thank you."

Fletcher took Simpson's hand. "Lieutenant, there were a lot of woods and a lot of brigades in that war." He smiled, a wide, warm smile that relieved the hard severity of his features. "But now I study on it some, I do recollect supporting a retreating brigade at Antietam. I was going backward myself that day, in what's called a recoil retreat. I bet they didn't teach you that at the Point."

Simpson shook his head, and Fletcher continued: "You let your guns recoil and you reload and fire them from their new position. Then you do the same thing over and over again as long as you're able. The cannons dictate the pace of the retreat, but the main thing is you keep your face to the enemy and continue firing." Fletcher's smile grew wider. "When you come right down to it, I guess we've all had our duty to do at one time or another."

"This is all very interesting, I'm sure," Stark said, in fact shrugging a complete lack of interest. "But we have to be going."

The lieutenant ignored Stark. "Good luck, Major." He was silent for a few moments, then added, "It's been an honor."

Fletcher stood with Stark and Slaughter, watching Simpson and his detail walk down the gangplank to disappear into the sleet-lashed gloom.

"Mr. Slaughter," Stark said, nodding in Fletcher's direction.

The gunman's smile never reached his eyes as he opened his coat and drew a long-barreled .45 Colt from a cross-draw holster. He pointed the gun at Fletcher's belly. "You," he said, "git going."

"Remember, Mr. Slaughter," Stark said, "always discretion. Keep that weapon under cover until we get into the carriage."

Stark at his side, Slaughter following a few steps behind, his gun concealed under his mackinaw, Fletcher left the *Rajah* and walked onto the dock, where a closed carriage stood waiting, its twin lanterns glowing orange in the darkness. A coughing, red-nosed driver was up on the seat, his breath smoking in the cold air, and the horse stamped, its iron shoes clanking loud on wet cobblestones.

"Just a word of warning, Fletcher," Stark said as he ushered the gunfighter into the carriage. "One wrong move, even blink in a way I don't like, and I'll order Mr. Slaughter to shoot you." He climbed into the carriage and sat beside Fletcher. "Do you understand?"

"Perfectly," Fletcher said.

Wes Slaughter, his narrow, rodent face eager, sat opposite Fletcher, his Colt across his knees. "Do something the senator don't like, Fletcher," he said. "Give me the chance to kill you."

After the cold of the boat deck, the carriage was reasonably warm. Fletcher settled back against the leather cushions and smiled.

"Go to hell," he said to Slaughter.